Praise for Sibella Giorello

". . . holds the reader in its powerful grip until the very last word. Sibella Giorello writes like a seasoned pro. No mystery lover should pass up this novel."

–Fred Chappell, author of *I Am One of You Forever*, on *The Stones Cry Out*

". . . an exceptionally skillful debut . . . readers will follow [Raleigh Harmon] eagerly through this adventure and hope for more to come."

–Ann McMillan, author of *Civil Blood*, on *The Stones Cry Out*

"With three-dimensional characters who could be your neighbors, fascinating forensic geology tidbits, and a rich attention to details, *The Stones Cry Out* is easily one of 2007's most compelling novels."

–Titletrakk

". . . creative descriptions . . . authentic dialogue . . . she has that certain X factor . . ."

–Novel Journey

". . . gifted novelist . . . more than once I found myself awed by her vivid word pictures."

–Crosswalk

the rivers run dry

Also by Sibella Giorello

The Stones Cry Out

the rivers run dry

A RALEIGH HARMON NOVEL

SIBELLA GIORELLO

THOMAS NELSON
Since 1798

NASHVILLE   DALLAS   MEXICO CITY   RIO DE JANEIRO   BEIJING

Portion of "The Sea and the Mirror" by W. H. Auden, © 1944 by W. H. Auden. Reprinted by permission of Curtis Brown, Ltd.

Published in Nashville, Tennessee, by Thomas Nelson. Thomas Nelson is a registered trademark of Thomas Nelson, Inc.

Thomas Nelson, Inc., titles may be purchased in bulk for educational, business, fund-raising, or sales promotional use.

ISBN-13: 978-1-61523-167-6

Printed in the United States of America

For Joe

Well, who in his own backyard
Has not opened his heart to the smiling
Secret he cannot quote?
Which goes to show that the Bard
Was sober when he wrote
That this world of fact we love
Is unsubstantial stuff:
All the rest is silence
On the other side of the wall;
And the silence ripeness,
And the ripeness all.

—W. H. Auden

chapter one

It was early October when I drove east toward the mountains outside Seattle with tainted emeralds on my mind. The autumn sun gilded birch leaves and the blue sky appeared polished by a crisp and steady wind. But the green in the trees stole the show.

Armies of cedar and fir and hemlock marched up the foothills of the Cascade Mountains, long limbs glowing with a peculiar shade of green I'd seen only once before: when a six-carat emerald rolled across a stainless steel examination tray in the FBI's materials analysis lab. That gem's green facets glowed with a hue so verdant, so luscious, it whispered sibilant promises in the ears of greedy men.

Just before the town of Issaquah, I turned south off Interstate 90 and followed Sunset Way to the western side of Cougar Mountain. My car windows were open and the air smelled of pine needles and dry curling leaves and iron-rich soil warmed by the sun. This was supposed to be a routine visit, a courtesy call by the FBI for the local PD. But I've learned not to judge anything by appearance; that gorgeous emerald in the FBI lab cost three men their lives.

I parked in a small gravel lot on the right side of the road and walked over to a gray Crown Vic idling beside a police cruiser, the drivers' windows lined up with each other. When I knocked on the Crown Vic's window, the glass lowered six inches.

I leaned down. "Detective Markel?"

"Yes . . ?" He raised his eyebrows.

"I'm Raleigh Harmon, FBI."

He blinked, then squinted as though the sun hurt his eyes. "Oh. I was expecting . . . when Jack Stephanson said your name . . . I thought . . ."

"Yes, sir, I understand."

Two weeks ago the FBI transferred me to Seattle from Richmond, Virginia, and although Southern women often carried family names forward as first names, here in the Northwest people kept assuming "Raleigh" meant I was a man.

"Not that there's a problem," the detective added.

He had driven six feet forward, far enough to open his door and climb out. The state trooper left his car where it was, walking over to where I stood.

"This is Trooper Ron Lowell," the detective said. "He's with the Washington State Patrol."

The trooper's blue uniform had vertical creases that looked as though the clothes were ironed on his body. A white braid circled the brim of his felt hat. Trooper Lowell smiled, dipping the hat toward me.

"Ma'am," he said. "Nice to meet you."

My heart squeezed with homesickness, for a place where all men had manners like his. Behind us, a car door slammed and a small woman walked toward us. She looked like an elf purged from a fairy tale. Her long red hair leaped over her shoulders in ropes of lava and her enormous black boots scuffed across the loose gravel shards, creating a sound like belligerent applause.

"This, this is Fern Valley," the detective said. "She works with Issaquah Parks Department. Fern, this is Special Agent Raleigh Harmon with the FBI."

Fern Valley's pinched expression silenced every question about her name.

The detective continued, "The vehicle in question belongs to one Courtney VanAlstyne. She lives in Kirkland. We called the residence, a roommate answered. She hasn't seen the girl since Sunday."

It was Tuesday, two days later, and the vehicle in question was an army green Land Rover parked perpendicular to a cedar log boom that ran the circumference of the gravel parking lot. Behind the log boom a bulletin board was mounted on plywood and displayed a map of hiking trails stretching across Cougar Mountain. A ring of maple, oak, and aspen trees dropped dying leaves on the Land Rover, smothering the windshield with a flat conglomerate of burnt oranges and bruised reds.

"Who found the vehicle?" I asked.

When no one answered, I asked again.

Fern Valley rolled her big blue eyes. "Sunday afternoons I clean the trailhead," she said.

"That doesn't answer my question."

She sighed, a sound like steam escaping a tight seal. "I come out here Sundays to clean the trailhead, okay? That's when I saw a car. I came back Monday; it was still here. So I called the cops. They said wait another day. I came back this morning, it's still here. I've been waiting for you to show up. Get this thing out of here, okay?"

I glanced at Detective Markel. He wore an expression that compressed his emotions into the diplomatic mask of law enforcement.

"We're exercising due caution," he explained. "We still haven't established what—"

"I'm tired of people treating the mountains like some football stadium," Fern Valley interrupted. "You know how many beer cans and condoms I pick up out here? It's sickening. Now we're supposed to run some Park and Ride? Nobody respects the land. Nobody."

Detective Markel waited, attempting to ensure the rant was over. For now. Then he turned to me. "We sometimes get people going on overnighters—hike all day, camp the night, drive home the next morning. But this particular trailhead isn't known for overnighters. It's more of a quick run. Most campers drive over to Tiger Mountain. Wouldn't you say, Ron?"

Trooper Lowell had his thumbs hooked into the wide black leather belt holding his holstered gun and a radio with a cord running to the mic clipped on his left shoulder. He reached up, brushing away a gnat, shifting his stance. The black shoes gleamed with an obsidian polish.

"Ma'am, we run plates on every vehicle that's left on park grounds more than twenty-four hours," he said. "Sometimes we get folks hiking to the trail's end, like Detective Markel said, but it's taking longer than they expected. Or maybe they get drunk and a friend takes the keys. Maybe the vehicle's out of gas. We hear 'em all."

"And if the car is left for more than twenty-four hours?" I asked.

"We tow it. That's after we run the plates, of course, see if it's stolen or any outstandings exist in the way of warrants. Issaquah PD handles the tow."

I glanced at the detective. His black hair was greased, combed, riding waves to the back of his head.

"But you didn't tow this car," I said.

"Well, no."

"Because?"

"Because it's not so cut-and-dried," the detective said. "After we phoned the roommate, we called the girl's parents—the title lists them as the vehicle's owners. The mother said she hasn't heard from the girl since Sunday. She begged us to launch a search, we ran the dog out here yesterday but he went around in circles. Up the trail just a ways, then circle back to the parking lot. The father came out, watching the whole thing. He was pretty upset, you can imagine. When the dog came up with nothing, we decided to call you guys for some forensics. You know, just in case."

"See?" Fern Valley hissed. "If I didn't say something they would've just let this thing sit here leaking oil into the land. Do you have any idea what motor oil does to the ecosystem, to the streams? The salmon? Like the salmon don't have enough problems."

I thanked Fern Valley for her time, gave her my card, and told her she could leave now. She spun, red hair scything the air, and stomped back to the white pickup parked at the edge of the gravel. The truck door read "Issaquah Parks Dept." I watched the truck pull onto Sunset Way, the tailpipe belching noxious clouds of exhaust.

The trooper, on the other hand, received my genuine smile and a business card with all my FBI contact numbers, including my cell number. But his reaction was more wounded than Fern's. He suddenly looked childlike, the most athletic boy dismissed early from the big game. There was no polite way to explain that evidence collection had a better chance of withstanding cross-examinations in court if only essential personnel were involved;

nobody wanted to be told they were inessential, particularly in law enforcement.

"You don't want me to stick around?" he said. "I can help. Really."

"Thank you, Officer Lowell. We appreciate your time. We'll be in touch."

"Ma'am, I'm happy to help."

"Yes, thank you. We will be in touch."

His brown eyes roamed my face, searching for some motive. Finally, he tipped the lapis blue hat, and his cruiser made a wide U-turn through the parking lot, disappearing down the two-lane road lined by trees with flaming leaves.

I walked to my car, popped the trunk. The detective followed.

"Did you notify the media?" I asked.

"The family wants to keep this very low-key," he said. "No media."

"That won't help you find her."

"What I told them. But they won't listen. The mother said, 'Publicity will only make her circumstances worse.'"

"What circumstances is she talking about?"

"They think she was kidnapped."

"Pardon?"

"For money," he said. "They're wealthy, like, really, really wealthy. They talk about kidnapping like nothing else could've happened. We told them it would still help if we went public, but they're adamant. All the time begging us to find her, with no media involved." He sighed.

"Fingerprints?" I asked.

"Just hers. On the steering wheel, door handles, stereo. The usual."

Before I headed out this morning, my new colleague, Special

Agent Jack Stephanson, had warned me the Issaquah PD would be skittish about disappearances like this. Several years earlier a local family sued the police department, alleging detectives hadn't responded diligently when their teenage daughter went missing. A chronic runaway with a known drug problem, the girl's case had received standard procedure from overworked and understaffed detectives. But when she surfaced as the second victim in a serial killing that stretched across Seattle's east side, the subsequent lawsuit raked millions from city coffers and lined the pockets of trial attorneys. These days even Seattle's smallest police departments called in the FBI for technical backup, asking for the kind of tests and procedures that might dissuade lawyers from trial. And whenever possible, they did what parents asked.

I snapped on latex gloves and squeezed my hand into the wheel well, carefully removing the soil nestled inside. The small grains crumbled between my fingers, a dirt dried by an August drought and a similarly rainless September. I deposited the sample into a sterile cotton bag, marking the paper tag with a Sharpie, pulling the drawstring tight. I ran an index finger across the tire treads. They were new tires, still holding extraneous molded rubber pieces from the factory. I found a slug of soil inside one of the treads and placed that in another cotton bag.

Then I glanced around the parking lot. The shards of gray granite were too large and loose for wheel impressions. Even if the tires had left an impression, the trooper drove directly behind the Rover, obliterating any trace. Kneeling down and opening my work bag, I took out a canister of fingerprint powder, one jar of Vaseline, and about twenty sheets of white card stock paper.

"Please pop the front doors," I said.

The detective shimmed a flat metal Slim Jim between the

door's frame and window, popping the lock. At the back of the car, I smeared Vaseline across the rear tires, coating the treads until they glistened, then laid the card stock on the gravel directly behind each wheel. Walking to the front of the car, where the doors were open, I could smell sun-soaked leather and a vanilla air freshener so heavy it powdered my tongue like talc.

"On the count of three," I said, "push it back."

We leaned into the door frame from opposite sides, pushing against the Rover until the rear wheels rolled across the paper with a crunching sound.

"Okay, that's good," I said.

I picked up the paper from under the car. The bottom sheets had torn against the rocks, but I needed only the top. With the small box of fingerprint powder, I gently blew magnetic fragments across the Vaseline. The black tread marks swept into view.

"Neat trick," the detective said. "It looks like the car drove over the paper."

I nodded, greasing the front tires, laying more paper on the gravel before we pushed the Rover forward into the log boom. I slipped all four tread impressions between separate vellum sheets and took photographs of each tire with a digital camera.

"Do we really need all four tires?" the detective asked, frowning. "No offense meant."

"None taken. Every shoe leaves a different print, depending on the manufacturer and wear. It's the same with tires."

He didn't look convinced.

"We once had a case where a suspect's vehicle had four different tires, all different makes. Each tire left a completely different tread mark at the scene. Because we had a record for each, when prosecutors showed the statistical anomaly, it sealed the verdict. You want legal protection, that's what I'm offering."

He nodded, but worry knotted his forehead. The FBI billed the local police departments for time, material, and expenses, and small town PDs were already strapped financially. The detective would have to defend every forensic procedure.

"I won't run any tests until I hear back from you," I said. "The soil analysis is the most expensive, save that for last, if y'all even need it."

"Y'all?"

"You and your department."

"Where are you from?"

"Virginia."

"That explains you calling me 'sir.' How long you been out here?"

"About two weeks."

"You enjoying our Indian Summer?"

"It's beautiful."

He lifted his head, the black hair sparkling with illumination, bright coal dust riding a crystal stream. "Yep, we've got some good weather. But when it starts raining, let me know what you think."

I shrugged. "It rains in Virginia."

"Sure it does. But do you feel like you've been in the shower for six months?"

I snapped off my gloves, told him to call if there was anything else, and drove back to the office with the windows down. My assigned government ride was a 1997 Buick Skylark. At first glance, it looked dark blue, but in the bright sun it revealed a peculiar shade of purple, a color that provoked my colleagues to dub it "The Barney Mobile" after the fake dinosaur on children's television. The color didn't bother me as much as the smell that came from the backseat, a rank stench of vomit that rose like an apparition, testifying to the fear and panic in every collared criminal who ever puked back there. As if that wasn't enough, the car's engine knocked too, a sound like spare parts coming loose under the hood. I checked; I couldn't find anything.

But for my foreseeable future, this was my car, and the Seattle field office was home base, courtesy of a disciplinary transfer that was requested by my former supervisor in Richmond. Disciplinary transfers were one way the Bureau dissuaded agents from disagreeing with orders, even when the order seemed wrong. Scratch that: *especially* when the order seemed wrong. My now former supervisor claimed I had placed myself in grave danger unnecessarily, that I continued to work the case even after she'd suspended me. The case closed with spectacular effects for the Bureau, the Feds looking like heroes, but my supervisor still thought I needed punishment. To her disappointment, Alaska didn't have an opening. She chose the next farthest office from Richmond.

Now I drove down Madison Street, heading toward Seattle's waterfront, descending the steep grade that rolled across downtown in an east-west pattern. Although the Bureau's field office perched atop Spring Street in a ten-story building with an underground garage, my assigned parking spot sat fifteen blocks away on a sliver of leased land above the barnacle-covered piers that buttressed the waterfront.

I left the windows cracked, locked my car, and loaded up my gear. Laptop, handheld radio, cell phone, gym bag for a lunch-time workout that never happened, and my briefcase. Then I slipped on a blazer that covered the Glock .22 holstered to my belt. In the distance, a ferryboat horned the air.

The first seven blocks weren't so bad. They ran parallel to Puget Sound, but the second half pitched near forty degrees. The sun burned on my back, my hands stung from twenty pounds of gear, and my thighs ached so badly that when I reached the corner of James and Spring Street, my hello to Mike at the front desk was nothing more than a hoarse whisper. I rode the elevator to the third floor, wiping sweat from my forehead. When the doors parted, a gruff voice barked my name.

"Harmon!"

Allen McLeod, my new supervisor.

I walked down the main corridor of the Violent Crimes unit, my gym bag bouncing off my right leg. Allen McLeod approached from the opposite side of the room, lumbering through a maze of cubicles with towering stacks of paper until he reached my desk. He rested one large hand on the column of cardboard boxes with case numbers scrawled across their sides. I still hadn't unpacked.

"Where've you been?" he asked.

A big man, he wore starched white shirts that looked pilfered from the closets of his superiors. The red suspenders were flecked with oily stains.

"Jack sent me out to Issaquah. They wanted legal backup on a missing." I explained that we'd taken tire impressions and soil samples.

"See if Jack needs anything else," he said. "And check with me end of day."

"Yes, sir."

He paused, about to say something, then walked away. I set my laptop and briefcase on my desk, rubbing a sweaty palm creased by the nylon straps. My desk phone blinked with unanswered messages. I punched in my numbered code for voice mail, writing down the information, and halfway through the second message, Jack Stephanson walked over and rested a muscular haunch on the edge of my desk.

"How'd it go, Harmon?"

I raised an index finger, indicating that I was still writing. He reached down, depressing the plastic triangle in the phone bed, severing the message.

"I asked you a question," he said.

Setting down the receiver as if it were made of glass, I described my visit to Issaquah. Jack's azure eyes were set close and they gave his face the focused intensity of a German shepherd. When he asked me to recount the evidence collection procedure again, I said, "Did I do something wrong?"

"No," he said. "File it."

"Pardon?"

"Send that thing down with the *Titanic*. It's another nowhere case. But that's just *my* opinion," he added. "*You* might choose to do something different. But I know you can handle the consequences."

"What are you saying, Jack?"

He stood up. "I need you to get to the courthouse."

"You just said file this."

"You need to pick up my paperwork," he said. "Pronto."

I counted to five. "I've got an interview scheduled in half an hour. McLeod wants a background check on a Federal applicant."

"Tell the clerk down at the courthouse that I want certified copies of all prior convictions on a guy named Bookman Landrow," he continued, as though I'd said nothing. "Case goes to trial Thursday. Keep that day open. I need an assist."

He adjusted his blue jeans; they groped his muscular legs. "Oh, and another thing, Harmon . . ."

I swiveled the chair, picking up the telephone, punching in my code again. It was only fair. He wasn't explaining why the VanAlstyne case was a dead end; I didn't need to listen. He stood behind me for several moments, then walked away. When I glanced down the aisle, watching his cowboy's swagger in lug-soled shoes, he suddenly turned around and raised his voice, making sure it crossed the cluttered room. "Harmon, I need those documents now. So quit pouting and get over to the clerk's office."

From the corner of my eye, I saw my supervisor lift his head. The phone stayed nestled between my shoulder and ear and I wrote down all eight messages, documenting the information, before logging onto the computer and checking e-mail. I replied to one message from a former colleague in the FBI's mineralogy lab in Washington DC, and ignored the Bureau's blanket request for agents willing to move to Iraq and investigate stolen antiquities. Twenty minutes later, I walked down the corridor to the squad's conference room and purchased a can of Coca-Cola and two bags of potato chips from the vending machine. Between bites, I returned two phone calls.

Forty-nine minutes later, I walked outside, heading toward the courthouse on Jack's orders. The sun was still shining and the west side of the city's skyscrapers reflected the view of Puget Sound. The glass panels made it look like the ferryboats were navigating vertical reaches, cruising up an ocean of concrete, sailing for the bright and distant sun.

chapter two

When I was assigned to Violent Crimes, I expected some hazing. The good intentions of the politically correct had assigned some unfortunate token women to the toughest unit of the FBI, the unit that called out SWAT more than any other branch. As much as anything else, necessity forced the Violent Crime units to develop their own proving grounds; these guys deserved to know whether I could cover their backs.

But Jack Stephanson wanted some torture beyond hazing. An alpha among alphas, Jack was assigned by my squad supervisor to be my training agent, the person who guides the newbie through her transfer, eases the transition, shows her the ropes. Instead, Jack was fashioning my noose.

Per his order, I found the King County Courthouse, a Beaux Arts-style building that swallowed a block between Jefferson and James streets. In the clerk's office, a homeless man stood at the public computer, pile-driving a soiled middle finger into the Return key. When the computer froze, he cursed the pretty woman standing behind the counter, spittle gathering at the corners of his chapped mouth. He picked up a rumpled paper bag from the floor, promised to return, and shambled down the hallway, leaving behind a scent of salt and paranoia.

I walked to the counter and asked the clerk for help.

"Can I see some ID?" she said.

Her blonde hair fell like liquid citrine, her bare tan shoulders dark against her yellow sundress. She wore high heels, and to read my credentials, she balanced herself by placing both manicured hands on the laminate counter. Then she tipped back on her heels.

"Jack just called me," she said. "You're an agent?"

"Yes, ma'am."

"You work with Jack."

"That's right."

She paused. "Like, side by side?"

"He's a colleague."

She repeated the word, a sharp pebble on her tongue. "Colleague. That means you go on stakeouts together. Stuff like that?"

"I'm not sure what you're asking."

"It's fifty cents a page for straight copies," she said. "We charge a fee for certifying every page."

"That's fine."

"Type the guy's name into that computer." She pointed a red fingernail at the computer terminal where the homeless man had been.

"But that computer's not working," I said.

"Guess you've got a problem."

Behind her, a computer rested on a long wooden desk. And behind that, a Xerox machine hummed idly against the far wall.

"Could you print out the copies for me?" I asked. "We would pay all the fees."

"You got cash?"

"Pardon?"

"Cash. We only take cash. No credit cards. With fees for

certifying and all, you're looking at fifty bucks easy. Jack says the guy has priors up the yin-yang."

"Okay. Do you know where I might find a cash machine?"

"Beats me." She smiled, her teeth white as petrified bone. "Be sure to tell Jack that Tiffany says hello."

She turned and walked back toward the metal cabinets, past the available computer and the Xerox machine, her high heels clicking across the marble floor, a sound like an empty chamber tumbling in a revolver.

≈

Later that evening, as dusk settled over Seattle in a series of stratus clouds that glowed like backlit amethyst, I opened the front door to my aunt's house on Capital Hill. A small black dog raced down the hallway to greet me. I dropped my briefcase and laptop, kneeling to stroke Madame's soft fur, whispering praise in her ears. Down the wainscoted hallway, I could hear my aunt's voice, the sound of the old South gone west, and the voice of my mother, a woman Virginia-born and bred and believing.

"Nadine," my aunt said, "here's another good one. See what you think."

"Oh, Charlotte, really, you believe I need it?"

With Madame by my side, I walked down the hall and found my mother and aunt in the kitchen with three long-haired cats hunched across the painted table. As Madame entered the room, the cats arched their backs, hissing, and my mother's dog crawled under the table, curling beside her feet.

"All you have to do is wear it," my aunt was saying. "Rub the crystals if the situation is particularly bad."

She draped the necklace of polished stones around my mother's neck.

"That's fuschite," I said.

She waved a plump hand, dismissing me. "Raleigh, forget all the geo-technobabble. Who cares? What matters is these stones can protect your mother."

"Protect her—from what?" I bit back the obvious point: fuschite wasn't protecting her from any nutty New Age ideas.

My mother leaned forward, allowing the light to catch the stones' green and silver veins. "My, Charlotte, this is beautiful," she said. "But I've never heard of such a thing. Have you, Raleigh?"

I shook my head. Charlotte Harmon had lived in Seattle twenty-one years, having fled Richmond in the wake of an acrimonious divorce. Back then, Seattle was a somewhat obscure city, particularly to Southerners, and I remember my mother wondering aloud why anyone would cross the Mason-Dixon Line if a gun wasn't at their back. But my aunt had found her true home.

And now we were living with her in an old Craftsman bungalow on the northeast edge of downtown. In the two weeks since we'd arrived, the tone of my mother's soft voice had changed from familiarity to uncertainty, as her sister-in-law revealed how far she'd fled from the South.

"Nadine, you will not regret wearing protection in this city," she said. "It's the best place in the world, but even the ghosts want to live here. You need to arm yourself, spiritually speaking."

"I just don't see how that's necessary, Charlotte." My mother turned to me, looking for help. "Raleigh?"

I opened my mouth but my aunt barreled forward.

"If you're worried about the necklace matching your outfit, just put it in your purse. You can touch the stones every now and then if you feel threatened. You won't believe the change that comes over you."

"This is nuts," I said.

"Raleigh Ann!" my mother said. "Don't be rude."

My aunt placed her hands on ample hips, her batiked silk tunic seeming to quiver.

"I'm telling you, Nadine, this city is the Grand Central Station of the spirit world. Every spirit comes through Seattle before going on to other dimensions. And some of them never leave."

"What are you talking about?" I said.

My mother threw me a harsh look, then smiled at Charlotte as though she were offering a free vacuum. "Go on, Charlotte."

"You remember when I moved to Seattle, I was as thin as Raleigh. Now look at me. I'm as wide as the Chesapeake and it's all because this city has a spirit of hunger. Food, food, it's all about food here. If you don't protect yourself, Nadine, you'll find twenty pounds landing on your hips by Christmas."

"Aunt Charlotte, this is—"

"Raleigh," my mother warned.

Holding up the plump hand, she severed my mother's scold. "You just watch, Raleigh. You won't be able to stop eating."

"I don't want to stop eating."

"That's what you think."

The last time I saw my aunt was at my father's funeral, four years earlier. She was an exotic character, the aunt who sent me rocks for birthdays and Christmas, and she had flown into Richmond with the smell of patchouli and rain and grief. She had been sensitive enough, or sufficiently devastated, that she did not raise any New Age ideas then, but now I recalled how she gripped a specimen of pink tourmaline during my father's funeral. At the time, my mind numbed with pain, I only saw a mineral the color of antique roses and a bosomy woman with tear-streaked cheeks whose pudgy fingers rubbed a rock with an agitation I mistook for misery. Her brother, my father, was dead, murdered in an alley near our house.

I saw pink tourmaline, not spiritual kryptonite.

"Speaking of hunger, what's for dinner?" I said, attempting to change the subject.

"How does tofu tetrazzini sound?" my mother said.

"You're asking me?"

"It sounds great!" my aunt said.

My mother shooed the cats off the table, and I walked upstairs to change clothes and search my closet for the stash of candy bars. My bedroom, barely used, was a shrine to my late father. Every morning before work, I locked the door with a brass skeleton key, hoping to shield my mother from the walls that held copies of his law degree from the University of Virginia, the official appointment to the state's Superior Court, the handwritten note from the governor, vowing every resource to solve a crime that to this day remained unsolved. Even the bookcases held his boyhood favorites—*Treasure Island, Pilgrim's Progress*—with prep school tennis trophies and blue ribbons for shag dancing contests.

I did not believe in ghosts, except one who was holy, but there was no mistaking that in this bedroom my father felt close, palpable. The feeling comforted and haunted me at the same time.

When my cell phone rang, I pulled the closet door behind me, leaving an inch open for air, and lifted the phone off my belt clip.

"Harmon?" My supervisor, Allen McLeod.

"Yes, sir."

He paused. "Jack sent you to Issaquah today. That right?"

"Yes, sir."

"Girl missing?"

"Correct."

"Go talk to the parents. Start making nice. We're in a bad game of hot tomato. The parents called a senator in Washington. He called our ASAC who called me. He wants to know what we were doing about her disappearance."

"I was told they wanted it kept quiet."

"You did that. I didn't know what the ASAC was talking about because you didn't explain it to me."

"Jack told me to file it, sir. He said it was a nothing case."

I heard the bedroom door open. My mother said, "Raleigh, do you know where my—" She stopped at the closet door, dropping her voice to a whisper. "Oh, you're on the phone. I'll wait."

"Jack meant file it *after* you checked with me," McLeod said. "I'm sure that's what he told you."

"Yes, sir." I watched my mother turn and take in the documents on the walls. The bedside table lamp cast gold into her dark curls. I heard her gasp.

"Get over to the parents right away. Tonight. And check in with me first thing tomorrow morning. We need to be on this like wet on rice."

My mother stood beside the bed, leaning into the black-and-white photograph of my father holding a tennis racket. He was smiling.

"Harmon?"

"Yes, sir."

"Are you listening to me?"

"Yes, sir."

"Full briefing tomorrow morning."

I closed the phone.

My mother was moving like somebody about to lift a dark veil. She went from photograph to document to the bookcase, her fingertips brushing the fringed blue ribbons. When she turned back to me, her face was porcelain.

"Have you seen my raincoat?" she asked.

I shook my head.

"Strange. I can't find it anywhere. I know I brought one. Do you think it's possible somebody stole it?"

"No. Of course not. You misplaced it. That's all."

"I hear things in this house. At night. Do you hear them?"

"The cats. They creep around."

She examined my face, her brown eyes changing to hazel. "It's going to rain. That's what they say."

"Yes, I heard that too."

"They say it rains all the time here. They say it never stops raining."

"Then plenty of raincoats for sale." I smiled.

She nodded.

"Don't be late for dinner." She closed the door behind her.

≈

A six-mile moraine of land ten minutes from downtown Seattle, Mercer Island boasted more millionaires per capita than any other city in Washington State. Later that night, after choking down tofu, I crossed the bridge that connected Mercer Island to the city. Lights from the waterfront mansions danced on the lake, glimmering like castle fires in a kingdom moat.

The VanAlstyne estate sat on the west side of the island at the end of a long winding descent, an iron gate guarding the property. I leaned out my car window, speaking into the rectangular metal box bolted to the ironwork. Moments later, the gate slid back and I drove toward what looked like a small hotel. In the circular driveway, my headlights brushed a black Porsche. I could hear water lapping against the rocky shore beyond the house, a wet percussive sound without detectible rhythm.

At the front door, a young woman stood waiting. She was dressed entirely in black, including massive eyeglasses that gave her a severe appearance, and her dark eyes swept over my credentials. I followed her efficient steps across a wide marble floor, a pink rock, probably from Italy. The woman, who had yet to introduce herself, walked up a curving staircase where her steps were suddenly muffled by white carpeting. We turned right at the top, her stiff back leading us down a gallery with brass sconces bowing over abstract paintings sealed under glass without glare. With one knuckle, she rapped on the final door, absently smoothed her short black hair, and at the word spoken within, turned the knob.

"This is Special Agent Raleigh Harmon with the FBI," she said. "Would you like me to stay?"

The king-sized bed was covered with gray silk pillows, dark and translucent as winter rain, and in the far corner, directly below a picture window that framed Seattle's nightline, a man and a woman ate dinner. The round table was covered by a starched white tablecloth. Steaks were on their plates.

"No, thank you, Sequoia," the man said. "We'll call you back."

Sequoia closed the door without looking at me.

The man lifted a decanter of red wine, refilling their glasses. The woman beside him had a languid posture that reminded me of a waterfall. She lifted her glass, staring at me over the crystal edge, while the man cut a bite from his rare steak, then pushed back his chair.

"Raleigh Harmon, was that it?" He was still chewing as he extended his hand.

"Yes, sir." His skin felt like pumice.

"Martin VanAlstyne."

"Nice to meet you, sir."

"This is my lovely wife, Alex."

Alex VanAlstyne lowered her sculpted chin just enough to acknowledge the introduction.

"Perhaps you'll be able to tell us what the FBI is doing to find our daughter," he said.

"Sir, the Issaquah police are in charge of this case. We were called in for forensic tests only." I carefully explained that unless a federal crime was committed, the case would remain in Issaquah's jurisdiction, although we would help in any way possible.

"But a federal crime has been committed," he said. "Our daughter was kidnapped."

"Did you receive a note?"

His body was wiry, younger than the face etched with furrows. He seemed to twist with coiled fury. "No, we don't have a note. But we have every reason to believe she's been kidnapped."

I glanced at the wife. Her wineglass poised in her hand, she watched her husband.

"And what reasons are those?" I asked.

"Money," he said. "What else? My daughter's life is worth a good deal of money, Miss Harmon."

I nodded, as if agreeing with his theory. "And the last time you saw your daughter was . . . when?"

"Saturday evening."

It was the woman who spoke. Her dull voice was somehow alluring, the sound of steady wind over an open field. "It was close to 6:00 p.m.," she continued. "We were getting ready for the symphony. Courtney stopped by. And then we went out."

"Why did she stop by?"

"No reason in particular. We talked. My husband and I left,

Courtney left after us. I spoke to her again Sunday morning, on her cell phone. She was on her way to the math library at the university."

"My wife and daughter speak to each other several times a day," Mr. VanAlstyne said. "Our daughter has never gone a single day without contacting us. It's been two days since we heard from her and her car is sitting at Cougar Mountain. Doesn't that strike you as suspicious?"

I assured him it was highly suspicious. "But in the eyes of the law your daughter is considered an adult. Which means she wasn't officially missing until yesterday, twenty-four hours after you spoke to her."

"This is complete idiocy," he said. "Your legalistic perception has nothing to do with what's actually happened. How can you stand here and say these things?"

"Sir, I understand your frustration, but until the evidence says otherwise, the Issaquah police will have to handle the case." I also explained that the FBI doesn't automatically get involved with kidnappings unless there's extortion or the kidnapper crosses state lines.

"You're telling me the FBI isn't going to help us?"

"Sir, is it possible that your daughter went—"

"No," he interrupted.

"She was going to the math library," the wife said. "She would have told me if she was going somewhere else."

"Perhaps somebody has seen her," I said. "The media can help publicize her disappear—"

"No," she interrupted. "Absolutely not. We know how the media works. They'll dig into our personal lives, creating scandals."

"Any attention like that will only put Courtney at greater risk. What if the kidnapper decides it's too risky to contact us, and he kills her? No, my wife and I agree. Publicity will make things worse for Courtney. We want this settled, quickly and quietly. We will pay whatever they ask."

"But you just said there was no ransom note."

"That's what we need the FBI for—to find her."

I counted to ten. "Sir, I—"

"Quit blowing smoke at us with all this feigned respect," he said. "What we need is a real search for our daughter. Forty-eight hours might not sound like much to you, but we know our daughter. Courtney has never—not once—been out of touch with us. Something is wrong. Somebody took her."

"Sir, I wish you would—"

"I told you to stop that."

He stepped across the white carpeting, his wiry body moving with an electric urgency. Beside the door, he pressed a tiny brass button set within the green wall. Sequoia appeared.

"See her out," Martin VanAlstyne said. "We're finished with her."

chapter three

Driving away from the VanAlstyne estate, I followed the narrow twists of island road, passing through a phalanx of mansions, each positioned for a commanding view of the water that mirrored city lights and all the bright skyscrapers shaped like crystals of smoky quartz.

In my hometown of Richmond, new money was relatively unknown. As in most of the old South, an ingrained caste system still played itself out among the tobacco and aluminum dynasties and the vast plantations that passed like an open secret from generation to generation. But during my years away from home, I had met new money similar to the VanAlstynes. One of the most memorable introductions came on my first day at Mt. Holyoke College in Massachusetts, after I found a new cell phone on my dorm room desk. By today's standards, the phone was enormous, but back in the 1990s it seemed as sleek and exotic as a python. The phone contained five hundred free minutes, part of the gift for every girl in the North Mandelle dormitory, courtesy of Mark Tomlinson.

Mr. Tomlinson's daughter Ashton was in my freshman class, and her father held the patent for a particular mechanism used on every cell phone. At the parents' reception that day, I went to thank Mr. Tomlinson for his generosity. He was a diminutive man who wore a baseball hat and torn tennis shoes to a formal gathering, and later that day his bright red Ferrari sped away from the dormitory, never to return. In the spring, after report cards had gone home to parents, I was walking down the dormitory hallway when I heard a keening sound, like the wail of some small animal caught in the teeth of a metal trap. It was coming from the showers. Ashton Tomlinson was crouched on the floor, her sobs echoing off the white subway tiles. She had been caught breaking the college's honor code, all of her term papers a plagiarized mess of aspirations. The next day Ashton Tomlinson took the bus home to Greenwich, to stay.

In all these encounters, I've learned that when people are unaccustomed to the transformations that great wealth brings, they tend to wear their new identity with peculiar self-consciousness. One moment gripped by an arrogant insulation against the daily rigors of making a living; the next so deeply needy and insecure, so profoundly fearful that the former definitions might surge forward and steal the recent foothold in their new strata, that their moral code disappears. But new money was still money, and the morning after my visit to the VanAlstynes, I was reminded of how it exerted influence where money mattered most.

"Harmon, in my office," my supervisor said.

Still sweating from the weighted climb from the car, I blotted my forehead with the back of my wrist. McLeod closed the door to his office. It was a glass cube. Every agent turned to watch our conversation.

"You went to the VanAlstyne's last night?"

"Yes, sir."

"Drop that 'sir' stuff."

"It's a habit."

"Break it," he said. "This morning I got a call from Washington, and I don't mean here. I mean DC. Soon as you left the VanAlstynes, they dialed the senator again. This time he called the director. The director, Harmon. The director called our SAC who called the ASAC who called me. You keeping up?"

"Yes—"

"This was 4:00 a.m. Are you still with me?"

I nodded.

"The ASAC asked—again—what we're doing with the VanAlstyne case. I didn't even know it was a case."

"It's not. The Issaquah PD called us when the girl was officially missing twenty-four hours. No sign of struggle at the vehicle. No blood evidence. No fingerprints but hers. Yet the VanAlstynes insist she was kidnapped. There's no evidence pointing to that. No phone calls, no ransom note. We're involved only to cover the local PD against trial attorneys."

Allen McLeod had hands like oversized mittens, and when he rubbed them over his face, they made *scritch*ing sounds against his whiskers. "We need to get all our ducks in the fire," he said.

I nodded as though that made sense.

"I can't tell headquarters these people are crazy until you give me something more to work with," he said. "No later than 2:00 p.m."

≈

By West Coast standards, Courtney VanAlstyne's condo building in Kirkland was practically prehistoric. The squat stucco structure, painted the color of sandstone, was built in 1948 with concrete pylons that sank into the edge of Lake Washington so that the front units perched over the water.

Standing in the living room, I stared at the water below and felt an imaginary shifting sensation, the feeling that usually comes from being aboard a boat. Beside me stood Courtney's roommate, a girl named Stacee Warner, a tiny twentysomething with olive skin that hinted of ethnic heritage.

"Did you come here alone?" she asked me.

"Yes. Why?"

"I don't know . . ." Her voice trailed off. It was 10:20 a.m. and my arrival had woken her up. "I just thought maybe somebody else would be with you, like you work in pairs. Like on TV."

The girls met as freshmen at the University of Washington, I had learned, and moved in together because the VanAlstynes refused to allow their daughter to live on campus unless she joined a sorority.

"Courtney refused," Stacee said with a drowsy smile. "It's not her style to hang out with a bunch of girls who spend all their time shopping and gossiping. She's way too cool for that. But the parents wouldn't even let her get an apartment near campus. They think the U-District is too grungy. Her dad owns this condo from way back when, maybe his bachelor days. And he gave it to her. *Gave* it to her. Free. She doesn't even charge me rent."

"You must be close."

"We have a lot in common. Like, we both think advanced algebra is easy. We both like working with numbers. Only Court's a math genius and I'm not. Did you know that?"

"No."

She stared out the window. The sunlight on the blue water shot oblong flashes of silver on the white walls. "It's not like her to be gone this long."

"That's what her parents said."

"She calls them every day. Sometimes her mom and her talk,

like, four or five times a day. About nothing." Her tone was a mixture of admiration and jealousy.

"Mr. and Mrs. VanAlstyne believe she was kidnapped. What do you think happened?"

She tucked short strands of dark hair behind her ears, her sleepy face suddenly gamine. "Alex—that's Mrs. VanAlstyne— she called here Sunday night looking for Court, because she wasn't answering her cell phone. I told her they make you turn it off in the library."

"How do you know Courtney was at the library?"

"That's where she said she was going."

"Has she ever left town suddenly, not told anybody?"

Her dark eyes darted toward the water. "Are you reporting back to her parents?"

"That depends."

"I want to tell you, 'cause I think you should know this, but I don't want to get Court in any trouble."

"What if she's already in trouble?"

"Sometimes she used to take off for Las Vegas with her boyfriend. She had me set up three-way phone calls, so her mother wouldn't see roaming charges on her cell phone. They pay all her bills, credit cards, everything. I had to hold my breath the whole time they were on the phone, waiting for the conversation to end so I could hang up." She laughed, then abruptly stopped. "But I'm not feeling like this is funny. I feel like this is really serious. Shouldn't you have a partner or something?"

I guessed it was my age throwing her off. She expected an older agent, a veteran.

"What time did she make those trips to Vegas?"

"After we first moved in together, like, two years ago. But she broke up with that guy."

"What time did she leave here on Sunday?"

"Ten. Maybe eleven. Actually, it could've been noon."

I waited for an explanation. In the bright sun, her eyes looked like dark seeds.

"I'm not much of a morning person," she explained. "My mind doesn't really function until the afternoon. Like, right now, my brain feels stuffed with socks."

"Tough if you're a student," I said.

"It was." She pursed her lips. "I dropped out last year. It just costs too much, you know? Besides, I make plenty of money now. So it's no big deal."

"What do you do?"

"I'm a waitress." Her brown eyes came to life. "I work nights. Nobody ever tips big at breakfast, so no loss for me."

"If Courtney went to the library, why was her car at Cougar Mountain?"

Without a word, she walked across the room and into the kitchen where a refrigerator stood like a stainless steel sentry and the black granite countertops were covered by a micron of dust. Above the desk tucked in one corner, a map from the United States Geologic Services showed green areas—state and federal lands—with swirls of fine lines for the altitudes. Someone had drawn in the roads with pencil. Pushpins punctured several summits.

"We have this bet," Stacee said. "Who can hike the most trails in one year. Winner takes all. We both love to hike."

"What's the prize?"

"No more laundry. The loser does all the laundry, like, forever."

The colorful pushpins marked several mountain summits, but the pins were only three colors—yellow, green, and blue.

When I asked if the colors meant anything, Stacee said yellow was for a trail Courtney hiked solo; blue meant Stacee hiked by herself.

"And green means we hiked together, because yellow and blue make green." She turned to me. "I really think Court went to Cougar Mountain to hike Clay Pit Road. She wanted to beat me to it."

"You didn't tell this to the parents?"

"If they think something happened to her because of our bet, they'll kill me. I drove out there Monday, looking for her. I walked over that mountain, screaming my head off. I stayed until it got dark."

"And the parents don't know?"

"About the bet?"

I nodded.

"They hate her gambling, on anything."

She led me to Courtney's bedroom. The room was about twenty feet square with walls covered by black-and-white photographs, each showing an image of stunning symmetry, and all the mahogany frames were hung so perfectly level they seemed like an abstract sculpture. The double bed's sheets were bunched at the bottom, like layers of ruptured gray silt.

"Does she have a new boyfriend?" I asked.

"She doesn't need a boyfriend. Guys hit on her like you would not believe. Even when they don't know she's rich. She's that beautiful. And when she didn't come home Sunday night, I thought maybe she met somebody at the library and you know . . ."

I peeked into the closet. Courtney VanAlstyne had organized her clothing by color and type. Every red blouse together in one section—all the white T-shirts, the black skirts, a section of pressed blue jeans. Her shoes stood floor to ceiling on cherrywood shelves, organized into groups of tennis shoes, flats, heels, sandals, and boots.

"Neat freak," Stacee said. "It has to do with the math-genius brain. She gets crabby when things aren't in perfect order."

On the bottom shelf, two pairs of hiking boots were separated by a wide space, presumably where another pair of boots belonged.

"Did she have another pair of boots?" I stepped toward the shelf.

"Yes."

I pulled two evidence bags from my back pocket, gently scraping soil from the soles, working dirt loose from the treads with the cap of my pen, letting the soil fall into the bag. It wasn't much to recover—the neat freak had dutifully cleaned the boots before shelving them—but at this point, procedure was as important as anything else.

"What are you doing?" she asked.

The tone of her voice sent a shiver down my spine, and I didn't turn around. She sounded like a small frightened child who had woken to find a parent doing something dangerous.

"This is just procedure. Do you know where she hiked before Sunday?"

She didn't reply, and when I turned the whites of her eyes were visible above the brown irises. My first impression of Stacee Warner was that she was a scrappy personality, even drowsiness couldn't disguise it. But now a fissure cracked open, revealing a vulnerability that made me want to insist Courtney VanAlstyne was fine; she probably flew to Vegas again. No ransom note, no body; no traces from the dogs. But I didn't. Once upon a time, I received my own bad news, and among the worst things people said were platitudes. *Your father is probably fine, there must be some mistake, I'm sure it's going to be okay.* Words of supposed comfort stung more than outright disregard, because in tragedy if you doubt the depths of darkness you run the risk of robbing the grieving of their love.

"You—you think she's dead."

"No, I don't."

After taking the samples, I replaced the boots on the wood shelf and marked the bags with a Sharpie. I thanked Stacee for her time, gave her my card.

It was 11:00 a.m.

And Stacee Warner was wide-awake.

≈

The University of Washington's campus stretched from one body of water to another, Lake Washington to Lake Union, forming one of the largest colleges in the Northwest. Known simply as "The U," it boasted top-ranked medical and law schools, and alumnae wore straight faces when they said God was a Husky.

The UW's math library was located in Padelford Hall and on Wednesday afternoon the only person inside was a young Asian man at the reference desk. He hadn't been working on Sunday, he told me, but agreed to find the librarian who was and have him or her call the number on my card.

I took the stairs one floor up. The halls were quiet, the students apparently outside for lunch in the sun. Professor Mark Wolper, Courtney's advisor, had his office door cracked six inches, and I could hear his voice rising and falling. When I glanced into the opening, he was hunched over a desk bisected by stacks of paper. His worn cotton T-shirt stretched across a rounded spine, his knobby vertebrae looking like a string of pillow lava. I stood in the hallway, waiting for the phone conversation to end, but after ten minutes, I knocked on the jamb to indicate my presence.

He stopped mid-sentence, head swiveling. "Yeah, what?"

I stepped inside. The phone rested in its base.

"Excuse me," I said. "I'd like to ask you some questions."

"Are you in the 102 class? Because we have tutors for you girls."

"No, sir. I'm with the FBI."

"The what?"

I opened my credentials case. "Special Agent Raleigh Harmon."

"FBI." He snorted. "You want to ask about my Arab students, that it? Well, I'm not talking."

His gray eyes were flat until I mentioned Courtney's name. Then the eyes flashed to life.

"When was the last time you saw her?"

"Friday afternoon." He picked up a paper clip, unwinding the metal. "What's this about anyway?"

"What did you two discuss on Friday?"

"Her project."

I waited. The paper clip turned into a jagged silver line. "What's her project?"

"She's writing a thesis. You wouldn't understand it."

"A thesis?"

"Yes."

"Isn't that unusual, a junior writing a thesis?"

"*She's* unusual."

"In what way?"

"For one thing, she's a female with a working brain." He tossed the damaged paper clip into the steel trash can, pinging the side. "That alone sets her above 99 percent of her sex."

"I see."

"Do you?" He snorted again. "Okay, FBI. You want to know whether she was plotting to blow up the campus?"

"Actually, I'm curious about this idea that women are dumb. Is it a theory, or a lemma on the way to empirical proof?"

"Are you mocking me?" he said.

"No, but the last time I checked both clinical science and deductive reasoning had yet to prove double X chromosomes hinder cerebral development. But if you've made a breakthrough on your own, I'd like to hear it."

He paused. "Your background is . . . ?"

"Geology."

"With the Feds? You're kidding me."

"Miss VanAlstyne?"

He glanced out the window. A column of sunlight sliced diagonally through the room, revealing dust mites dancing in entropy. Her thesis, he explained, focused on ideas of probability and the statistical quantities that characteristically defied mathematical definitions.

"Courtney wants to prove that quantitative boundaries exist for luck." His face broke into a ragged grin. "Her math . . . it's like poetry."

"Nobody's heard from the poet since Sunday morning." I watched his reaction.

His long fingers reached for another paper clip, unwinding again. "She wasn't in class Monday. Or today. I was going to call."

"Any idea where she might be?"

He shook his head.

"None. You're sure?"

"She takes research trips. Sometimes."

"Does this research take her out of the area?"

He tossed the second paper clip, missing the trash can. "Let me ask you, Miss Geology. If you were studying luck, where would you go?"

"Where it doesn't show up."

"Why?"

"Because some of the best definitions come from studying the opposite quality."

"Interesting. She goes to Las Vegas to study gambling. It's fantastic material. Winners, losers, both in abundance, and everybody inside a casino wants to talk about luck. Here's Courtney, quantifying anecdotes with mathematical equations. I'm telling you, it's poetry."

"I thought the house always wins."

"That's just it!" he exclaimed. "The house wins *most* of the time, in order to recoup its money, to stay in business. But what about the rest of time? That's the area Courtney's working on. She's quantifying what we colloquially refer to as 'luck.'"

"If you believe luck exists."

"Let me guess. You don't believe in luck."

"No, sir, I don't."

"Well then." He snorted. "You won't have to bother your pretty little head reading her thesis, will you?"

≈

On the drive back to the office, down Montlake Boulevard, I called the Bureau's special agent at Sea-Tac Airport, a guy named Marvin Larsen. According to Jack, Marvin was "a troglodyte." But even a dinosaur could help.

"We got no Courtney VanAlstyne on any outbound flights," Marvin Larsen told me. "Unless she got hold of some fake ID, or cooked up a fraudulent passport, she didn't board any planes out of here. I even checked Saturday. No goes."

At 2:45 p.m., still sweating from the climb, I explained all this to Allen McLeod as we sat in his glassed-in office and he scribbled notes on a white legal pad, doubling back over my details and circling key phrases.

"Sounds like we have a rich girl disobeying her parents," he said. "And they can't admit their princess would do anything wrong. Maybe she's sleeping around. Maybe she's getting away from them. But let's not screw ourselves in the foot. Write up 302s for all the interviews and I'll take them up to the ASAC for a paper trail."

"Yes, sir." I caught myself. "And what about the parents?"

"The senator wants to call them personally. He made that clear to the ASAC. Let 'em know they're getting full bang for the buck. Big donors, big favors."

"And we let the Issaquah PD handle the case?" I asked.

"Right."

I stood to leave.

"Harmon?" he said. "Check with Jack. He was wondering where you ran off to."

chapter four

No Barney Mobile for him. No stinking backseat. No
engine that rattled.

Jack Stephanson drove a black Jeep with a removable
hardtop, the gray leather seats soft as driving gloves, and the
nubby tires squealed as he sped through the underground garage.
At the solid steel gate, he flicked his index finger, signaling the
guard. The gate lifted and the Jeep shot up Spring Street.

"The witness is Felicia Kunkel," he said. "Felicia's got some
kids but they belong to the state now—hey, buddy, move it!"
Jack honked the horn.

At the edge of the Jeep's bumper, an elderly Chinese man
shuffled on the white crosswalk, his black satin slippers frayed at
the heels. He stepped with an odd tenderness, his shoulders
curled, as though his reedy weight might injure the pavement.

"Somebody get this guy a wheelchair," Jack mumbled.

When the horn honked again, the man's head swung on his
neck like a dandelion dangling from its stem. His dry lips uttered
something unintelligible, and the moment his feet cleared the
car's path, the Jeep rocketed down Fourth Avenue.

"Felicia might try to run," Jack said. "She's scared. She doesn't
want to testify. You're going to sit on this one, Harmon. Do not
let Felicia get away. Without her, our entire case collapses. We

spent ten months nailing these pervs. You blow this one—imagine *that* on your record."

It was 4:00 p.m. and Seattle's office workers were purging from buildings in an anxious exodus to beat rush-hour traffic. I watched the women stride down the sidewalks in sharp slacks and jewel-toned blouses, their blonde hair cut in angles that refracted sunlight like successive shelves of gold. The men were broad-shouldered, lantern-jawed. Even the suits couldn't disguise direct Viking descent.

When the light turned green, Jack swung the Jeep down to the waterfront along the piers, to the Bureau's leased parking lot.

"Jack," I said, "lay off the torture routine. It's already old."

"I'm not torturing you, Harmon," he grinned. "You're doing that all by yourself."

I gathered my gear from the backseat, slammed the Jeep's door, and climbed into the stinking Barney Mobile.

≈

Felicia Kunkel lived in a two-bedroom yellow rambler six blocks east of Sea-Tac Airport. Jack and I waited in our separate cars with the Bureau radios on while the tactical squad scoped the house. They wore flak jackets and gripped MP5s. Within six minutes, they radioed that Felicia's "employer" was not home.

As the tactical team took silent places within the ragged camellia bushes on either side of the front door, Jack and I walked across the dirt lawn. Suddenly the air vibrated with a sizzle like heat lightning. The sun disappeared. When I looked up, I saw grease-ringed bolt seams riveted to the underbelly of a 757. Moments later, the roar kicked in.

Jack stood on the front stoop, waiting for the jet engines to fade before knocking on the door. Waxy green leaves were scattered across the steps, creased by boot impressions. The concrete stoop miscalculated the foundation by four inches, causing the front door to appear raised.

Jack knocked again. "Hey, Felicia! You ready?"

She opened the door. "I'm havin' second thoughts."

Her pale face was freckled with small red sores. Dun-colored hair hung in greasy curtains to her ribs, to the precise point where her torso changed shape and her bottom swelled like an inverted funnel.

"Felicia, you're not going to let me down, are you?" Jack said. "C'mon. We had a deal. You help us; we help you."

She flicked her eyes toward me. "Who's this?"

"This?" He turned, as though surprised to discover someone standing behind him. "This is just Raleigh. She works in the office."

"What's she doing here?"

"Raleigh's going to take you to the hotel. She'll stay with you through the night, make sure you're okay for tomorrow. You can order all the room service you want. Hey, raid the minibar, have a pajama party. Then tomorrow morning Raleigh will drive you to the courthouse. And you can get your kids back."

Felicia's green eyes shifted. She was the nervous type who couldn't hold a stare long, but her glance over my shoulder seemed forced. The bushes never rustled.

"Bookman could come back any minute," she said.

"So what're you waiting for, another beating? That's all he's got for you, Felicia. Pain and more pain. How much more abuse do you want to put up with?"

Her eyes filled with tears so suddenly it was as if a water pipe had broken inside her neck. "You're sure this is gonna work?" she said.

"Felicia." He said her name in a whisper. "Felicia."

Her green eyes rested on Jack's mouth.

"Anybody in your situation would be scared. Somebody tells you different, they're lying. Let me help you, Felicia. I want to help you."

Then he reached up, wiping a tear from her mottled cheek.

≈

Our double room at the Edgewater Hotel, courtesy of the FBI, had two queen beds, one desk, a chair, and a well-stocked mini-bar that Felicia raided while I checked the closet and bathroom, then under the bed.

"Hey, look," she said. "They got Grey Goose in here."

I stood at the window, wondering whether to draw the curtains. The hotel room hung over Puget Sound like a ship's deck, Seattle being a city that gathered its waterfront in both arms. I hated to lose the view, but I worried Felicia's "employer" might be ambitious enough to hire a boat and fire into a hotel room. I pulled the curtains halfway, leaving enough view to fire back.

"You want a drink?" Felicia bent over the small refrigerator's open door.

"No, thank you."

"Well, I need a drink, that's for sure. Where's the ice?"

I picked up the phone on the nightstand between the two beds and dialed 0 for the front desk. The clerk informed me that the ice machine was just down the hall from our room, for my convenience. I informed her that my convenience required a bellboy with a bucket of ice, pronto, or we'd call the manager. I hung up.

Felicia stared at me. "You need a drink."

"No, thanks."

She shrugged. "More for me."

Clutching tiny bottles of vodka to her narrow chest, she upended a drinking glass from the paper doily beside the sink and poured two bottles into the glass, followed by the briefest splash of orange juice. She downed it, then poured another and walked to the window, yanking back the navy chintz drapes. A gloaming twilight drifted into the room, filtering the furniture with a rosy quartz glow.

"Come away from the window, please." I picked up the phone and dialed room service. Two cheeseburgers, extra fries, onion rings, two chocolate milkshakes, two cans of Coca-Cola, cheesecake, and a thermos of black coffee, extra sugar. And the ice bucket.

"You want anything?" I asked Felicia.

"Now you're talking."

When the rolling table arrived, it was covered by a white tablecloth that brought the VanAlstynes back to my mind, wealthy people who ate dinner in their bedroom. I tipped the bellboy in the hallway, lifted the tablecloth, then removed the knives from the stiff swaddles of white napkins. I rolled the table into the room.

Felicia picked up the plate covers, uttering curses that I assumed meant appreciation. Golden steak-cut fries, perfectly salted. Toasted burger buns cradling green butter lettuce. Thick red tomatoes, glistening slices of red onion.

I locked the door, positioning Felicia at the far side of the table, blocking her path to the exit. She washed down every third bite with another double vodka and OJ.

"You eat like this all the time?" she asked.

"In hotels?"

"I was more thinking this kind of food. You're kind of skinny."

"I'd eat this meal three times a day if I could."

"You don't get to eat what you want?" She nibbled on her burger, plucking the crust from the edges.

"I live with my mother—she's a health fanatic. She cooks tofu and organic bean sprouts. Red meat freaks her out."

"Get out."

"Her food tastes like old newspapers."

She dropped her head, the greasy dun hair falling forward, and laughter came soundless, a soft interior rumble that shook her shoulders, a girl used to hiding her joy. When she looked up, the light in her green eyes was bright with alcohol. She finished her drink, then walked to the luggage rack and pulled a pair of yellow pajamas from her torn duffel bag.

"I'm gonna get changed," she said.

She walked to the bathroom and I set the untouched cheese-cakes on the desk with the thermos of coffee, then backed the table into the hall, locking the door again.

"Felicia." I knocked on the bathroom door. "You need to keep the door open."

She cracked it a foot.

I walked over to the big window, glancing back and forth between the bathroom and the view outside. Night had swal-lowed dusk, and two ferries were crossing the Sound like hovering plates of candles. Picking up one of the cheesecakes, red ribbons of syrup swirling across its creamy surface, I watched her step out of the bathroom wearing Mickey and Minnie Mouse pajamas.

She made another drink. "You sure you don't want one?"

"Yes, ma'am."

She threw ice into the glass, half of it landing on the floor. "My daddy was stationed in Georgia. He made us say 'sir' and 'ma'am' all the time. He said it showed respect. If we screwed up, we got the belt. One time he beat me—I'll never forget it. All I asked was could I go to the bathroom. I was six, about to pee my pants. That buckle had my legs scabbed up for weeks."

She plunked down on the bed, scooting herself back against the headboard, holding the remote in one hand, the drink in the other. She channel surfed before settling on a show that switched scenes with a sound like jail doors clanging.

"I love these crime shows, don't you?"

"Not particularly." I ate the other cheesecake she didn't want.

"Yeah, you probably see this stuff in real life, huh. I bet they get it all wrong."

"That's part of it."

The other part, the greater part, was that I resented how residents of Hollywood's gated communities profited from tragic lives—lives like Felicia's—all the while shaking their heads sadly as though genuine concern was a legitimate part of their commerce. The only learning these shows provided went to the cons who picked up new tricks from prison.

"Can I ask you something?" she said suddenly.

"Sure."

"They'll put Bookman away for good. Right?"

"That depends on you, from what I hear."

Bookman, I learned, had been Felicia's pimp since she was fourteen, luring her out of Portland, taking her away from the nice Christian father who wielded a belt buckle for paternal respect. But Bookman turned out to be worse, far worse, and Felicia worked the streets of Seattle with fresh beatings that made the buckle feel like a feather by comparison. Now twenty-two, Felicia had the face and figure of a middle-aged woman.

"He'll kill me," she said. "You guys know that?"

"When you see him in court, don't feel sorry for him. Don't hold anything back. Put him away for good, Felicia."

Rape, extortion, battery, kidnapping a minor, crossing state lines—all the man's offenses before Felicia described the meth lab inside the house and the back door that rotated junkies through the kitchen.

On the TV, a pedophile received a long lecture from two inordinately good-looking actors wearing fake badges clipped to designer shirts. Felicia set her glass on the nightstand, bumping the telephone, and stumbled across the room to the luggage rack. She rifled through her duffel bag again, then shambled back to bed holding a plastic picture frame with a photo of two small mulatto boys and a baby girl with blonde hair as fine as corn silk. The baby looked dazed, her green eyes vague. Felicia set the frame on the table, bumping her drink.

"Cute kids," I said.

She climbed under the covers, rolling onto her side away from me. The television program concluded with the sound of cell doors, and another crime show followed featuring sexual assault victims. I glanced over, about to ask if we could please change the channel, when I heard a snore.

I walked over to the bed. Felicia's mouth had fallen open and I could see missing teeth among her back molars, small red caves in her gums. Her heart-shaped face looked almost pretty, her eyelashes dark crescents on the white skin. But she had been crying, as silently as she had laughed, and the salty rivulets ran like dry streams down her cheeks.

I turned down the TV's volume and walked to the desk, picking up the phone and dialing Aunt Charlotte's house.

"Raleigh, where are you?" she said. "It's past ten o'clock."

"I won't be home until tomorrow."

"Are you in danger?"

"No. I'm on assignment."

"You're in danger—I can hear it in your voice. You need one of my necklaces."

"No, really, Aunt Charlotte. I'm fine."

She lowered her voice. "What should I tell your mother?"

When my disciplinary transfer to Seattle became official, I called Aunt Charlotte. She was thrilled we were moving and invited us to live with her. Plenty of room, she insisted. But I explained my caveat: my mother must never know I work for the FBI; she would only worry, become even more paranoid. As far as my mother knew, I was a geologist. Aunt Charlotte promised she wouldn't slip. "Honey," she told me at the time, "working for the FBI is not something I'd broadcast around this city anyway. Remember the WTO riots?"

"Tell Mom I'm out of town. Tell her the geology firm needs a rush study done in Yakima. I should be home tomorrow."

There was a long pause. "You're sure you're not in any danger?"

"I'm sure."

"Where are you? I'll bring you one of my necklaces. You need protection."

"That's the gun's job."

"That is not funny."

"You're right," I said. "I'll call you if there's an emergency."

I carried the thermal carafe of coffee to the bed, stretching out. I didn't have pajamas, since Jack pulled me for duty so quickly, and sleep was risky, considering Bookman's criminal ambitions. I drank two cups of coffee staring at the muted television, then turned it off and switched on the light between our beds. Felicia mumbled incoherently as though waking up, so I draped a white bath towel over the sconce, dimming the light.

In the nightstand drawer, I found a red Bible courtesy of the Gideons. This copy was dedicated to a woman named Jacqueline Harris from her four children, and when I turned to the book of Luke, the spine crackled as though never opened. I read about the woman at the well and kept reading through the night until a dove-gray dawn spread across the sky outside and the clouds curdled the way they do just before heavy rain.

chapter five

Felicia slept like a lobotomized rock. In the morning, she was still facing the photograph of her children on the nightstand. Except for that one brief moment, I had not seen her stir once.

I cleaned my face with a washcloth, not wanting to risk a shower, then walked to her bed.

"Felicia." My voice sounded hoarse from no sleep and too much coffee. "Felicia, time to get up."

I called her name a third time. She didn't react. I walked over to the window and turned on the air-conditioning unit, twisting the plastic knob to the coolest setting. I switched on every light in the room.

"Felicia."

Her skin was the color of the dawn—dark milky gray—and when I yanked back the blanket, her fetal position had the desperate and fearful appearance of human remains excavated from ancient volcanic ash. I shook her shoulder. No response.

With a stab of panic, I pressed my fingers into her thick neck. Her pulse throbbed against my skin, slow and steady, the yellow Disney pajamas lifting and lowering on her narrow rib cage. I leaned down, speaking directly into her ear. Not even a startle.

I picked up the clock radio, scanning the stations until a guitar screamed. Cranking the volume, I placed the radio beside her head.

Not even a flicker across the eyelids.

I turned on the television, where the early morning news offered a litany of depressing events. I raised the volume until every word from the pretty blonde newscaster shot through my brain like a dull arrow. Felicia didn't react, but the light on the nightstand phone vibrated red; the phone was ringing. Felicia smacked her lips, uttering a low bovine moan. Her eyelids fluttered.

"Hello?" I said into the phone.

"This is the front desk." The woman's voice sounded angry. "We have quiet hours."

I looked down. Felicia was gone again.

"Do me a favor," I said. "Call this room until a woman answers."

I hung up, turned down the TV, and walked into the bathroom. When the phone rang, I turned on the sink faucet, soaking a white washcloth under cold water until my fingers numbed. The phone rang and rang, then suddenly stopped. I stepped out, cradling the washcloth in both hands, and saw Felicia still in bed with the telephone receiver pressed against her left ear. Her eyes were closed, her elbow bent, wavering above her face.

"Mmmm, who is this?" she mumbled.

I watched her listen to the aggrieved voice on the other end. Her eyes flew open, enlarged and sightless and fired by interior panic. When she looked at me, standing beside the bed with a dripping washcloth, another flicker of light crossed her face.

"What—?" She pulled herself up. "What—where am I?"

I hung up the phone, turned down the radio, and dropped

the washcloth into the sink. I tossed Felicia's duffel bag onto the bed. "Get dressed."

She pulled the nylon blanket up to her shoulders, scooting down into the bed. "It's cold. Why is it so cold in here?"

"Get up, Felicia." I yanked off the blanket.

"What's your problem?"

"Get out of that bed now. Or you'll find out what cold really feels like."

"Leave me alone."

I walked to the sink, picking up the dripping washcloth, and started back toward her.

She sat up, holding both hands in front of her. "What is with you?"

I threw the washcloth back into the sink and yanked jeans and a T-shirt from the duffel. "We're going to be late."

"You should have gotten me up earlier," she said.

"Felicia . . ."

"I'm going!"

She started with the jeans, one foot creeping as though into a tunnel full of spiders. She rested before the next leg, eyes closing.

"Felicia!"

"Lay off!"

I counted to fifteen—because ten was never long enough—and took several deep breaths. "Jack wants us at the courthouse at seven thirty. If we're not there, it's a problem. For both of us."

She yawned, smacking her lips. "I got cotton mouth. Can I get a soda?"

"No."

"Reach in that little refrigerator. The soda's right there."

When I didn't move, she scowled.

"I got a headache," she said.

She shimmied into a red T-shirt with the words "I'm the Princess" spread across the chest in pink glitter. She yawned again and tried to run her fingers through her long hair. Her hand kept missing, combing the air, and my anger evaporated.

"Do you always sleep like that?" I asked.

"Like what?"

"Dead to the world."

She bent down for her socks. Red, the heels worn to nothing but threads.

"Where I come from," she said, "dead to the world keeps you alive."

~

Thirty minutes later, in the happy plastic seats at the McDonald's beside the ferry dock, we ate breakfast under fluorescent lights. Felicia's skin looked sallow, but she ate three hash browns and sucked down a supersized Diet Coke. Her eyes watched the exits.

"By this afternoon," I said, "it'll all be over."

"That's what I'm afraid of."

I drove the Barney Mobile east from the waterfront into Pioneer Square and parked in a lot where the windshields reflected gunmetal clouds like bars of lead. When I climbed out, I had to turn sideways to shrug into the reserve blazer from the hanger in back. It didn't smell great. I checked my gun and cell phone and watch. We had ten minutes.

Felicia was still in the passenger seat, staring at a brick wall.

I leaned down, speaking across the front seat. "You okay?"

She shook her head. "I ate too many of them hash browns. I think I'm gonna throw up."

I raced around the car, squeezing between bumpers, and yanked open her door at the precise moment the hash browns and Diet Coke hurled toward the dashboard, a brown heap of masticated food. It dripped off the blue vinyl and plopped on the plastic floor mat. The sound was like a finger at the back of my throat.

"Oh, Felicia."

She coughed, wept. Then threw up again.

I opened the back door, grabbing her duffel, tossing the tattered clothes on the seat. At the bottom of her bag, I found the large white towel with Edgewater Hotel embroidered on it.

"We'd be in a real mess if you didn't steal this towel," I said, wiping her face. "That was real planning on your part."

"I'm sorry," she sobbed. "I'm so sorry."

"I was joking, Felicia. It's not a big deal. We'll get you cleaned up and ready to go."

"I wish I could kill myself."

"Felicia, relax. My car already smelled like puke. What's more of the same?"

But she didn't hear me. Or couldn't. She rocked on the seat, forward and back, her plaintive apology circling into a chant that rose from the car with the sickly smell. I lifted her legs, swiveling her body to wipe vomit from her shoes, and suddenly realized her apologies were not meant for me. They were larger, wider. Messier than early morning vomit in an ugly car. The words continued to search for solace or wisdom or grace, falling from her lips like shattered glass. I eased her from the car and leaned her against the brick wall. She grew quieter, sniffing back tears, but the pink glitter words on her shirt were ringed with dark stains, the word *princess* mocking her. Despite the possibility of rain, I cracked all four windows, then tossed the towel in a green Dumpster behind the parking lot. Taking her elbow, I walked Felicia to the court-house for a date with justice.

Jack Stephanson waited inside. He wore a three-button navy suit, a green silk tie the color of weathered copper, and a face creased with fury.

"What happened to her?" he said.

"She had breakfast twice. Down and up."

Felicia dropped her head. "I'm sorry."

Jack stepped forward, then caught a whiff. Revulsion swept across his face. But his voice purred.

"Felicia, honey, you're nervous. I'd be nervous too. But we'll take care of everything. Stay here, don't move. I'll be right back." He placed a shoebox in her hands. "I got you something special for the big day. Brand-new shoes."

Felicia wiped her nose with the back of one hand and opened the box.

"Atta girl," Jack said.

He pushed me to the side. "This is how you babysit a wit-ness? No wonder they booted you out of Richmond."

"Don't you dare pin this on me, Jack. *You* told her to raid the minibar. *You* told her to have some drunken pajama party. Guess what? She did what you said."

"Get her in the bathroom, clean her up. I had the guard hang a dress in the third stall. She wears panty hose too. They're in the shoe box."

I looked at him. "You knew she'd do this."

"Clean her up."

"You wanted her to do this, on my watch."

"I want her looking like Mary Poppins," he said. "If you can't handle that, I'll find somebody who can. Got it?"

"Oh, I got it, Jack. Believe me, I got it."

~

Bookman Landrow turned out to be a wiry black man, and the blaze orange jumpsuit courtesy of the King County Sheriff's Department made his long dark arms look like burnt twigs. Indistinct tattoos swirled across his skin, looking more like bruises than ink, and when he turned to look at Felicia, the expression in his almond-shaped eyes iced my spine.

"He's going to kill me," Felicia gasped. "I told you, he's going to kill me."

"Don't give him the chance. Put him away for good."

We sat directly behind the prosecutor's table, the first wooden bench from the small gate that provided the only barrier between Felicia and the man who wanted to kill her. Bookman's defense attorney was a compact, intense man named Joe Morrisson who kept pressing a manicured hand to his charcoal pin-striped suit as he conferred with Bookman, whispering asides that Bookman took for opportunities to send Felicia the dead look.

"Keep your eyes off him," I told her. "Especially when you get on the stand. If they ask you to identify him, point, but stare at his forehead."

Her skin was chalk white and the sores on her face glowed in contrast, aggravated by the scratchy paper towels I'd used on her in the bathroom. Combined with the outfit Jack picked out— navy rayon dress with ecru lace collar and blue pumps—Felicia looked lost and depressed, like a polygamous Mormon wife on suicide watch. In an attempt to avoid Bookman's stares, Felicia opened her purse. It was a fashion detail Jack had overlooked and she pawed through the cracked leather pouch mumbling to herself. I listened in a distracted way, watching Jack finish his conversation with the U.S. attorney on the case. My head felt weighted, the way it did just before a bad cold set in, but each time Felicia's arm brushed against mine, I felt a jolt of the anxiety coursing through her veins.

"I'm never drinking again," she said, still digging. "I'm never having another drink so long as I live. No more drugs neither. I'm gonna get my kids back, get a job. Soon as I'm done here, that's what I'm doing."

"Good girl," I said. "Way to go."

"I'm serious."

"So am I."

Her head dropped over the purse again, her murmured words falling into the bag. "Me and alcohol, it's as bad as me and Bookman. Me and everything is bad." She looked up. "Hey, you want this?"

I looked over. She held a green plastic disk the size of a quarter, with white lettering embossed around the crimped edges.

"What is it?"

"It's a free token. You know that Indian casino, out I-90?"

I shook my head.

"I'm never going there again neither. I just go broke out there. The slots. What do they say? If I didn't have bad luck I'd have no luck at all. That's me."

Before I could tell her there was no such thing as luck, the bailiff told us to rise. Felicia dropped the green disk into my hand.

chapter six

Friday morning Allen McLeod called me into his glass box of an office. Jack Stephanson leaned against the cube's far wall, one ankle crossed over the other. A slender woman with sloe-brown eyes and dark hair like polished tiger's eye sat in one of the available chairs. I took the seat beside her.

"Harmon, meet Lucia Lutini." McLeod dropped into the big chair behind his desk. "Lucia's our victim support coordinator. You two can talk later. Right now, we've got to deal with this other mess." He clasped his hands, laying them on his stomach. "I don't want to go barking up a horse's mouth, but it looks like we've got a serious situation here."

Yesterday afternoon a King County Superior Court judge sent Bookman Landrow far, far away. Felicia, relieved and joyful, asked me to drive her to the Department of Social Services. Wearing her new dress, she sat in the backseat to avoid soiling her new blue pumps, the floorboard still tacky with vomit. She did not want me to come inside when she made her appearance to the social worker handling her case, and I didn't argue. Felicia needed to stand on her own. I needed sleep.

But now I realized I should have stayed with her. One blue dress wouldn't wipe out a file as thick as my wrist.

Jack uncrossed his legs. "From the get-go, Harmon's been the point person on this. Take it up with her."

"Jack asked me to help him," I said, the defensiveness ruining my voice. "I followed his orders."

"He's your training agent, Harmon. You do what he says, when he says it." McLeod unclasped his hands, the fingers opening like falling fence rails. "But you're still expected to make decent judgment calls."

I nodded, giving myself time to bring my anger down a notch. "I'm not aware of what went wrong."

"Maybe down South they don't know how to talk to a victim's family," McLeod said. "So I brought in Lutini—she'll handle it from here. Meanwhile you and Jack get to work on this missing."

"Courtney VanAlstyne?" I said. "That's what this is about?"

Jack said, "Harmon made a rat's nest out of the VanAlstyne situation, not me. Let her clean it up."

"Jack, this is urgent," McLeod said.

"Urgent is a bomb strapped to an Arab's body. My counter-terrorism work trumps any alleged disappearance of a rich girl. Let Harmon work this by herself."

"Headquarters called us, Jack. This jumps to priority," McLeod said. "You find out what happened or you find a way to throw it back to Issaquah PD, I don't care which, but I'm tired of 4:00 a.m. calls from the ASAC asking what we're doing about this kidnapping when we don't think she was kidnapped. And the parents won't go public. The whole thing's nuts. I want write-ups on everything from this minute forward, every *t* crossed, every *i* spotted."

"Dotted," said Lucia Lutini.

"What?" McLeod said.

"The correct phrase is every *t* crossed, every *i* dotted." Her voice sounded like melted butter.

"What did I say?"

"Spotted."

"Fine," McLeod growled. "Dot the *i*'s."

Jack leaned forward, placing his hands on the desk. I could see condensation gathering on the varnished shine, his skin hot with anger. "What am I supposed to tell counterterrorism, it's time for recess?"

"You'll figure it out, Jack." McLeod said. "You've got a sliver tongue."

"Silver," Lutini said.

McLeod stared at her, his expression frozen. "Anybody else, Lutini, I'd have them transferred to Alaska."

"I know," she said.

≈

Back at my desk, I called Detective Markel at the Issaquah PD, leaving a message to explain our sudden interest in the VanAlstyne case. I would be on Cougar Mountain tomorrow, I said, looking into the crime scene on behalf of the Bureau. We would not charge his department for time and tests. I hung up and ran a background check on Courtney VanAlstyne's former boyfriend, the name the roommate gave me, printing out the information and copying it for McLeod.

Just after 1:30 p.m., Lucia Lutini asked me to lunch.

Cumulus clouds bumped across the mottled blue sky as we walked down First Avenue, heading south. She wore a wool cape the color of moist moss, her black boots tapering to deadly points. In the air I felt the first bite of fall.

"I spoke with the VanAlstynes this morning," she said in her buttery voice, the words keeping a rhythm that sounded like a melody. "Separately. The wife first, then the husband."

"What's your impression?"

She tilted her head one degree left, then one degree right. "She's hiding something."

"About the disappearance?"

"At this point, I don't know. The only certainty is that Mrs. VanAlstyne is a lovely woman with a firm grip on her own neck."

We crossed at Yesler Way and a man in a ragged coat with a face like a skinned plum stumbled toward Lucia. When he opened his mouth, his breath smelled like butane.

"Lucia," he said. "How about some change?"

"Hello, Red. I'm going to tell you the same thing I always tell you. The mission is two blocks over. They serve hot meals. Why doesn't that sound good to you?"

"Lucia," he moaned.

Her hands were tucked inside the green cape, but she took one out and wagged a finger at him. "Ah, I see. You think you can embarrass me with my companion. You're a smart guy, Red. Very smart."

"C'mon. Give me some money."

"You want to come to lunch with us? Best sandwich in Seattle."

"I got a stomach virus. I can't eat nothing."

"The mission treats that too." She smiled, walking again. "Have a wonderful day, Red."

"No thanks to you!" he yelled.

In Occidental Square iron grates caged the root-balls of deciduous trees. The red leaves remained on the branches, and the dead brown leaves scattered across the bricks, creating a susurrus that revealed the unpredictable wind.

"Red's been down here for years," Lucia said, by way of

explanation. "I first encountered him when his hair was blond instead of gray. How time accelerates for those people."

"Why 'Red'?" I asked. "His skin?"

"His eyes. Even back then."

We walked two blocks south where a line of people waited outside a brick building. The air smelled of garlic and onions and seared meat. Lucia turned down an alley and keyed open a black door, walking into a steam-filled room. At a large sink, a young man washed pots, his dark hair curling from the moisture, one forelock dropping like a comma to his brown eyes.

"Buon Giorno, Lucia."

"Buon Giorno, Pietro."

She unwrapped the green cape, walking into a tight kitchen where bottles of translucent green olive oil and russet vinegars hovered above a blackened grill. A round man with a laurel of white hair stood with his back to us, the frayed strings of his apron hanging from his circular torso. With the roaring hood and sizzling meat, he didn't hear us approach. Lucia reached out, gently touching him on the shoulder. He turned, a pair of tongs in his right hand snapping like crab claws.

"Lucia!" he cried. "Why you didn't call? Mario, he was just here!"

She shook her head and shrugged her shoulders at the same time, a seamless gesture that said Mario was not for her. "Papa, I want you to meet Raleigh Harmon. Raleigh, this is my father, Danato Lutini. Raleigh works with me, Papa."

Danato Lutini shook my hand, and my arm undulated like a rag doll.

"You a crime fighter like my daughter, yeah? I feed you anything you want. Anything!"

Lucia kissed his cheek and I followed her back to a storeroom no bigger than a closet. She overturned two five-gallon buckets, hanging my blazer and her cape on the door hinge. Danato appeared with sausage sandwiches on paper plates, the long roll cradling roasted pork bedded with tomato sauce and sautéed onions. My first bite exploded fennel and black pepper and garlic without a trace of bitterness and just when I caught those flavors, the roasted tomato kicked in behind it.

I swallowed. "Wow."

Lucia wiped sauce from her lips with a paper napkin. "It's literally a hole in the wall, this place. One window on South Jackson. But that line out there? Goes around the block every day. Papa won't hire waiters, won't buy tables. He stays at the grill, my Uncle Carmine shuffles back to give him the orders. People wait forty-five minutes for a sandwich."

"It's worth it."

Danato appeared in the door again, this time holding two demitasse cups.

"Eh, Raleigh, you like my sandwich?" His voice had a sing-song accent.

"Loved it."

He smiled, lifting his head with a nod, a gesture of yes and thank-you and I-knew-you-would. When he glanced at his daughter, warm light filled his face.

"Lucia, you drink the espresso. Take your time. A good lunch, yeah? None of this hurrying business. It's bad on the stomach."

"Thank you, Papa."

We sipped the coffee. It had the sharp challenge of bitter chocolate. I stared at the boxes along the shelves, the imports marked *Italia*, trying to find the courage to ask.

"What does McLeod want you to tell me?"

She set her cup in the saucer. "Our beloved supervisor has the idea you don't know how to handle rich people."

I didn't respond.

"Personally, I disagree," she said. "In fact, I believe you come from that same tribe."

"You think I'm rich?"

"Old wealth, most of it gone. That once-upon-a-time circumstance of money."

I sipped the espresso.

"Yes, what I thought. Gentrified poverty. Which is lovely—consider yourself doubly blessed. You received what money's mostly good for, education and high culture, but your boundaries broadened. McLeod, who is determined to rise in the ranks by playing by every rule, is fairly obtuse. The malaprops, for instance. But I noticed you never flinch when he mangles the mother tongue. That's Southern, partly. But also cultured."

"I would appreciate your advice."

"Well, you've already surmised Jack is a raving egomaniac. What else do you need to know?"

"Your best advice."

"Watch your back."

"How long have you worked for the Bureau?"

"Eleven years," she said. "All of them in Seattle. My background is accounting; I'm a CPA. After eight years with white collar I didn't want to go to Quantico for personal reasons. Three years ago I requested victim's assistance. They complied. Other duties are thrown in occasionally, such as profiling."

I guessed she was a master at profiling. "How do you like this squad?"

"My father has a phrase: Eat for the hunger that's coming."

"Pardon?"

"Don't let yourself go empty. Keep some fuel in the tank."

"All right."

"Now, the VanAlstynes," she said, "they present a curious puzzle. Why the need for privacy when they're so worried their daughter has been kidnapped? Perhaps they've been victims of extortion in the past, and they don't want us or the public to know about it. I'll find out what I can, and I'll help you as much as possible, but . . ." She tilted her head, shrugging, the same gesture she gave about Mario. "After that, I'm hoping you'll know what to do."

≈

Friday rush hour began with a drive north to the University District. The sky had sealed itself with gray clouds that sank toward the horizon as though weighted with silver pellets. Just off Roosevelt Avenue, I found Mama Mia's Pizza, the plate-glass window jaundiced by cooking oil fumes.

Behind a chipped white counter, a clutch of Asian men wore clean green uniforms and chattered in their native language, paddling pizzas into the mouth of a false brick oven. Where Danato's smelled of Italy through the centuries, Mama Mia's smelled of wet cardboard, powdered milk, and bleached flour. A dozen teenagers waited at the counter, forking over ten bucks for an all-you-can-eat Friday buffet. Youth wasn't the only thing wasted on the young.

In the far back, I found Kermit Simms. He was wiping down a series of small round tables, the wrought-iron type found in French cafés, and when I introduced myself, the skin on his face turned a hue resembling the soiled rag in his damp hand.

"Do you have a moment?" I asked.

"What's this about anyway?"

"When was the last time you saw Courtney VanAlstyne?"

"I knew it. Her old man put you up to this. I haven't gone near her, so take a hike."

The teenagers pushed several tables together, scraping the iron legs across the beige linoleum that was gritty with soil. Kermit began tossing the dingy rag back and forth between his hands, his sinewy forearms twisting with each catch. He smiled suddenly, for no particular reason. "So, yeah, thanks for stopping by," he said.

"We're not done."

He glanced at the Asian men near the front door. They were hollering at each other in some foreign language as more teenagers streamed in the door.

"I got one minute," Kermit said. "That's it."

I followed him toward the bathrooms in back, where a chrome pay phone was bolted to a wall with names and numbers scrawled across it, including what looked like slate-blue eyeliner proclaiming "Lauren loves Chris."

"When was the last time you saw her?" I asked again.

The rag dangled from his fingers. "I just told you. Not for a while."

"What's a while, Kermit?"

"Two months, at least. You heard something else, it's a lie."

"Why would somebody lie about it?"

"You got wax in your ears? She broke up with me. I was upset. But I'm over her. History. Done. Take the *l* off lover, that's what we got."

"Why'd she take out the restraining order?"

"Her old man put her up to that! Marty VanAlstyne wanted it to be one mile, get the idea? Even the police said I got a right to get to classes like anybody else. I told you, the guy's just waiting to pounce. And have I bothered her? No."

"But you did. At one time."

"She broke up with me and wouldn't tell me why. I got a right to know why she was kicking me to the curb."

"Why was she?"

His neck was cabled with ligaments, steel cords holding the suspension bridge of his shoulders. "Normal people, people with class they let you down easy. But she's spoiled. That girl's nothing but a spoiled brat."

"Nobody's seen her since Sunday. Her parents are worried."

He paused. "Nobody's seen her?"

"She hasn't been home. She missed her classes. No phone calls. Any idea where she might be?"

He shook his head.

"I heard you two made trips to Vegas."

"You think I have something to do with this?" His face darkened. "Hey, she's a big girl. She can handle herself."

"You're sure?"

"Leave me alone."

"Was she in any trouble, Kermit?"

"Trouble?" He sneered. "Her daddy takes care of 'trouble.'"

"You mean like when an ex stalks her? That kind of trouble?"

His hand squeezed the rag, making a fist. "One night in Vegas I watched her run up a hundred and eighty grand in bad bets. When she couldn't pay, she called Daddy, and the next thing you know Steve Wynn's comping us another night at his casino. She's spoiled."

A burly college kid with a two-day skid of beard across his chin squeezed past us into a narrow door marked "Restaroom." When the bathroom door closed, Kermit lowered his voice.

"Look, unless you're arresting me, I don't have to talk to you."

Even if I were arresting him he didn't have to talk to me. But why ruin a good thing? I gave him my card, asked him to call if he thought of anything.

Anything, I wanted to add, that came to light under the torch he still carried for Courtney VanAlstyne.

chapter seven

The next day was Saturday, and in the morning Aunt Charlotte shuffled into the kitchen wearing a set of lustrous pajamas decorated with burnt sienna butterflies. The color matched her short auburn hair, stiff and dyed, flattened in back. She poured herself coffee, grabbed toasted bread made from unsprouted wheat, and plunked down at the turquoise table, letting out a sigh.

She asked me if I was sleeping all right.

Fine, I told her.

"Your mother's kind of a night owl, isn't she?"

"She keeping you up?"

"I'm just not used to noise at night. Living in the city, I start thinking we're having a break in."

"I'll talk to her about it."

"No, no," she said quickly. "Don't make her uncomfortable. I love having the both of you here. I was thinking maybe if she came to work in my store . . ."

"Give her something to do during the day?"

"That's the thought. My only concern is about the dog, here alone with the cats all day."

"Madame can come with me today. That's one down."

Her face brightened. "You can take your dog to work?"

"I'm hiking in Issaquah today."

Her face dropped. "For fun or for work?"

"Work."

She set down the mug. "Raleigh, you need one of my necklaces."

"No. Really."

"Where are you hiking?"

"Cougar Mountain."

"What don't you get?"

"About what?"

"Why they named it Cougar Mountain."

"Okay, why?"

"Cougars? Animals?" she said. "They attack."

"Again, this is the gun's job."

"You're walking around without any kind of spiritual protection."

I started to explain that I did have spiritual backup, but she held up the hand.

"Stop. Don't bother," she said. "Don't tell me who watches over you. Your mother already gave me that lecture, thank you very much. Fortunately, after twenty years in the Episcopal church, I'm immune to conversion."

≈

In the gravel parking lot where Courtney VanAlstyne's vehicle once sat, I studied the map of trails that snaked across Cougar Mountain, and I waited for Jack Stephanson. The trails crossed the hilly topography with a sort of meandering purpose, eventually leading to various overlooks and destinations. Pinned beside the map was a notice warning about bobcats, cougars, and bears.

Thirty minutes later, after Madame had investigated every

bit of flora in the parking area, I started up the trail without Jack. The autumn wind smelled of faded chlorophyll and sandy soil, and every gust sent yellow aspen leaves fluttering in slow spirals that landed on red-tipped ferns. But the narrow trail was rocky and without vistas, and I tried to imagine the long-legged child of privilege stepping over the rounded outcroppings of rock. After a mile I came to a fork in the trail, where a weathered wooden sign hammered to an oak tree pointed to the Clay Pit Road, the trail Stacee Warner mentioned. I took the turnoff, scanning the humus shoulders for disheveled leaves, stray footprints, one shred of evidence that might back up the kidnapping allegations of the VanAlstynes. Madame raced ahead.

I wondered again about the girl.

Did she climb to contemplate math theories? Did she relish conquering steep hills, ticking off the trails on her way to winning a bet with her roommate? And her parents, the man and woman at a bedroom table, tense and frightened, his competitive drive honed as buffed quartz. If the old boyfriend could be believed, the father knew his daughter took risks. Maybe his daughter assumed a net was always under her high-wire act.

But would that girl simply walk away?

"I found you!"

Madame barked. I jumped. My right hand reflexively reached for my Glock.

"I'm exhausted." The woman came up behind me, panting, then bent to Madame. "Oh, that's a good doggie. Good doggie. Yes, you're a nice doggie." She straightened. "I've been calling your name, 'Yoo-hoo, Raleigh.' Just about to go home. But now I've found you."

Her platinum blonde hair was cut into spikes that stood on her small head like asbestos fibers. Her facial features—tiny eyes, button nose, pink mouth shaped like a bow—gathered in the center of her face, as though fearing proximity to the hair. Her short legs were sheathed in bright red leggings, the elastic shining with the stretch.

"Do I know you?" I said.

"I'm Claire. Your aunt called me. She said you were out here by yourself with no protection." She stuck out her hand, a lump of clay. "I'm a clairvoyant."

"Excuse me?"

"Charlotte and me, we go way back." Panting between sentences, she unzipped a blue fanny pack that hung from her abdomen like a marsupial pouch. "Here's my card."

The card showed a drawing of a head, both eyes closed, with one open eye in the forehead. *Claire the Clairvoyant*, it read. *I see what you mean.*

"Charlotte Harmon sent you here?"

"Yuh-huh. You're in danger. Your aunt's getting a strong vibe of danger. And she thinks I can crack this case wide open."

"What case?"

"She said you're always in trouble with your bosses."

"Wait a minute. What did my aunt tell you?"

"You're looking for someone. Or something. She didn't know which, but I don't need much to put two and two together."

I handed back her card. "Thank you for your concern, Claire. If you're really interested in helping, contact the Issaquah police."

"The whole way up here I was picking up very strong signals. Definite harm, bodily harm. It's in the force fields. And fire."

"Fire?"

"Yuh-huh. I keep picking up the word *fire*."

"There's a drought."

She grabbed my arm, gasping.

"What's wrong?" I asked.

"Listen! Somebody's coming!" She released my arm and scrambled into the thick brush beside the dirt trail, kicking at the undergrowth of grass and fern and fallen leaves. When she crouched in the alder bushes, her crimson knees were skirted by red-tipped ferns.

"Get over here," she hissed. "Danger's coming!"

Madame trotted over to her, wagging her tail, ready to play the game. Claire shooed her away.

I continued to look down the trail, the wind gusting, the leaves filling with sibilant whispers. But the bend in the trail prevented me from seeing more than ten yards back.

Suddenly a man emerged. I heard Claire gasp.

Madame barked.

"Where've you been?" Jack Stephanson demanded. "And your cell phone—you turned it off?"

"It must not get a signal up here," I said.

Claire slogged from the sidelines, brushing fern fronds from her leggings. One red maple leaf clung to the shards of hair, a jaunty feather in a spiked cap.

"You *know* this guy?" she asked.

"Who's this?" Jack said.

Claire placed her hands on her hips. "I am Claire the Clairvoyant. Who are *you*?"

"None of your business."

She pointed at him, turning to me. "This is the dangerous force I was picking up. *He* took the person you're looking for."

"What?" Jack said.

"Dark energy is pouring out of him, Raleigh. See it? Oh! I can't breathe." She placed one hand over her heart, closing her eyes. She began to hum, a low monotonous tone like somebody imitating an electrical transformer.

"Who is this freak?" Jack asked.

"I am Claire the Clairvoyant." Her voice continued the monotone, her eyes still closed.

"Clairvoyant." Jack looked at me. "This is how you work?"

"She came out here by herself," I said.

Claire's blue eyes flashed open. "I'll have you know I've worked with detectives in Seattle. They all know Claire."

"I'll bet," Jack said.

"Claire, we appreciate your offer," I said, "But you need to leave."

"I understand much more than you do, Raleigh." Her eyes danced between my face and Jack's. "You will hear from me when the channels clear again. And I won't tell Charlotte about this . . . man. It will only worry her more. But you have my word. I will crack this case wide open."

She picked her way down the striated boulders and broken bark, moving like a red beetle afraid of getting dirty.

"Now why didn't I think of a clairvoyant?" Jack said.

"Somebody sent her out here."

"You're talking to people about your cases?"

"No."

"Must be how they work down South. Call the old ladies, see if their bunions hurt. Maybe the clairvoyant's a step up for you."

I counted to twenty—fifteen never being long enough—but Jack jumped into the silence. .

"You said K-9's already been through here."

"Yes, but they couldn't get a continuous scent. The dog ran in circles. The girl was on the trail, then she was gone."

"Abducted by aliens," he said. "Write up the 302 on the whack job and pass the case to the CIA. That'll impress the rich parents. Put some spooks on the trail."

"Jack, go home."

"Harmon, I get it. Barbie didn't call her parents and they're worried. But some rich girl deciding to run away doesn't rank with terrorists who want to wipe out thousands of people in a split second. When the entire town of North Bend gets nuked by some crazy Arab, see what kind of calls McLeod gets from headquarters."

I started up the trail, Madame fell in beside me.

"Yeah," he said to my back, "go find Barbie. Forget the terrorists, they're a figment of my imagination. I'm leaving. Good luck, Raleigh."

"I don't believe in luck," I said over my shoulder.

"Figures," he said.

≈

Two hours later I still wasn't ready to surrender and admit Jack Stephanson might be right. And the very real possibility that he was kept me hiking the mountain trails until the sky turned dark opal and gold leaked out of aspens. My eyes ached from watching loose rocks under my feet. Madame's dark shape was nearly invisible, her movements heard among the ferns rather than seen. She rustled out the juncos and robins who chirped the close of day, and when a soft rain began to fall, it was more mist than anything. My mind wandered, traveling from Courtney VanAlstyne to Jack Stephanson to Claire the Clairvoyant to whether Jack would report her weird appearance to McLeod. My heart clutched with anger, at all the relentless hazing, this disciplinary status, this unwanted move west. Harsh words filled my mind, fierce retorts that would put Jack in his place, and just then my right heel slid across wet rock and I fell, landing on my back, the hard ground shoving the air out of my lungs.

For several moments, I lay still, feeling my tailbone throb. And my fingers burned, the skin raked by a branch I tried to grab on the way down. When Madame ran over, licking my face, I rolled on my side and crawled to stand. There was a massive scrape on my right thigh, numb, just beginning to bleed. My breath came ragged. For several moments I stood still, trying to gather myself. I looked around at the trees and my first thought was that I was seeing just another leaf. An odd autumn leaf. But even in the failing light, the color didn't look right. It wasn't red or orange or yellow. It was white. And blue. When I stepped closer, I saw the knot cinching the fabric to the branch. It was one turn, hastily tied. The fabric's edges frayed from fresh ripping.

Adrenaline pumped through my heart as I pulled a pair of latex gloves from my back pocket, snapping them on my stinging fingers. I dropped the fabric swatch into an evidence bag and searched the area, found nothing more, then carefully made my way to the parking lot.

A dusty white Corolla with a radiating crack across the windshield was parked ten feet from the trailhead. The car hadn't been there this morning, and I hadn't seen anyone on the trail. I took down the license number, just in case, then I drove into Seattle.

The Metro buses ran empty down abandoned streets, looking destined for ghost towns, and a spittle of rain fell on my windshield, barely enough for wipers. Below the FBI office the garage was empty and I took a spot marked for visitors, cracking the windows and telling Madame to stay. I rode the elevator to the Violent Crimes unit, similarly purged for the weekend. I boxed soil samples from the trail, then e-mailed a former colleague in the mineralogy lab in DC, notifying him about the soil coming through Bureau mail.

To my surprise, Eric Duncan e-mailed back.

I dialed the lab long distance. He picked up on the second ring.

"What are you doing in there on a Saturday night?" I asked.

"I could ask you the same thing," he said.

Eric Duncan had worked in the mineralogy lab for more than twenty years, not all of them by choice. About ten years ago, he went to Quantico to become a special agent. But during his second week of training, he noticed his left hand losing strength. Before long he was struggling to wash his hair. Bureau physicians ran a battery of tests and Eric Duncan was diagnosed with early stage Multiple Sclerosis. He returned to the mineralogy lab. When I left the lab for Quantico, he was my biggest cheerleader.

"You saw my e-mail," I said. "I'm working. What's your excuse?"

"I'm cleaning out my desk. Monday's my last day."

"What?"

"When you came up here this summer, you saw the crutches. I said the wheelchair was next—"

"But—"

"Raleigh, when they built this behemoth of a building, the government didn't hire cripples. You think my MS is waiting around for the Bureau to match the Americans with Disabilities Act?"

I searched for words. My mind came up empty.

"Did you read my e-mail?" he asked.

"Yes."

"The guy's in Spokane, which, unlike the rest of the East Coast, I realize is on the other side of the state. I can even pronounce it correctly. He's an excellent geologist, among the best at forensics. Send him your samples. Better yet, drive out and meet him." He paused. "How's the move anyway?"

"I saw rain today."

"What I'd give for a walk in the rain."

"I didn't mean—"

"No, you didn't mean that. And I'm not feeling sorry for myself."

"Really?"

"Maybe just a little."

We laughed, but my heart was filled with an aching sensation. I swallowed. "Eric, I'm really sorry this is happening to you."

He was sighing, I thought.

But after several long moments, when all I heard was air moving, air crossing an invisible network of wires from one side of the continent to the other, I felt my heart open. And the feeling seemed more real, more tangible, than the phone I held in my hand.

≈

When Aunt Charlotte moved to Seattle, she carried with her a massive financial payoff from an alcoholic ex-husband. Her departure was preferable to a nasty public divorce concerning infidelity and physical abuse on the husband's part, particularly when Charlotte's brother sat on Virginia's Superior Court, roundly admired by every attorney in town.

Several years later she opened a small store called Seattle Stones, which I always assumed was a geological store, the same way that I mistook the pink tourmaline at my father's funeral. But just after 6:00 p.m. on Saturday, I walked down University Avenue, five blocks south of Mama Mia's pizza, and followed three slouchy teenagers through the door of Seattle Stones. A series of Himalayan mule bells rang as the door opened, startling one of the slouchers to grab at his jeans, which were the size of elephant feed bags.

"Raleigh!" Aunt Charlotte said. "Nadine, look, it's Raleigh."

My mother was packing a corrugated brown box, wearing a circle of tape like a bracelet. Around her neck was a series of polished red stones. She offered me a smile.

One of the teenagers scuffed to the glass counter where Aunt Charlotte stood extinguishing a stick of incense. He stared down into the glass, the halogen lights illuminating displays of geodes and amulets and silver jewelry twisted around crystals. When he looked up, his blue eyes were stagnant ponds surrounded by rivulets of blood.

"You got any, like, paraphernalia?" he said.

"Sure do," said Aunt Charlotte. "All my paranormal stuff is in that far corner. UFOs, telekinetics, it's all there. And check out that moon rock. Looks exactly like the Montana granite next to it, which just goes to prove we never were on the moon."

He blinked. A slow blink. A momentary hiccup in a brain medicated for deep sleep.

"No, um, smoke stuff?"

"Séance candles come in next week. Just in time for Halloween."

I watched his mind click into gear. He shifted his red eyes toward the other two who were curled like fossil ammonites over the moon rock and matching Montana granite. At his signal they walked out the door, in search of a real bong shop.

"That happen often?" I asked.

"Not having what somebody wants?"

"Never mind." There was no polite way to explain that the sign outside could be read "Seattle Stoned."

"Last week," she said, "I had a woman come in asking about kitchens. She thought I sold granite countertops. I told her, 'Honey, granite is for sissies. What you need is some nephrite. That'll get you cooking.'"

Around 6:30 p.m., Aunt Charlotte closed the shop and I followed her wheezing black Volvo wagon home, driving down Montlake Boulevard, reading her tailgate bumper stickers that looked like a political version of Tourette's Syndrome. Sharp declarations about animal testing, war, authority, and women who needed men like fish needed bicycles, a sentiment that made no sense to me since aquatic life would be a whole lot more interesting on wheels.

We drove up the east side of Capitol Hill, and as soon as we got home I climbed into the claw-footed bathtub upstairs, soaking with my eyes closed until my muscles released. When the water cooled I dried off, wrapped myself in a robe, and fell on the bed, hair wet on the pillow.

My memory of the details surrounding my father's murder had a staccato quality, like misshapen chips knocked off a large tumbling boulder. I remembered working at my desk in the FBI's mineralogy lab, a plagioclase specimen resting under my microscope. And I remembered the phone ringing. But my next memory was sitting in a car outside my parents' house in Richmond. How I got there, who drove, it was lost to me. So were the words spoken during the memorial service. Yet I could still recall the white hands of the mortician at Bliley's Funeral Home, the bird-shaped tie tack he wore, and most clearly of all, a series of extended nights on the couch in the den, wrapped in my father's favorite sweaters, breathing his warm, safe scent and realizing that with every passing second, the scent was fading.

And after my bath, I had a dream in which my father appeared so vividly I later doubted it was a dream. He was standing in the forest I had just hiked, his arms open. He was smiling, about to say something, when Aunt Charlotte walked into my bedroom.

"Did I wake you?" she asked.

"What's wrong?"

She wore an expectant expression, like someone who offered a present and wanted to hear the recipient's gratitude.

"Aunt Charlotte, about Claire . . ."

"Raleigh, she once told me something was wrong in my house and right there Beryl choked on a hairball."

"Beryl, the cat?"

"She went into cardiac arrest."

"Claire?"

"Beryl. I started screaming and Claire just picked her up, laid her on the table and started CPR. She blew the breath of life into that animal. I'm telling you that woman can sense trouble. That's why I asked her to go find you."

"I appreciate the thought, but Claire's interfering with my work."

She drew herself up. "What do you mean?"

"She's a civilian, Aunt Charlotte. She can compromise an investigation." I didn't have the energy to explain how defense attorneys salivated over something like this. And the media that seized any opportunity to make the Bureau look chaotic or cracked. "Please don't ask her to help me."

In the broad plain above her eyes, I saw my father's face, his thoughtful countenance. But then she looked away, staring at the bookcase directly across from the bed. The smell of incense from her store, an oily musk, clung to her cerulean blue tunic.

"Actually, I'm more concerned about your mother right now," she said.

I froze. "Why is that?"

"This morning she told me her spirit's dying. I said, 'Honey, you come work with me at the store. It'll lift your mood.' You know, like we said, give her something to do. I thought she was enjoying herself today, meeting people, helping ship orders. But in the car on the way home she asked if I wanted to go to church with her. 'Nadine,' I said, 'I haven't set foot in a church since David died and I only went in there because he was my brother.' After what the Episcopals put me through with my divorce? No more."

"Where is she now?" I pushed myself off the bed.

"She's putting on fancy clothes. Now I ask you, what kind of a church holds Saturday night services?"

≈

I drove the rusting black Volvo down Broadway, feeling the warmth from my bath dissipate into a misty rain that shrouded street lights and produced amber halos like visible half-lives of radioactive minerals. On the sidewalks, men and women clad in fleece and jeans talked and laughed and ducked into restaurants. Nobody carried an umbrella.

Except my mother. I parked on Fifteenth Avenue and locked Aunt Charlotte's car, running to catch up to the umbrella that was a brutal shade of orange, a napalmed Caribbean sunset, that matched the flame-hued toreador pants and the high heels that gave her a mincing step.

"The sign said it's a Holy Spirit church," she told me. "I was driving by with Charlotte the other day and realized I'm suffering a bad case of the ordinaries."

"I'm sorry to hear that."

"Have you noticed how people dress in this city? It's like living inside the L.L.Bean catalogue."

"I like L.L.Bean."

"Please, do not tell me that. Those clothes are for women who can't dance."

A rainbow of tempera paint smothered the front window, the finger-painted words proclaiming "He lives!" The aluminum edge of the window was torn, as though pried with a screwdriver, and next door was a Thai restaurant where a homeless man slumped against the building. He looked as if he had fainted on the spot. I opened the church door and my mother closed her umbrella, shaking loose the light mist of rain. For several moments, she stared at the homeless man, then walked in her tiny steps to where he lay and tucked dollar bills into his torn coat pocket. The man never stirred. As we stepped inside the church, I could smell curry and lemongrass and the moist troubled breath of people who have been crying. The room was crowded with swaying bodies and lifted arms and voices singing "Holy, holy, holy."

"Thank you, Jesus!" somebody shouted.

My mother handed me the umbrella and clicked toward the front of the crowd. I took a seat in back on a metal folding chair, stretching my feet out. The row in front of me was empty.

My father used to say there were two kinds of people in the world: those who believed in coincidence, and those who had the courage to recognize God. Believing in coincidence, he said, was like a baby in its crib, staring up at a mobile, continually surprised by the objects that floated past. The person who recognized God also admired the beauty of the mobile, but with a more refined perception; they acknowledged the same delight while realizing that such order only comes from creative design.

So I should not have been surprised when the tinny electric organ died down and the crowd swayed to repeating refrains in minor keys and the preacher began speaking about water. He was a man of indeterminate age. Thirty, perhaps fifty. This preacher's brown skin was soft and pliable and his dark eyes shone with a luminosity often seen in small children. He wore pale blue slacks, and his determined strides crossed the abbreviated room, his arms flying as he thanked God for the rain, for a break in the drought, for whatever fell from the sky.

"The Bible says rain is a blessing," he said. "And it says drought is a curse. Most of the time Seattle is very, very blessed."

"Amen!" somebody hollered.

"But this city's been operating under a curse. That's why we had us a drought. We got to pray through the spiritual battle."

"Tell it, preacher!"

"That's right, I'm tellin' it. And I'm gonna remind you tonight about water, about the blessing of water. Because no matter what the weather, no matter rain or no rain, we got water that don't never run dry. And to get that water, all you gotta do is *believe*. That's right. Believe. When the rivers run dry, you call on him. He fills you up again. Can I hear an amen?"

"Amen!"

My mother's hand shot up, the familiar gold jewelry sparkling, her fingers splaying like a student with the correct answer. She cried, "Amen!"

"Jesus came to that woman at the well," the preacher said, "and how did he talk to her? Did he say, 'You filthy Samarian, go on home'? Did he say, 'How dare you take five husbands, what's wrong with you?' No, he didn't shame that woman for her life."

"Praise Jesus!"

"Jesus said, 'Woman, go ahead, get some water from this here well. And after you drink it, you gonna be thirsty all over again.' Because that's how it works with earthly things: you get some, then you want more. Jesus said, 'I am the *living* water. You believe in me, you won't never thirst again. That drought in your soul? That place inside where the rivers run dry? I'll wash it clean and you won't *ever* thirst again.'"

"Hallelujah!"

"God is good!"

"Now, let me ask you," said the preacher, lowering his voice, "which of those waters you gonna choose?"

"Gimme the good water!"

And then the preacher's voice stretched out all the syllables, his tone rising and falling, hill and valley and hill again, and within his voice I heard the South, a background in Alabama or Georgia. I glanced at my mother. She was enraptured.

I closed my eyes.

"I'm telling you, you gotta choose," the preacher was saying. "You gotta choose where you get your water. Don't be relying on some weatherman. He can't quench your thirst. It don't work like that. You gotta call on *the one*, you gotta ask for the *living* water. And guess what? He's gonna carry it to you!"

The organ hit a high note and when I opened my eyes, the crowd's arms were waving. I could still see my mother's black curls, bouncing between the brown limbs. She was praising God, shaking off the ordinaries, and I knew there was no coincidence between this moment and the one two nights ago when I held a Gideon Bible in my hands and read this same story while Felicia

Kunkel snored in the next bed. And still I felt the powerful undertow of coincidence tugging at my mind, a temptation to chalk everything up to accident. I yearned for rational fact, for certainty. It was the reason my father felt compelled to tell me about the two kinds of people in this world.

I closed my eyes again. The preacher kept going, hours left in him. I listened to people sing out "Hallelujah!" and "Amen!" and the melodic voices of black people washed over me, rinsing away some of my homesickness, carrying me back, way back, all the way back to Virginia.

chapter eight

On Sunday morning, my mother slept in and I found Aunt Charlotte in the parlor, sitting in a green wing chair, reading the *Seattle Times*. The cats slumbered in her lap and the paper was draped over the high wing behind her right ear. The floor around her feet looked like the bottom of a birdcage. Rather than disturb the cats, she was releasing the paper as she finished the stories, letting it sail to the floor before reaching behind for another section.

"Good morning," I said.

"Good morning." She held out her coffee cup. "Get me another cup? I don't want to disturb the cats."

I was in the kitchen when the phone rang.

"I'm busy!" Aunt Charlotte called out.

I picked up the phone. "Hello?"

"Did you find anything on Cougar Mountain?" Jack asked.

I blew across the dark surface of my coffee. "What do you care?"

"I don't, actually," he admitted. "But make sure you check with your clairvoyant. Maybe she got a signal from space."

"Jack, what do you want?"

He wanted to know whether I'd seen the videotape of Osama bin Laden, the one where he's sitting in front of a gray rock. "Yes,

I've seen it." The tape showed the terrorist leader looking like a malevolent third-world shepherd expounding on why the West must be wiped off the map and Israel shoved into the sea. "The tape came out after 9/11."

"Yeah, that's the one," he said. "I heard a geologist watched that tape and pinpointed bin Laden's location in Afghanistan, just by those rocks behind him."

"That's true."

"I need you to get to North Bend," he said. "I'll be waiting in the parking lot at Mount Si."

Then he hung up.

I replaced the phone, leaning against the kitchen counter for several long moments considering my options. When I picked up my coffee, it tasted cold.

"Raleigh," my aunt called out. "How's that coffee coming?"

≈

Mount Si stood like a geologic outburst, a dark and looming rock that rose more than four thousand feet from the middle of a placid green valley where farmers once grew hops. The evident release of an invisible fault line, Mount Si's western end had the craggy face of an ill-tempered barrister, his misshapen head graduating to a humpback on the eastern end where an evergreen forest extended to the Cascade Mountains.

The day was bright, with clouds high and distant as wisps, and I decided the best way to deal with weather in the Northwest was to remember mood swings of a manic depressive. At the base of Mount Si, I parked next to Jack's Jeep and turned off the engine. The car knocked, shook, hissed, and I waited until the convulsions were over before opening the door. Madame leaped out.

Jack stood at his black Jeep, his wide back blocking the sun.

On the Jeep's seamed hood lay one quadrant of a USGS map. I stood beside him. He didn't turn, he didn't speak.

"Jack?"

"The dog again. You take that mutt on all your assignments?"

"Fake some gratitude. I'm here. On a Sunday."

He folded the map. The trailhead's path was strewn with dry needles that crunched softly under my boots, releasing a crisp scent of pine. My muscles still ached from yesterday's hike, each step tight, kneading lactic acid through my legs, and within minutes Jack's back had disappeared. I struggled to climb the mountain's face, a series of switchbacks crossing higher into the forest. After the first mile, the trees' emerald boughs changed to lean brown trunks, the bark stripped and polished. Sunlight carved into the woods, flickering between the thin stands, and when I finally caught Jack, it was at the two-mile mark. He was flinging bright cusps of tangerine peel toward the brown trees. I pulled the water bottle from my pack, hands shaking, and filled a nylon dog dish I'd brought for Madame, setting it on the ground. She lapped until the water was gone, then turned for the shade, panting.

From this plateau, I could see the town of North Bend below. Train tracks curved through lush fields, houses gathered on narrow country roads that wandered like river tributaries. The small town had a peaceful appearance, like a Christmas village waiting for its first snow.

"Nice place, huh?" Jack said.

I nodded.

"That's why the nut jobs want to blow it up." He finished chewing, ran the tip of his tongue over his white teeth, and told me that several weeks ago a hiker was coming down the trail at dusk just as some men were starting to climb up.

"It's almost dark," he said, "and these guys are hiking up the trail from the bottom. Weird enough, but it gets weirder. They walked in twos, each pair spaced about ten minutes apart. The hiker coming down sees one set, then another, and another."

They wore synthetic slacks and collared shirts buttoned high, he said, and the soles of their street shoes slipped on the steep path. They carried large aluminum-frame packs, the weight of which caused them to lean forward like men moving pianos, sweating profusely.

"Pay attention to this last detail, Harmon. It's important. They were all Middle Eastern. Every single one of them."

He waited for my response. I reached down, pouring more water into Madame's bowl. "What's this got to do with me, Jack?"

"The hiker gets to the parking lot. No cars. Not one. The bus doesn't run out here. Are you catching my drift?"

"I'm not playing twenty questions with you, Jack. Tell me what you need."

"Shoulder-launched missiles dismantle into small pieces that fit in backpacks. The summit of this mountain puts a shooter one mile closer to air traffic. If this still isn't rattling your brain, think about the flight pattern from New York or DC into Sea-Tac. It crosses right over North Bend. Taking down a commercial jet from here is like picking off ducks at the penny arcade. Imagine how many extra virgins they get for wiping out the infidels."

I closed my water bottle, placing it in my pack. "What do you need from me?"

"I want a lynchpin for this case. I want evidence linking the suspects to this summit, just like that geologist did with bin Laden. They say you're a smart girl. Figure it out."

Forty minutes later I reached the summit of Mount Si, a

desolate cone of metamorphic rock, wind-stripped and ice-sheared. Jack stood beside a haystack-shaped precipice, the village below looking distant as if seen through the wrong end of a telescope.

"Over here," he said.

I walked across the loose gray rocks to the haystack formation then kneeled for a closer look. The rocks' sharp edges dug into my knee. This was tortured earth, rock that had been heated, cooled, sheared, and fractured, all before it was exposed to summit weather. Geologists would label this stuff *mélange*—the French word for *mixture*—because it contained everything from pale markers of marine sediment to dense volcanic crystals. And it was friable, eroded by the elements. I took several samples, placing them in an evidence bag.

"This too," Jack said.

I walked over. On the ground near his feet, scraps of what appeared to be an old fire huddled in the jagged rocks, the twigs as wiry as pipe tobacco. I kneeled again, collecting pieces, wondering if this fire was just somebody's bad attempt at a romantic moment. As I was collecting the pieces, Madame came around my side, licking my hand. I gently pushed her away.

But she came around the other side. Again, she licked my hand.

"Is that dog going to contaminate my evidence?" Jack asked.

"Go on, girl," I said.

But Madame would not quit.

She pushed her snout under my forearm, raising her head, flicking my hand off the rocks.

"Madame, stop it!" My voice was harsh and she ran away, her claws scrabbling across the loose stones. I watched her turn behind the haystack outcropping. She started barking.

"Here's what I'm having trouble with," Jack said. "You're on assignment and you bring a clairvoyant, and you bring the dog—"

"I didn't bring the clairvoyant. And the dog won't hurt anything."

I marked the evidence bag, placing it inside my pack, then stood. Madame was still barking from behind the rock, a sound that the wind captured and threw off the side of the mountain.

"What's her problem?" Jack said, seething.

I walked across the stones, around the haystack, and found Madame at the summit's lone tree. It had spindly limbs, the lopsided appearance of a divining rod, a shape cultivated by wind and rain and snow.

"Madame, quiet," I said.

But she continued to bark. I saw a small bird, its dark talons clutching one of the tree's emaciated branches.

"Madame, hush."

At the sound of my voice, the bird tilted its head, the lidless eyes like polished ebony. It did not fly away as I approached. Its charcoal gray feathers were camouflage among the rocks. At the breast, the feathers turned white as fog.

"That's a Camp Robber." Jack came up behind me. "Just a stupid gray jay but they'll steal a sandwich out of your hand."

I stepped closer. The bird tilted its head again, black eyes clicking over the scene. Something cracked under my feet, the bird flew away.

"I might've guessed," Jack said, "you'd be the first person to scare one of those birds."

I glanced down, trying to see what I'd stepped on. The fragments gathered between the rocks, a sandy detritus produced by erosion. But when I kneeled down, I could see plastic pieces, their concave fractures forming along unnatural planes. I picked up a piece. Madame licked my wrist again.

"You better say something nice about my dog." I held out the plastic fragments.

He leaned down, placing his large hands on his knees. I collected pieces of burnt plastic and dented shell casings, and when I lifted a pile of rocks behind the haystack that were gathered in a mound that defied gravity and erosion, I found a black plastic bag. The corners were sealed with duct tape. I cut it open with a pen knife and held it out for Jack to inspect.

He tapped his fingers against the granules, rubbing the substance between his fingertips before touching it to the tip of his tongue.

"Gunpowder," he said.

I looked at Madame. She wagged her tail.

"She's a search dog," he said. "Why didn't you say so?"

chapter nine

D ry volcanic basalt drawled all the way across eastern Washington and on Monday morning I drove across it on Interstate 90, headed for the forensic geologist in Spokane. I carried with me the torn piece of fabric and the soil samples from Cougar Mountain, along with Jack's evidence for counterterrorism from Mount Si.

Although the highway ran straight as string across the desert, I could feel the road lifting and lowering, the rise so gentle, the descent so quiet that most people probably missed it. But those subtle shifts marked an earth-shaking scientific controversy, one that crystallized my views about science and man, and how we pursue the truth.

For most of the twentieth century, geologists assumed gradual erosion over millions of years created the landscape of eastern Washington. The relatively flat desert is interrupted by dramatic canyons, or what the locals call coulees. The most famous one was sealed with rebar and concrete, then filled with water—the Grand Coulee Dam. These channels extended for miles and stretched hundreds of feet across.

Only one geologist disagreed with the theory of gradual erosion. His name was J Harlan Bretz, an individualist who rejected punctuation with his first initial. Bretz held a PhD in geology from the University of Chicago and spent years studying eastern Washington. In 1929 he concluded that the coulees could only have been formed by a catastrophic flood because the sides were almost perpendicular and the bottoms were wide and flat, not narrow winding channels produced by slow trickling water. Bretz thought the flood came quickly and carved the solid basalt within days, maybe even hours.

By all accounts, Bretz was not a professing Christian—he never mentioned Noah—but every scientist in the world suddenly characterized him as a crackpot, heaping peer-reviewed abuse on his flood theory. But decades later, when aerial photographs were taken of the area, engineers noticed how the solid land rippled. The waves in the rock couldn't be seen from the ground, but from the sky the evidence was obvious. A lot of water crossed the Columbia Plateau, all at once. When the engineers calculated the hydraulics necessary to cut several hundred feet through solid rock, one solid estimate was a million cubic feet of water—per second. Water that could toss forty-foot boulders like Ping-Pong balls.

Bretz's evidence, it turned out, was impeccable, and geologists started putting the pieces of the puzzle together. A massive glacier once blanketed what is now western Montana, but the glacier had melted suddenly—nobody knew why—and now they realized where all that melt went. It was as if a giant bucket had been tipped on its side, a flood bursting across the Columbia Plateau, cutting basalt like a buzz saw.

And it happened in hours. Not millions of years.

J Harlan Bretz was ninety-six years old when he was awarded the Penrose Medal, geology's highest honor, and now as I stared out my windshield, watching sagebrush tumble across a desert with no evidence of moisture, I was reminded of the crucial characteristic linking my science work in the lab to my work as an agent in the field. Preconceived notions were not my friend; they were my avowed enemy; they blinded me to the truth. Six days had passed since anybody had seen Courtney VanAlstyne, and I no longer discounted any theory about what happened to her, including her parents' idea that she could have been kidnapped.

At the exit for Eastern Washington University, I drove past an empty football stadium, circled behind it, and parked outside a corrugated steel building. Inside, I offered my ID to the guard at the front desk and walked under exposed air ducts that ran along the ceiling. Beside the door marked Microanalysis Unit, a tall man with a black moustache waited. He wore cowboy boots and offered his right hand. It was the size of a baseball mitt.

"Howdy, I'm Peter Rosser," he said. "How ya doin'?"

The lab was filled with the natural weapons of enemy-occupied territory: samples of minerals, tree barks, leaves, seeds, pollen, animal pelts, paw prints, and a series of ropes that hung from the ceiling made of cotton and hemp.

"Nice lab," I said.

"When your state gets to tax Microsoft and Starbucks, you wind up with a surplus on the books." He grinned. "For a while, at least."

We walked toward the back of the lab, passing a stainless steel table with a car door propped against sawhorses. The door was riddled with bullet holes, and plastic straws had been shoved through the holes to show ballistic angles of entry and exit. Behind the door, a crash test dummy sat on a vinyl bench seat wearing a beanie.

"Let's see what ya got." Rosser threw me a raft of paper.

I signed the custody and release forms, telling him which samples were urgent. He opened each bag, marked the contents and case numbers, then poured each sample into a separate stack of sieves before locking the canisters together. They looked like brass wedding cakes. Opening a door under his desk, he slipped the first stack into the shaker, then flipped the switch. He turned to me.

"Eric Duncan says you're a forensic geologist."

"I was. I went to Quantico, now I'm a special agent."

"You're still a rock head." He grinned. "Most people gawk at the ropes. I saw you rubbernecking the minerals."

"Guilty."

"Why'd you leave the lab?" he asked.

"There were good days, when I couldn't believe they paid me to look at rocks all day." I hesitated.

"But?"

"But the stories behind the rocks got to me. I decided to help find some happy endings."

"So how's that working?" He tugged on the end of his moustache.

Before I could answer, the sifter beeped and Rosser turned, opening the door. He took out the canister, replacing it with another, turning the machine on again. He was lost to the puzzle before him, no longer needing a reply. I waited as he carried the soil to a picture window on the north side of the room, writing down corresponding colors and textures, before extracting one sample and placing it on a glass slide. He slipped it under the Polarizing Light Microscope. Since the scope was attached to his computer monitor, I could see the minerals forming a reverse view of the night sky, black stars sparkling against a white background. Rosser wrote down the details.

When he finished, he carried the torn fabric into a small back room. It was filled with peculiar sounds—whirs and squeals of refrigerators working overtime—and he cut a small piece from the cloth and placed it on a stub of carbon adhesive no wider than a pencil eraser. When he slid it into the Scanning Electron Microscope, the Gateway monitor jumped to life. A colored bar graph, the X-ray analysis, showed various chemical elements divided into relative ratios. The chemicals were S, Fe, and As.

"Sulfur, iron, arsenic," Rosser said. "Hey, check out that arsenic ratio. You got longitude and latitude for this stuff?"

"No, but I can show you the quadrant on the map. I was on Cougar Mountain."

Back at his desk, he pushed aside blood splatter samples turning brown from oxidation, and opened a map drawer, pulling out the Issaquah Quadrangle. He ran his finger down the right side, where the text explained the rock formations.

"Yep, what I thought." He looked up. "Bituminous coal, which accounts for the high sulfur content. And a trace of arsenic."

"Trace," I repeated. "That wasn't what I saw on the X-ray. The arsenic ratio was pretty high."

"You see the problem already. There's enough arsenic on that fabric to poison a Clydesdale. The stuff on Cougar Mountain usually isn't that potent."

I stared at the DMV dummy, sitting behind the shot-out door. Somebody had drawn hair on the cottony chest. "Any idea where the arsenic might come from?"

He twirled the ends of his moustache. "There are some old mine shafts up there."

"Mine shafts."

"Cougar Mountain had a lot of coal mining, way back at the turn of the century. But the shafts are all closed."

"Anything else?"

He shook his head. "I wish I could give you an answer, but . . ."

But the truth exceeded an easy reach.

"You want me to run this other sample now?" he asked.

He meant Jack's evidence, the rocks and gunpowder from Mount Si. I told him yes and waited for some of the preliminary findings, enough information to get Jack off my back for a while. The other tests—tracing the manufacturer of the plastic, sourcing the gunpowder—that hunt would take more time.

Before I left, I asked Rosser for a piece of the fabric.

"You want to send it to the Bureau lab in DC?" he asked.

"I trust your analysis," I said.

He twirled the moustache, watching me. "Hoping to find some match in the field, that it?"

I nodded.

"You never know," he said. "You never know."

≈

On the drive back to Seattle, I tried to think of all the ways arsenic could creep into ordinary life, anything that might explain how that much arsenic got on a piece of fabric tied to a tree on the mountain where a girl had gone missing.

Back in the old days, arsenic was used for rat poison. Today, ammunition factories added arsenic to bullets, fortifying the ammo. What also bothered me was the sulfur. Left alone, arsenic wasn't terribly poisonous. But the mineral paired up in some of the most toxic marriages on Earth, and if arsenic combined with sulfur, even small doses were deadly.

When my cell phone rang, I was grateful for the distraction.

Until I flipped the phone open. Jack.

"Harmon, where are you?"

"I'm on my way back from Spokane."

"Spokane, who told you to go there?"

"I took the soil samples to the state geologist. He gave us an expedite. I've got trace evidence on your Mount Si material."

He paused. I thought that would shut him up.

Not for long. "How far are you from Seattle?" he asked.

"The last exit said something about Lake Chelan."

"You're hours away."

"So?"

"So what're you doing—taking the scenic route?"

"No, Jack, I'm driving a car. Wonder Woman's invisible plane wasn't available. What's so urgent?"

"It's Felicia."

I waited. A green Suburban passed on my left. I flicked on my blinker, stepping on the gas, slipping in behind the speeder because Felicia had done something horrendous and it would get pinned on me. I watched the speedometer hit 65, then 70, then I realized how long it had been since he'd said anything.

"Hello, Jack? Are you there?"

"Yes." His voice sounded as flat as the desert beyond my windshield.

I felt a stab of panic. "Let me have it, Jack."

"She's gone."

I leaned forward, gripping the steering wheel so tightly my knuckles turned white. Another exit washed past my right window.

"Gone where?" I said.

"She's just gone, I don't know where."

When it hit me, when I realized what was happening, I felt a wave of relief—followed by a mean temptation to torture Jack.

"Wait, Jack Stephanson cares? You're worried about her. That's what this is about?"

"Knock it off, Harmon." His voice still sounded flat, but now there was something mean beneath it, like molten magma ready to blow. "We need Felicia for appeals, that's all. Find her. Tonight. Don't bother coming into the office unless you locate her."

Then he hung up.

chapter ten

I decided Jack was serious about finding Felicia and when I
reached the town of Snoqualmie, I pulled off the interstate
and followed the big neon signs that filled the dusky sky
with a strange orange light.

If there was one thing I knew about addicts, it was that their
habits exerted supernatural force over their lives. It was the dinner hour when I walked into the casino, and men in oversized
T-shirts clouded the poker and blackjack tables, leaning their
elbows on the green felt, their eyes glazed with interior motives.
I circled the area twice before heading over to the slot machines.
They ran in phalanxes of chrome and glass and ringing bells, and
when the long levers were pulled they sounded like trapdoors
opening. Brass tokens tumbled through the machinery in metallic waterfalls, pooling in hollow steel baskets that amplified the
sound of money. I found Felicia in the third row.

With one arm, she clutched a white paper bucket, her plump
bottom swelling like pillows on either side of the chair. I waited
for her to finish a losing bid, then tapped her on the shoulder.

She didn't turn. She reached for an empty glass beside the
machine and held it out, eyes fixed on the rolling figures. "Rum
and coke with a cherry," she said.

When her glass wasn't taken, she turned around.

"Oh. It's you." She went back to the machine, setting down the glass, staring at the bright triptych of loss. "What're you doing here?"

I told her Jack wanted to talk to her.

"The last person I want to talk to is Jack Stephanson," she said.

I understood the sentiment but held my tongue. "Felicia, he just wants to know you're okay. Are you?"

She took one brass token from the white bucket and rolled it into the machine. I didn't even bother watching. I glanced along the row where an elderly woman three stools down was pulling the long lever with an arthritic hand. She let go and covered her mouth, coughing wetly, a deep rheumy cough that didn't sound finished. Her silver and turquoise rings depicted ancient tribal symbols—the Thunderbird, the Raven—and when her spin came up empty, she rolled another coin into the machine.

"How'd you find me?" Felicia asked.

I held up the plastic disk. "Remember? You gave it to me in the courtroom. You were going to quit drinking and get your kids back."

She sucked in her lower lip and yanked the lever, hard. It swung up, calm and slow.

Ace . . . Ace . . . Ace.

A red siren on top of the machine ignited. The light whipped crimson beams around the room. And brass tokens tumbled, plummeting into the hollow tray. Felicia's eyes were bright as cut gems, her lips pulled back into a smile that revealed all her missing teeth. But the other players weren't smiling. Their faces held level expressions, like people sensing betrayal.

"Yeah, baby!" Felicia cried.

She scooped the tokens into the bucket, the coins hitting the paper bottom with a sound like a snare drum, then slithering over each other like glittery chimes. Lifting herself off the stool, she walked down the aisle, head held high, and carried the bucket to a bullet-proofed kiosk at the far end of the casino. An emaciated Native American man dumped the tokens into a mechanical counter that spit out a paper receipt. He extracted $25 from a drawer, sliding the two bills toward Felicia under a thick partition of bulletproof Plexiglas. His bony fingers did not release the bills until Felicia picked them up.

She turned to me, grinning. "I'm going to buy you a cheeseburger."

"That's not necessary."

"But I want to."

"Hang on to your money."

Her smile evaporated. "You're too good for it?"

The restaurant had brown vinyl booths, and from where we sat I could see the gambling floor and hear the parabolic ticking of the roulette wheels. The menu was a laminated sheet between ketchup bottles and a wood-paneled wall where Chilkat blankets furred with dust.

"What happened to getting your kids back?"

Felicia shrugged her narrow shoulders. The waitress came. "Two of my usual," Felicia said.

I put the menu back.

"My *new* usual," she said, as the waitress left. "Cheeseburger, fries, chocolate shake. That's what I can thank the FBI for. And that's all."

"Jack helped you out of a bad situation," I said. "Believe it or not, he actually cares about you."

"Yeah? Bookman's got people waiting to kill me if I show up anywhere near the house. The lady down at social services told me I gotta get a job before I can see my kids, and every job has drug testing. My cell phone got shut off because I can't pay the bill. How stupid do I look to you? I saw how Jack *helped* me."

I glanced across the gambling floor.

"Get my kids back," she continued. "Where am I gonna raise them, in here?"

The cheeseburgers arrived. Pink grease filled the buns, the bread disintegrated in my hands. The lettuce was wilted, the French fries arced flaccidly. And I ate everything. When the check arrived, I got there first. Felicia didn't protest; I didn't think she should. Buying Felicia Kunkel one bad meal before she went back to the casino floor didn't seem anywhere near sufficient. I fought the sudden urge to grab her small hand and lead her back to social services where we could set up visits with three children who wondered what happened to their mom.

But the road to hell was paved with good intentions. Once upon a time, I had raised chickens in our backyard, a ten-year-old girl who thought the anticipation of eggs hatching surpassed the emotion on Christmas Eve. As soon as one egg showed hairline fractures, as soon as I heard the cries inside that shell, I reached into the coop and flicked away the hard pieces, coaxing the blind and bleating chick from their casing. A swelling benevolence filled my heart, so powerful that I helped all the scrawny birds from their shells. They came out pitching beak-first into the dry sawdust, their triangular bony wings covered with wet down that trembled at their sides. I set the baby chicks under the warm red heat lamp and went to bed.

The next morning, every chick was dead.

Struggle had its purpose. Struggle exercised some crucial muscles. It prepared young life for the world outside a shell, a world full of even greater challenges.

But knowing the rules of hardship did not silence the howls wailing through my heart as I walked Felicia back to the slot machines and watched her sit at a new spot, cradling another paper bucket, this one full of fresh tokens. She held the bucket as though it were a baby, and when I gave her another of my cards, I wrapped both of my hands around her palm. She nodded absently, slipping the card into the back pocket of her jeans.

I wormed my way across the gambling floor. A frown collected on my forehead. My eyes wandered the room. Perhaps I was searching for one small signal of hope, one item that might convince me Felicia's life would improve, eventually, at some point. I sent up one of those wordless prayers, the kind where you resign yourself to not having all the answers, and the green felt tables seemed to open like fans, the people seated on the ends suddenly appearing like abstract ornamentation. That's when I saw the cocktail waitress moving among them. She was a dark-haired girl who wore a white blouse tied at her slim waist, and she held a raft of drinks on a round tray, smiling happily as a man handed her a twenty dollar tip and patted her rear end.

I stopped. The chill running down my back seized my breath.

Her lithe figure bent to set another round of highballs beside men seated at the next poker table. An older man with an unnatural shade of black hair handed her a twenty, and just like the last guy, patted her rear end. Stacee Warner gave him the identical smile.

I watched her walk back toward the bar, her steps springy even in black stilettos.

No, I didn't believe in luck. But the safest bet in here was that I was the luckiest girl.

In the bar, she was placing dollar bills in a thin black pouch and her head was down. She looked up, ready with the automatic smile. But then she blanched and glanced over one shoulder. Down the shellacked wooden bar four men and a stick-thin woman stared at a flat-screen TV. The woman clutched her drink with hands like claws.

"What . . . why . . . " she was whispering, "what are you doing here?"

"I just dropped by to say hello."

She stared at me. "You can't call? I've got a phone."

"I do too. And anytime you want to tell the truth, call me."

"What?" Her voice was obviously louder than intended. She glanced down the bar again. The barflies didn't hear. Or care.

"Why didn't you tell me you worked here?" I asked.

"I told you I'm a waitress," she hissed. "What's it matter where?"

"It mattered enough for you not to tell me."

She set the tray on the bar between two vertical brass rails. She nodded at the bartender. He walked over, taking her orders, glancing at me. I smiled.

He walked back down the bar. Stacee turned around.

"I'm working. I can't talk to you. You're going to have to leave."

"Does Courtney gamble here?"

"Listen," she hissed, "it's totally uncool for you to just show up like this."

The bartender glanced over. He was upending a bottle of gin, squirting soda in the other glasses. He carried over the drinks, setting them on her tray, stabbing through the ice with little plastic stirrers. Stacee picked up the tray, pivoting, and carried the drinks to the poker floor, her smile locked in place.

"Can I get you something?" the bartender asked.

"Coke, no crushed ice."

The television played a horse race with closed-captioning across the top of the screen, only the hooves were visible, tearing up the track's brown dirt. I waited for Stacee and eavesdropped on the sporadic non sequiturs erupting from the barflies. Five minutes later, the bartender asked if I wanted a refill.

"Where's the waitress?" I asked.

"She's on break."

"How long?"

He slid a damp rag across the bar. "You an old friend?"

"Something like that."

He glanced over my shoulder. "Maybe Mr. Suggs here can help you."

The man standing behind me had an elongated torso and a compact head, sort of like a meerkat. His silver bolo necktie was imprinted with the image of an Indian chief.

"You need something?" he said.

"I'm just waiting for Stacee."

"You already saw her." His voice sounded pinched, as though the bolo was strangling him. "Now you can leave."

"Why's that?"

"Because I said it's time to go." He tossed his chin toward the bartender who picked up my drink and dumped the ice cubes under the bar. "I'll see you out."

He walked me to the exit and held open the door. He pulled the door shut behind me.

The wind lifted a stale scent of hamburger grease from my clothing. The parking lot was full. And in the distance, gray evening clouds hung over a brilliant sunset, like ashes clinging to dying embers.

chapter eleven

Early the next morning, resisting every protestation from an aching body, I pulled on sweats and a T-shirt and jogged down Broadway with Madame at my side.

Last night's wind had delivered new clouds, and their bright cumulus shapes tumbled across the sky like fresh laundry on an invisible line. We passed a homeless man sleeping in the doorway of a Chinese restaurant that was closed until lunch. Madame lifted her nose, catching his scent without changing pace. I began counting the fire hydrants. After twelve, I stopped. A raven swooped down in front of us, its oily black wings whipping the air with a sound like a furling flag, but Madame refused the chase. The bird clutched the metal rim of a municipal trash bin, *caw-caw-caw*ing its conquest of dented soda cans and candy bar wrappers, and when I glanced down, Madame's dark gaze stayed on the black bird, though she never left my side.

At the urban campus of Seattle University, I circled back, jogging the narrow east-of-Broadway streets before slowing to a walk as we approached Aunt Charlotte's. Madame suddenly shot ahead, leaping the brick steps to the postage stamp lawn, relieving herself on the drought-dead grass.

Inside the house, I filled her bowls with food and water, replacing them under the window, and drank my coffee, leaning against the window sill, staring at the cats across the room. Beryl, Opal, and Sapphire were curled on the ceramic tile beside the refrigerator, blinking bejeweled eyes layered with unreadable intentions.

When Aunt Charlotte flumed into the room, her reddish brown hair looked tornado-spun. Pillow folds creased her face. Beryl let out a yowl, sounding like a warped harmonica, while the other two cats arched their backs, languorous, pawing toward the fridge. Madame stopped eating her food.

"Are we hung-gwee?" Aunt Charlotte baby talked, opening the refrigerator door. The cats rubbed against the appliance, their long fur floating off their bodies before getting sucked into the cold draft of the fridge.

She shut the door.

"You are da most bee-yoo-tee-full cats in da whole world!" she continued. "Oh, yes you are! Oh yes you are!"

I glanced down. Madame was gazing up at me. I didn't care what skeptical intellectuals said about anthropomorphism: love an animal, you see it. I lifted my foot, gently rubbing it along her back.

"Oh, dis looks gooood!" She dumped three small tins of what appeared to be foie gras into the cat bowls, except foie gras was a high ethical crime around here. At least for humans.

"I'm so late," she said, turning to me. "Your mother and I stayed up talking."

When I came in last night, it was past 8:00 p.m., and my mother and aunt were sitting in the front parlor drinking herbal tea. I went straight into the shower, then bed.

"How late did you stay up?" I asked.

"Three in the morning. I haven't done that in years. Not sober. I'll pay for it today. Better break out the onyx."

"Onyx because . . . ?"

"Onyx stays in harmony with the first, third, and sixth chakras. It gets your energy balanced."

I had to ask. "What did you talk about?"

"Your father." She poured a mug of coffee. "I've spent the last four years missing him all by myself and now I don't have to. I am so glad you got in trouble and had to move out here."

I smiled. She meant well.

Beryl yowled; her bowl was empty. Aunt Charlotte scooped up the cat, setting her on the table, dropping herself into one of the kitchen chairs. She blew on her coffee.

"Nadine told me Helen is becoming famous," she said.

Helen was my sister, a professor of art at a university in Richmond. She was an expert on Vincent van Gogh. "Helen's fine," I said. "Helen's always fine."

"Still don't get along, huh? That's okay. Once upon a time I thought I hated David." She stared into her mug. "Now I'd give anything to have him back."

I carried my mug to the sink, squeezing her shoulder as I passed.

"Here's what I want to know," she said. "Where's this God of yours when you need him?"

I rinsed my mug in the sink. My hands were shaking. I needed food.

"You think God's listening to your prayers," she continued. "But it's more like calling a big corporation about a problem and getting put on hold. You hang on the line, listening to some harp music, but nobody ever picks up. Me? I finally came to my senses and hung up."

I set my mug inside the dishwasher, using both hands to close the door. Clasping both hands together, I reminded myself that she loved us. She intended well; she was an injured soul navigating the world with self-propulsion and an insufficient compass.

"Aunt Charlotte, it's not a good idea to stroll down memory lane with Mom. She can get lost back there."

"Don't be silly, Raleigh. It's cathartic. I should know. I've lived through pain."

"Yes, you have. But Mom's built differently."

"Bottling up emotion is not healthy. My friend Iona? Her husband left her for another man and she got so bitter. She wouldn't even talk about it. I told her, 'Iona, my husband had a torrid ten-year love affair with a man named Jack Daniels but I got over it.' Not two years later she came down with breast cancer. *That's* what bitterness does to women."

I took a deep breath. "If Mom got mad it would be an improvement. She gets depressed. And her depressions last for weeks."

She waved me off, a fly at her picnic. "That was before she had me. Mark my words, Raleigh. After living with me, your mother will be a brand-new person."

≈

Traffic was heavy on my way to work, and the only distraction came from Trooper Ron Lowell, calling my cell phone to ask if he could help on the VanAlstyne case.

"Sounds like you guys need it," he said.

"Why do you say that?"

"The story in the paper."

"What story?"

"You didn't see it? Front page of the *Seattle Times*. All about how Issaquah PD called in the FBI to find the missing girl. It says you guys have nothing."

I flipped on my blinker, swinging toward the James Street exit under the Convention Center. The concrete overpass threw the road into sudden darkness.

"Thanks for calling, Officer Lowell. I'll let you know if we need your help."

"Did I do something wrong?"

He was a foot soldier in the war on crime; another person who meant well, like my aunt. And I was being rude. "We appreciate your offer to help," I said. "Thanks for staying in touch."

I started to hang up but he said, "Can I ask you something?"

"If it's quick."

"I'm thinking of applying to Quantico. You know, become an FBI agent."

I might have guessed. "Good for you."

"I was wondering if I could take you to dinner. Talk to you about the Bureau, find out what I should do."

In front of me, a Toyota Prius hit the brakes. I missed the sloping back bumper by inches.

"I'm a little busy right now," I said. "Call the main number. We have recruitment guys. They can tell you everything."

"I'd rather get the inside scoop from you," he said. "Or maybe we could do both."

"Both what?"

"I can help you with this case; you can tell me about the Bureau. Fair trade and all that."

"Like I said, we'll be in touch. Good-bye." I tossed the phone on the passenger seat, feeling annoyed, and pulled into my parking spot near the waterfront. When I got out of the car, the air smelled of kelp and driftwood, and Puget Sound was painted with mutable blues and grays. I started my hike.

At my desk, I dropped my gear and walked the maze of

cubicles to Jack's desk. He wasn't there and I decided to accept Miracle Number One for the day. I walked to the conference room, dreading the thought that he was holding court in there. But he wasn't. Miracle Two. I bought a Coke and bag of chips from the vending machine and returned to his desk. The blue Hawaiian shirt with the rioting white hibiscus flowers was missing from its hanger, meaning he was on surveillance. He'd already explained the reverse psychology to me: "Harmon, if I'm wearing a loud shirt that draws attention, the perps know I'm not undercover." Hey, his life on the line; let him believe it.

I took a yellow Post-It note from the pad beside his phone and jotted down what I'd found out about Felicia, then stuck the note on his computer monitor. As I turned to leave, I noticed some framed photographs, each showing snow-capped peaks with a horizon so far back it was nothing but blue. In each picture, Jack had thrown a muscular arm around some attractive woman. Long-haired girls with nice smiles, pretty even with smears of zinc oxide on their noses.

"Like what you see?" he asked.

"I was leaving you a note. About Felicia." I pointed to the Post-It.

Under the short-sleeved Hawaiian shirt, he wore a white thermal undershirt that fit his arms like second skin. Reaching past me, brushing against my shoulder, he lifted the Post-It from the computer monitor.

"Is she okay?" he said.

"No."

"What's wrong?"

"Bookman hired hit men, the Indian casino out on I-90 is giving her free drinks, since all her money goes back to the house, and she looks worse than before, if that's possible."

He lifted the Post-It off his finger, then touched the adhesive again. Then pulled it off again.

"And you're the last person she wants to see," I said. "Her words, not mine."

There was no challenge in his eyes. No spark, no rebuttal.

I walked away, my face burning, and checked e-mail at my desk with a numb distraction. Manners were such simple things, provided your heart was swept clean. When it wasn't, even the simplest conversations became convoluted.

I read my e-mail—more incentives for Iraq, still not enough—and returned four calls, including one to a dean at the University of Washington, a woman named Nita Wells who spoke without the cumbersome restraints of punctuation.

"Miss VanAlstyne was taking twenty-two credits all in math but she hasn't registered for the spring semester we feel just terrible about her disappearance that they talked about in the paper this morning as you can imagine."

"Aside from her advisor," I said slowly, "are there any professors whose classes she signs up for on a regular basis?"

"What are you asking for us to tell you something confidential?"

"No, ma'am. We're simply trying to find out more about Miss VanAlstyne, in order to locate her."

"You want me to ask around do you think she's dead?"

"Ma'am, that question will alarm people. Please do not ask that."

"What are you *saying* how dare you I simply asked if *you* thought she was dead and I'm shocked you would even *think* I could go around asking such a thing I'm a *dean* you know what that means it means I *know* about confidentiality it's part of my *job*."

I paused, allowing my mind to retrofit the commas and periods. "Yes, thank you for clarifying, Dean Wells. I'm not at liberty to discuss details. But the FBI greatly appreciates the university's assistance."

With a fluttering good-bye, she hung up. I typed a memo updating McLeod on the trip to Spokane, the soil samples submitted, and in particular the arsenopyrite from the torn fabric tied to a tree on Cougar Mountain. It was more information than McLeod needed at this point, but I wanted to load him with ammo for when the ASAC called again, at the behest of the senator or the director or the VanAlstynes. I wrote a search warrant request for the casino, asking permission to send it to the U.S. Attorney's office, then deposited everything in the bin outside McLeod's office, which was empty, and drove back to the university district, all four windows down in the Barney Mobile. As I crossed over Lake Union, the water looked like a sheet of hammered steel.

Kermit Simms, the former boyfriend of Courtney VanAlstyne, was unlocking the filthy door at Mama Mia's pizza. I pulled into the loading zone, hopping out.

"Hey, you can't come in here," he said.

"Wanna bet?"

He shifted his body behind the door, using it as a shield. "Get lost."

"How much poker did you and Courtney play at that casino on I-90?"

"I don't know what you're talking about."

"I'm guessing you spent some quality time out there because last night I ran into Stacee Warner and she just about jumped out of her stilettos. Any idea why?"

He yanked on the key, still in the lock. He wiggled it back and forth, tugging. He gripped the door between his skinny legs and pulled with both hands. His fingernails were ragged, the cuticles ripped.

I took one step forward and wrapped my hands around his fingers, squeezing them against the metal key. His knees went soft. I squeezed harder.

"That hurts!"

"That's why I'm doing it. It's going to hurt even more if you don't start telling me the truth about Courtney."

"Okay, okay! Let go!"

I gave another squeeze, reinforcing my promise, then released his hands.

He shook out his fingers. "Why'd you do that?"

"Because the first time I asked, you didn't seem to understand. The second time, you mouthed off. You're a slow learner, Kermit. But now we have an understanding. You tell me the truth, the whole truth and nothing but, and I will leave you alone."

Down the avenue, some midmorning pedestrians passed in loose clutches, bedraggled students and dusty bohemians. Kermit glanced at them as they passed, feigning a casual expression, before leaping behind the door, pulling it closed. I threw my right foot against the jamb, grabbed the door, yanking it open and shoving Kermit inside.

"Hey, listen," he said, backing up, "I need this job. Maybe you don't understand."

"No, you don't understand, Kermit. Your girlfriend's missing. Quit playing games with me."

"I'm not playing games, man. It's the code violations in this place. These guys think you're some health inspector, trying to get me to narc."

"Tell them I'm a friend."

"Right. They've seen *Terminator*. You look like Linda Hamilton hunting down the cyborg. For all I know you've got some sawed-off pump action in the car waiting to take somebody's head off."

"You're right," I said. Why ruin a good thing? "Now tell me why Stacee freaked out or you'll see my bad side."

The light inside the restaurant was dim, a combination of gray clouds outside and the anemic glow from the EXIT sign above the door. Kermit's eyes looked like caverns.

"Look, I don't talk to Stacee, not since Courtney broke it off with me. But I can guess why she got upset. Management isn't gonna let her explain who you are. They'll just can her, same as me. If her dad wasn't an Indian, she wouldn't be pulling down bucks shuttling drinks to losers."

"How bad is Courtney's gambling problem?"

"Not that bad."

"Kermit . . ."

"Okay. It wasn't that bad at first."

"That's not enough."

"The Vegas trips got out of hand, so when Stacee got the job, it seemed like a fun place."

"Still not enough."

"I told you about Steve Wynn in Vegas, how Daddy took care of things down there. It was a full repeat. Daddy did the same thing at the Indian casino."

"I take it you've got fake IDs."

"No. We, uh, we . . ."

"Stacee made sure you got in?"

"I'm old enough. We're all old enough."

"Kermit, you're barely old enough to vote." I didn't really care about the fake IDs, not at this point. But he did and it gave me leverage. "I'll come back to the IDs," I said. "What I'm wondering is, did Daddy pay your debt too?"

"You're a jerk."

"It must have been humiliating."

"I'm over her, I told you. If she wants to play the big leagues, what do I care? Let somebody else clean up after her."

"Big leagues—you mean Vegas? She went back to Vegas?"

"She doesn't need Vegas. She shot to the top right here."

"At the casino?"

"Are you paying me for this?"

"How's the hand?"

"You're a mean woman."

"Kermit, you have no idea."

He sniffed, making me wait. But he described a secret high-roller poker game that played every other week near Sea-Tac Airport. The minimum wager was $10K and players closed out the night with hundreds of thousands in the pot, or in the hole. Seats were by invitation only.

"Courtney plays in this game?"

Even in the murky light, his wistfulness was evident, washing over his face like a bright unsatisfied hope. "She's the second girl to make the table."

"Does she win or lose?"

"I don't know," he said.

"She broke up with you when she got in there?"

He didn't reply.

"Or because you couldn't pay your own debt?"

"Are you done?"

"No," I said. "If Courtney's the second girl in the game, who's the first?"

"Kit Carson."

"Kit Carson—that's a woman?"

"Far as we know."

"What's that supposed to mean?"

"You've never heard of her?"

I shook my head.

"Then you're the only one," he said. "She's the Queen of Queen Anne Hill."

chapter twelve

I used the white pages hanging under the pay phone in Mama Mia's while Kermit Simms danced in agitation behind me, asking me to leave. Under the name Carson, I found seven Kathleens, eleven Kathys, six Kathies, and sixteen K. Carsons. One K. Carson had the word *unlisted* after it.

"Is that her?" I asked.

"How would I know?" Kermit said.

Back outside, I used my cell phone to call the FBI agent at Sea-Tac Airport, the so-called troglodyte named Marvin Larsen. He sounded happy to hear from me.

"I see those vultures at the *Times* got a hold of your missing," he said. "Maybe it'll scare up some clues. Why're the parents saying no to the media anyway?"

"We're not sure," I said. "They seem to think it will make her kidnapper torture her."

"Kidnapped? Who said anything about kidnapped?"

"Nobody. Listen, Marvin, speaking of help . . ." I described the high-stakes poker game, how the girl played at the table, and how it was a secret gathering. "It's every other week, down near the airport."

"You want me to check it out?"

I could hear the thrill in his gravelly voice and it triggered mixed emotions. Mostly, the hope that I would never have to find out what it was like to spend every day asking harried travelers if they'd left their luggage unattended at any time.

"Maybe later," I said. "Right now I need to locate the only other female in the game. Kit Carson, she lives in the Queen Anne area. I found one K. Carson, unlisted, in the phone book. Any chance you can do a quick rundown?"

"Give me ten minutes." He hung up.

I found a Mexican drive-thru just down the street and ordered something with "supreme" and "combo" in the name because it sounded like my cheeseburger gone south of the border, Coke, no crushed ice, and before I'd opened the bag, Marvin Larsen called back.

"Home phone and address," he said. "You need directions to get there?"

"I really appreciate this, Marvin. Thank you."

"One call to my buddy in the county tax office. He owes me."

"I'm guessing you've got contacts all over this city."

"And you," he said, "can call me anytime."

～

Kit Carson lived in the shadow of the Space Needle, in a neighborhood that spread like a tree skirt over the hilly terrain with a jumble of houses that ranged from French Chateaux to Prairie to Colonial Revivals. But Kit Carson's condo building, just off Denny Avenue, was a five-story brick structure with a lobby that smelled of lemon oil and dust. The front desk guard wore a blue uniform the color of a robin's egg, her black hair buzzed within a quarter-inch of her scalp. Her eyes were crystal gray.

"I'm here to see Kit Carson," I said.

"You got an appointment?" Her voice sounded like sand sluicing through an oak barrel.

When I flashed my Bureau credentials, she picked up the phone on the desk and punched in two numbers. She told whoever was on the other end that the FBI was in the lobby. "FBI" came with a sneer. Then she lowered the phone several inches. "What's this about, Ms. Carson wants to know."

"I need to ask her some questions."

"She ain't saying," the guard said into the phone. "Thinks she's cute or something."

Ten minutes later, after I'd had examined the sepia photos on the walls that showed half-naked women from the early 1900s wearing whale-bone bustiers and expressions of longing, the elevator began descending. It was a whirring, clanking antiquity, and its progress was recorded by a tarnished brass arrow above the polished brass doors. Inside, a tall female held the door open, her hair bleached to a shade so pale the strands had the transparent quality of dead quills.

"There isn't gonna be another car," she said. "You getting in or not?"

She punched a black enamel button marked "Penthouse," and we clattered to the top floor. The elevator opened in a living room. No hallway, no entrance. Just a wide expanse of wood and windows that framed ferryboats crossing Puget Sound like toy ships in an enormous pond.

"Take a seat. Ms. Carson'll be with you momentarily."

The last word was pronounced carefully, as though adverbs rarely tread on her tongue, and she waited for me to sit. Three red leather chairs faced a white suede couch under the windows, a zebra rug thrown between them. I took one of the chairs.

Outside, clouds marbled the sky and the wind brushed the water with an invisible hand.

Kit Carson walked into the room wearing silk pajamas, the material alternating between blue and green, glimmering against her slender body. Her handshake was powerful but her dark brown hair was cut into a delicate shag, like the one Jane Fonda kissed good-bye thirty years ago. She held a cigarillo and smiled, her teeth gleaming like polished alabaster. She sat on the white couch.

"I presume you checked out my background, so you know I give generously to police funds. What can I do for you, Miss Harmon?"

"Special Agent Harmon."

"Yes, of course. Agent Harmon."

"Ma'am, can you tell me the last time you saw Courtney VanAlstyne?"

Her brown eyes gazed up at the coffered ceiling. It was painted pink, with hidden lights illuminating the corners. "Ma'am." She turned the word over. "Well, I've been called worse."

"Have you seen Courtney VanAlstyne in the last week?"

"No. And I read the story in today's paper, about her going missing. I called her parents, offering my sympathies. Naturally, they hung up."

"Naturally?"

"Don't pretend to be obtuse. It doesn't become you."

"Why do you say 'naturally'?"

"Be that way." She puffed the cigarillo twice. "I don't qualify as even a distant satellite in the VanAlstyne universe."

"Miss VanAlstyne plays in a high-stakes game down at Sea-Tac. But you were there first."

"Who told you?"

"Does her father know about the game?"

"It isn't *that* big a secret, if you want to know the truth. We've been paying off the local cops for years, and, really, what's the harm? Police officers don't make enough to feed their house plants. And it's not like we're pushing crack on babies."

"About her father . . . ?"

"Yes, Daddy knew everything."

When I asked about the other players, Kit Carson spoke as though they were nothing more than some loosely affiliated church congregation—paroled embezzlers, money launderers, drug mules, rich kids with gambling addictions—and as I listened to her throaty voice, I admired her nerve. A federal agent showed up at her home, asking questions about an illegal game that could've brought double-digit years behind bars, and she pretended to tip her hand by mentioning all the other players. But that was her bluff, because if we already knew about the table and Courtney VanAlstyne's involvement, any information Kit Carson offered now would play to her advantage later, when she would need to beat the other guys to the plea agreement.

I wrote down the names she offered and tried to guess how many years she'd been clawing her way to the top. Surgical updates made her face appear close to forty-five, but the liver spots on her hands were the size of nickels. Nearer to sixty-five, I guessed.

"Let me offer a wager," she said. "The FBI thinks one of these players had something to do with Courtney's disappearance."

I didn't reply.

"And odds are you don't suspect me, or you wouldn't be here asking the early questions. You could be tailing me or bugging my phone or putting the squeeze on one of my bodyguards, perhaps with incriminating photos from my private life." She tapped the cigarillo against the cut crystal ashtray. "You'd be right to suspect the men. They're pigs, every last one." She smiled. "Of course, I've made a fortune playing with swine. But they're still pigs. All men are."

"When's the next game?"

"They called me this morning, after the story ran in the paper. They're assuming Courtney won't show. The game must go on. Swine, I tell you, pure swine."

"The game?"

"Tomorrow night." She arched an eyebrow, a painted feature resting above her eye as though applied by template. "I will gladly forfeit my place so you can stare into the trough."

"I've never played poker."

"Are you good with numbers?"

"Not particularly."

"Pity. You're cute enough to make a killing." She revealed the perfect teeth again. "Bad choice of words. But the offer stands. I'm not particularly eager to play. I leave for Monte Carlo later this month."

"Business or pleasure?"

"There's a difference?"

When I stood, offering my business card, Kit Carson remained seated on the white couch. She looked up at me, placing the cigarillo in the ashtray, tilting her head coquettishly.

"Have you ever shot anybody?"

"No."

"I'm disappointed," she said, almost pouting.

The female bodyguard escorted me to the elevator, the rattling metal dropping to the lobby. She held the door for my exit, bracing the brass lattice with her forearm, where a blue tattoo shaped like a cross stretched down her arm. As I passed the desk, the security guard wished me a good afternoon.

The light on Denny Way felt dreamlike, intangible. Traffic roared down the street, but the sound was muted, as though the automobiles were nothing more than schools of fish passing silently underwater, the metallic doors flashing like scales. I climbed into my car, the surreal sensation pervading my mind, as though I'd just stepped off a legendary Greek island where all the warrior women had perished.

≈

At 2:40 p.m., Lucia Lutini whipped the Italian wool cape around her shoulders and walked past the dusty cubicles, the stacks of worn paper, the bulletin boards layered with curling memos. She looked like Mediterranean nobility gliding through the bean fields full of serfs.

I shrugged into my blazer and followed her out to Spring Street. In front of us, two administrative clerks walked twenty-five feet from the building's entrance, per the law, and stopped where crushed cigarette butts littered the sidewalk.

"Ah," Lucia said as we passed. "They're gone."

"Smoke bothers you?" I asked.

"On the contrary. I enjoy a good cigarette now and then. What I don't care for is the company of young female smokers. They smoke cheap brands, use cigarettes for dieting, and it's tiresome watching such a futile struggle."

I glanced over my shoulder. One of the clerks was leaning against a parking meter, the other crossed her arms over a paunch of stomach. They were squeezed into straight skirts, their stretchy blouses gripping all the wrong places. They puffed like locomotives.

"This is what I wanted to talk to you about," I said.

"Smoking?"

"Profiling."

As we crossed Pioneer Square, I told her about the poker game and that a seat was open for us in tomorrow night's game. The wind was swirling dry leaves, stirring, stopping, stirring again. We crossed South Jackson Street where the sign in Danato's window said CLOSED. But Lucia keyed open the side door, waving to the Italian dishwasher with the smoldering eyes, and called out to her father.

"Lucia!" He said her name with five syllables. "And you bring your friend with you. So good, so good!"

In the back room, we sat on the upturned buckets. Lucia's elderly uncle shuffled past, a gaunt man with the bent posture of perpetual suffering. After she introduced me, the two of them spoke in rapid Italian while I wondered about my experience with great meals. They could never be repeated. And yet when Danato Lutini carried in the sausage sandwiches, the sheer fragrance caused me to reconsider.

"Mangia!" he said.

The first bite closed my eyes. A hum fluttered from the back of my throat, involuntary as a moan. Danato laughed, then left, and Lucia and I ate without words. When we finished, he brought espresso and almond biscotti. I tried to beg off. But he lifted his hands, the fingers gathering on each thumb, the wrists circling the air. A small emphatic gesture.

"Eh, Raleigh," he said. "You gotta eat for the hunger that's coming."

I snapped the biscotti, hints of lemon and cinnamon dancing on my tongue. I watched Lucia, elegant even on an upturned plastic bucket.

"You know who Kit Carson is?" I asked.

"First female to take the World Poker Championship. May 1989."

"One night at that poker table, Lucia, you could read all those guys. You'd have them profiled before the first hand was over."

"You really believe they have something to do with the girl's disappearance?"

"She's a gambling addict, from what I can tell." I pulled out the green plastic disk from the casino, telling Lucia about the roommate's reaction when she saw me, what the ex-boyfriend said about Courtney playing the big leagues. "There's something wrong here, I just can't figure out what."

"So, why not check out the casino?" Lucia said. "Why bother with this high roller game?"

"I put in a request for a search on the casino," I said. "But the poker game is tomorrow night and there won't be another for two weeks. Kit Carson might not be in that game. And after that, she leaves for Monte Carlo. In the meantime, the girl is still missing and I've got nothing else. Lucia, it has to be this game, this week. I can't play it. But you can."

We finished our espresso and walked back to the kitchen. Danato was scraping down the wide steel grill with a metal brush, his short thick torso working under the chef's jacket. Lucia leaned down, kissing his forehead.

"My Lucia." He looked at me. "She needs a good friend."

"Papa!"

"The truth, Lucia. You work too much crime, nobody gets close. You gonna wind up a rose with only the thorns. And Raleigh, she got the same problem."

Lucia's uncle sat on a kitchen stool beneath the pot rack,

scorched pans and old tongs hanging over his head. He read a folded newspaper in his lap and Lucia stepped over to him, kissing his cheek. He didn't react, except to mutter under his breath, his eyes remaining on the newspaper, his thick brows pulled down in concentration.

Danato shrugged his shoulders.

"Family," he said, "what're you gonna do?"

chapter thirteen

You, my dear, will have an enormous advantage at the table," Kit Carson was saying to Lucia. "These men either idolize you or hate you, or they want you in bed. Any of those motivations will help you beat them. Are you with me?"

It was Tuesday night and Kit Carson had changed from her aqua pajamas into a black tuxedo with a satin cummerbund red as polished rubies. A full-size poker table was set up in her loft, and Kit Carson stood in the divot of the dealer's position. Behind her the windows framed the night, the saltwater below spreading like ink, the city lights twinkling along the waterfront.

My cell phone rang.

She glared at me.

My aunt's number was displayed on the caller ID. I silenced the phone's ring. "Sorry."

"As I was saying," Kit Carson growled, giving me a sharp look before turning to Lucia. Her expression softened. "You're going to manipulate their emotions."

Lucia was sitting next to the bodyguard with the bleached hair. Next to her was an Asian girl introduced as Jonna. She wore a tank top with a yellow road sign advertising "Bad Girl on Board." I sat at the other end of the table's crescent.

"Now, let's talk money," Kit Carson said. "One reason that Courtney plays this table so well is because whatever happens, it doesn't change her financial status. If she wins $200,000, so what? She loses that much, big deal. Act like that, like the beloved sister of Bill Gates. Or maybe cousin. You're too good-looking to be his sister."

Jonna laughed, exposing teeth like canine incisors. Kit Carson threw her a glance, silencing her before dealing a round. The cards sifted from her manicured hands and after two hits, I folded with a pair of threes. Jonna and the bodyguard remained. But Lucia finally took them out with a "wheel"—Ace, 2, 3, 4, 5.

The skin on Kit Carson's face relaxed, as much as it could after years of tightening. She dealt another game. None of my cards matched, and when I tried to bluff, the bodyguard called my hand.

Kit Carson looked at Lucia. "Did you see it too?"

Lucia turned to me. "You're a terrible liar, Raleigh. You looked at your cards, hesitated, then made the bet."

"What's wrong with that?"

"The hesitation means you don't like to lie. After you made the bet, your hand went up, resting near your mouth. Women who don't like lying always put a hand near their mouth when they're forced to do it."

Kit Carson restrained her smile. "I'm glad you didn't try to read it in her eyes. Half these guys are going to wear sunglasses all night. You'll be forced to look for other tells." She described the player whose pulse throbbed in his neck when he bluffed; the one who pretended to check his cards incessantly, but only when he wasn't bluffing. "And if Pusan Paul starts to exaggerate, be careful. Like all male exaggerations, it's about seduction. I bat my eyes, but the seduction doesn't work on me."

The bodyguard nudged Jonna. Jonna grinned. Lucia's expression remained implacable.

"That's what I thought," Kit Carson said. "Seduction won't work on you either." She sighed. "I wish I could be there. It's like sending Mona Lisa to the table."

≈

The next day, after our late-night tutorial with Kit Carson, my nerves jangled as a half-dozen chairs scraped across the linoleum in the Violent Crimes conference room.

At the front of the room Brian Basker, our SWAT team coordinator, stood like a bulky ninja, his black Kevlar armor and leather boots matching those of six more SWAT guys, all of whom stood along the back wall. Basker waited while the agents sat down at the conference room table, among them Lucia Lutini, Jack Stephanson, and Byron Ngo, who was part of the organized crime squad.

Allen McLeod stood to my right, wearing his usual outfit of pious bureaucracy—white shirt heavily starched, dark slacks, red suspenders, red tie. But the expression on McLeod's face showed focused concern and his eyes continually drifted toward the one person at the table I didn't recognize—a lean, midthirties guy wearing a similar climb-the-ladder outfit. Nobody introduced him either, although he was taking notes, shielding his tablet from the agents around him.

Basker, lantern-jawed and large, clasped muscular hands at his waist, a soldier's version of "at rest."

"We sent Harford down to the warehouse with some business cards this morning," he said, referring to one of the SWAT guys. "He posed as a carpet wholesaler and they gave him a tour of the warehouse. It's standard-issue commercial space downstairs, concrete floor, twenty-five foot ceilings." He turned to the white board behind him, picking up the marker that rested on the ledge, stabbing at a blue rectangle on the board. "Our biggest issue is the stacks of rolled carpet on the main level. They run in a north-south pattern."

He drew lines inside the rectangle that represented the carpet warehouse that was the front for the card game.

"The rolls of carpet could easily conceal a shooter. Should a problem emerge, we plan to use this challenge to our advantage. But our hope is this will be a nonissue."

He glanced at Lucia. She looked fresh, rested, even though we'd left Kit Carson's condominium sometime after 2:00 a.m., having played every version of poker that might get thrown on tonight's table. After a restless night trying to sleep, I stumbled into the office to meet with McLeod, who told me management was assigning full SWAT and tech staff to tonight's surveillance, along with the agent from organized crime. And the VanAlstynes offered to cover Lucia's bets, no limit.

"Lutini will be carrying a titanium briefcase with a hundred grand inside," Basker said.

Jack whistled.

"The VanAlstynes provided the cash," McLeod quickly explained.

"I was wondering," Jack said. "The Bureau gripes if I spend ten bucks on a good narc."

McLeod glanced nervously at the man taking notes. The man tapped his pen on the pad, offering Jack a stiff smile. Jack smiled back, the tan skin crinkling around his eyes.

"Upstairs, two business offices," Basker continued. "Harford got into the first one by asking about purchase orders. But that's not where the poker game's played. Harmon's source says it's the next room. They keep a game table set up in there." He jabbed the white board with his marker, leaving a bat-shaped blue spot. "Players enter through an alley door, walk upstairs with one guy, then another guy greets them. I got that right, Harmon?"

I nodded.

"What did you call him?" he asked.

"The brush."

"Yeah, the brush. The brush is a guy who walks the players over to the poker table, asks them what they'd like to drink, takes care of the money, so forth. A ceremony kind of guy. Harmon's source said they also position two bodyguards at the office door and two more by the main entrance in the alley." Two more jabs at the white board. "But there could be more. Radio if you see them."

Byron Ngo raised his hand. As usual, the organized crime unit wasn't revealing why they wanted to join our surveillance, but my guess was they were interested in the Korean high roller named Pusan Paul. Kit Carson claimed he kept homes both here and across the Pacific and never talked about his work.

"Ngo, question," Basker said.

Byron Ngo's narrow face carried old acne scars and a wary expression, like he'd never gotten over being teased. "Where are you taping the wire on the UCA?"

UCA, or undercover agent.

Basker looked at Lucia. "Lutini, you got a preference?"

She turned her sloe dark eyes, evaluating Ngo for one brief moment. "You're wondering about the brush, when he escorts me to the poker table."

Ngo remained still, his eyes clouding.

Lucia looked back at Basker. "The game takes place in a warehouse, but these people want an atmosphere of sophistication, even legitimacy. And I'm a woman. This means the brush will escort me from the door to the table, likely placing a hand on the small of my back. Agent Ngo wonders whether the brush will feel the transmitter taped there."

Basker glanced at Ngo.

Ngo nodded, once.

"I've already considered this," Lucia said. "I'm wearing a black pantsuit with boots. The wire and transmitter will be taped to my lower leg. The boots will conceal both."

"What if they frisk you?" Jack interjected, glancing at Ngo for approval.

"They won't frisk me," Lucia said.

Ngo said, "What makes you so sure?"

"Frisking a high roller would be a tremendous insult. An insult that might cause me to leave," she said. "Furthermore, frisking would telegraph to the other players that the game makers didn't know who I was. Fear restrains greed. They can't have that."

Ngo and Jack were silent a moment.

Then Jack said, "You're, what, some high roller nobody's heard of—in Seattle? Yeah, that's plausible."

Lucia tossed her brown hair over her shoulder. "My name is Maria Labello. I'm a wealthy Italian-American who inherited substantial reserves of money from my family. They live in the Midwest. My grandfather was a meatpacker in Milwaukee, my father went into beer distributing, and I'm an old friend of Ms. Carson, who vouches for my identity *and* my bank account. I live in Italy most of the year, no children, and I've come to Seattle for a wedding of family friends. Ms. Carson has developed a sudden case of flu and offered me her seat. Based on Ms. Carson's reputation, the players agreed."

"What wedding?" Jack said.

"There is no wedding," she said.

"Great, Lutini. They start asking questions about the wedding, what're you going to say?"

"They won't ask questions," she said.

"They're sharks, they'll ask questions."

"Jack, men never ask for details about weddings." She tilted her head five degrees. "But perhaps you do?"

Basker coughed into his fist. "Back to the surveillance," he said.

In every single case, undercover surveillance was a strain on manpower. It meant long rotten hours and an astronomical number of x-factors because theoretically everything could go wrong. Devising contingency plans for each potential problem produced an anxiety that ran like an alternating current through every agent's bloodstream. Tonight's x-factors included disguising a surveillance van and several other vehicles full of FBI agents in an industrial neighborhood that was usually deserted.

"Five vehicles," Basker said. "Cars will rotate through the neighborhood. I want continual drive-bys on a five- to eight-minute interval." The panel van with surveillance equipment would be parked at the end of the block, stationary unless something went wrong. "Phone number on the outside of the van goes to an electrical supply company. The line rings silently inside the van."

"Answering service?" Ngo said.

"We want to know who's looking at us. Answer the call 'Basker Electric.'" He grinned. "Now, inside the van, we'll have Harmon, Stephanson, Ngo, and the Tweedles."

The Tweedles were seated at the back of the room, looking as though they'd been captured by the SWAT guys. The twin brothers had small blond heads and pink skin and brown belts crossing their stout torsos like equators circumnavigating globes. They came to the Bureau from Microsoft, computer security experts who were soon dubbed Tweedledata and Tweedledump for their abilities at saving crashed hard drives and wiping out viruses. Surveillance tape failures happened, wrecking an entire case. The fact that the Tweedles were coming tonight meant the suits upstairs were very interested in what we found. That also explained the man with the notepad.

"SWAT will be positioned at the following locations." Basker pointed at various spots on the white board. "A sniper on the roof across the street with a read on the poker room. The UCA's body recorder will be transmitting to all units. Keep the lines clear." He looked at Lucia. "All we need is your code word, Lutini."

The code word was a prearranged emergency signal, something Lucia could remember under dire stress. If we heard it during the surveillance, it meant one thing and one thing only: "Come get me, now, weapons drawn."

"Danato," she said.

"Danato," Basker repeated. "Everybody got it? Code word is Danato." He looked around the room. "Any questions?"

Nobody spoke. The gentleman writing notes clicked his pen closed.

"Then let's roll," Basker said.

A pungent smell filled the panel van, a strange combination of tar and unbathed skin, making the air feel close, stripped of oxygen. We had been in the van over an hour, parked across the street and down the block from Cosmi Carpet Warehouse, and the Tweedles were sweating.

"All the money you two got from Microsoft, you can't buy deodorant?" Jack yanked his black turtleneck, covering his nose and mouth. "You stink, both of you."

The Tweedles glanced at each other, the expression on their pink faces saying, what's *his* problem? They sat on separate swivel chairs wearing gray cotton shirts already ringed with sweat. Over their ears they wore headphones tethered to a monitor board that showed levels of tone and pitch, while a digital recorder ticked along, keeping track of time elapsed. On the live feed, I could hear Lucia on the transmitter, talking to the driver who carried her in a black Lincoln to the alley behind the warehouse.

"She's going in," Basker's voice came from the handheld radio. "All units acknowledge."

The "10-4s" came back, including Jack speaking into the radio through his turtleneck.

Ngo sat on a metal bench facing the computer monitor, bookended by Tweedles. Apparently the smell didn't bother him.

I heard Lucia greeting somebody, her voice perfectly inflected with a slight Italian accent.

"Buona sera."

The hellos coming back sounded throat-choked. Ngo smirked. I imagined the men's surprise when a woman as beautiful as Lucia walked in, the Giaconda in Armani, and I wanted to sigh with relief, but a sigh meant taking a deep breath and my nose was only accepting small pulselike pieces of what little air was available.

The brush introduced the players—beginning with Maria Labello—and I wrote down three names that matched those Kit Carson had given me, including Paul Lee, aka Pusan Paul. But I did not recognize a fourth name and wrote down a phonetic spelling, circling the words as a sensation like déjà vu climbed along the back of my mind. Perhaps it was Tweedle fumes. Too little oxygen. But against every natural inclination, I took a full breath, repressing the gag reflex. When the brush introduced the dealer, a guy named Tony, the déjà vu sensation returned, stronger.

"I know that voice," I said.

"No kidding, Harmon," Jack said. "It's Lutini."

I shook my head. The brush was explaining the night's game—Texas Hold 'Em—and minimum raises and bids and how bathroom breaks worked, and his voice sounded pinched, the nasal tones of New Jersey sandpapering edges from certain words.

"We got yer drinks, top-shelf only," he said.

"I've heard this guy before," I said. "In the casino."

"What casino?" Ngo said.

"The one off I-90." I turned to Jack. "When I went looking for Felicia, this guy was the bar manager."

Jack yanked down his turtleneck. "What's Felicia got to do with this?"

"I don't know, probably nothing. But the VanAlstyne girl's roommate works for this guy. She's a cocktail waitress. He's her boss."

"Fill me in, now," Ngo said. "I want all the details."

I told him about the roommate working at the casino, then described her reaction and how the manager ran me out of the place. "I swear it's this same guy, the brush."

Ngo frowned. "You're sure?"

"I'd have to see him to confirm, but that voice is dead-on."

Jack kept his eyes on the light display. "Did you flash your credentials out there?"

"No," I said. "We were just talking. Then this guy told me to leave."

"Did he know you were with the Bureau?"

"I didn't give him my card, Jack. But the girl was rattled."

Tweedledata swiveled on his chair. "Will you please shut up? We're having trouble hearing."

Ngo leaned in, whispering, "You have the guy's name?"

I closed my eyes. The voice was gone now and the transmitter was broadcasting a series of sounds I recognized from Kit Carson's tutorial: cellophane crinkling off a fresh deck; cards slapping through a shuffling machine; papery clicks as the cards slid across the felt, falling into pairs. In my mind, I could see the man's elongated torso, how he held his arms close, the small head perched like a meerkat's. His name badge was pinned over his left shirt pocket and the small black plastic rectangle said . . .

"Ernie. Ernie . . . something."

"Probably the fumes in here," Jack mumbled.

Ngo wrote the name "Ernie" in his notebook. "Any letters on the last name?"

Tweedledump swiveled, imperious. "Do you mind?"

As a matter of fact, I did, because as much as the tape would provide, I had learned last night that poker was a game of body language and facial expression and no tape would ever match Lucia Lutini watching these guys call, raise, fold, bluff, and otherwise reveal themselves. Maybe that was what was frustrating the Tweedles—the minimal speech of this operation.

"Try to get us a last name," Ngo said.

I nodded. And in the absence of anything to listen to, I stoop-walked across the van and slid open the black partition that connected to the cab. Through the windshield I could see amber halos around the street lights, a deserted road where one car was circling the block at a steady speed, stopping slightly longer than normal at the corner before disappearing again.

The view in the rectangular side mirrors showed an unhitched flat-bed trailer languishing next to a chain-link fence. I turned my body sideways, flattening the bulletproof vest, and pulled myself through the narrow opening between the seats, dropping on the passenger side palms first. I slouched against the door, my forehead aligned with the panel, and flicked open the dashboard air vent. The cab smelled of motor oil and vinyl, perfume compared to the odors in back.

Ngo stuck his head through the partition, his face above my left shoulder. "Don't blow our cover, Harmon."

Several responses flickered through my mind. The wisest was, *Don't answer a fool according to his folly*. The most practical was, *Don't argue with agents in organized crime*. J. Edgar had grandfathered them into a secrecy that made the KGB look like it operated under the Sunshine Laws.

I smiled at Ngo, patting the MP5, the machine gun's muzzle pointed toward the floor. A white towel covered the gun's butt.

"We'll be fine," I said. "Thanks for your concern."

Ngo slammed the partition shut.

I closed my eyes, drawing several deep breaths, searching for the name tag. Ernie . . . Ernie . . . I saw an *S*. Then a vowel. *O*? *I*? When my cell phone vibrated on my hip, his name slipped away and I yanked the phone off my belt clip, cupping my left hand over the light emitted by the LCD.

Aunt Charlotte.

Last night at Kit Carson's I'd shut off the phone, and today I'd been too busy to check in with my family.

Sinking lower in the seat, I whispered into the phone, "Hi, Aunt Charlotte."

"Raleigh, is that you?"

"Yes. Is this an emergency?"

"I can barely hear you!"

"I can hear you fine. Is Mom okay?"

"YOUR MOTHER WENT TO CHURCH!"

I clicked down the volume. "Please don't yell."

"Claire is here! She needs to talk to you!"

"I can't—"

"Raleigh, Claire here. I had a dream last night. About this girl, the one missing? I saw fire again. Rocks on fire!"

"Claire, this is not a good time—"

"Big round rocks, all piled up. Flames, just burning them up."

"Claire—"

"There's your clue. Fire. Can you hear me? You sound far away."

The partition slid open, Ngo stuck his head out. "Harmon, off the phone."

I closed the phone on Claire's voice.

"They just went on break," Ngo said. "You need to hear this."

I glanced at the side mirrors, then slid through the partition. The smell was worse. Tweedledata was waving me over. Jack cursed into his turtleneck.

"I got a digital copy for you to listen to," Tweedledata said. "Listen, listen. Listen to this."

While Tweedledump monitored the live transmission, Tweedledata handed me his headphones. The black plastic earpieces were slick with sweat. I leaned down, holding the piece near my right ear. I heard a rustle like crinoline. When I glanced at Tweedledata, he said, "That's her walking. Keep listening."

I heard Lucia greet someone. She asked for club soda with lime. Ice cubes clinked into a glass. Fizzing sound of soda. She thanked the bartender in Italian. More rustling.

"Nice game." A man's voice.

The rustling stopped. There was a brief exchange, and the man asked Lucia what brought her to Seattle. When she mentioned the wedding, his questions died on a dime.

She said, "How nice there was an opening for me tonight."

The man grunted. "It'll be open for a while."

"Oh? I can come back, yes?"

Another grunt. "You should. You're a better player."

"Really?"

"She was way over her head."

"Too bad. Though not for you."

He laughed. "They let her in for the money. But she was trouble."

"Was?"

"She's not coming back."

Lucia started to speak, but the brush's voice interrupted. "Let's get back to yer seats."

More rustling. Lucia walking. Then the sounds of cards sifting, thumps on the felt, the click of plastic chips. I glanced at Tweedledump, the twin listening live with Jack.

"Anything else?" I asked.

Tweedledump's blue eyes held a distracted expression. "Not yet. But I think Lutini's winning."

I checked my watch. At least thirty minutes to the next break, and the stench had gone beyond the Tweedles. It was the oppressive odor of men hunting, the predatory scent that pervaded locker rooms at half-time.

"Suggs," I said to Ngo.

"What?" He flinched.

"Suggs, Ernie Suggs. His name just came to me. The brush's name is Ernie Suggs."

He wrote it down. "You're sure?"

"Ninety percent. Let's see what Lutini says after the game."

I climbed back through the partition, slouching into place. The Kevlar vest rose against my chin. I took a deep breath, and let it out.

chapter fourteen

The sky had the appearance of indigo lace. My eyes roamed over the dappled blues as languid as a cloud spotter. The shapes shifted and bled and twisted with the fluidity of wild horses, but when my eyes came to the center of the sky my heart suddenly skipped a beat. The color had deepened. It was magnetic blue, the hypnotic darkness of winter in the far north, and a cold breeze brushed my skin. I realized what I was seeing: the greatest of the great beyonds. The place where time and space emerged. The end to every mystery, the beginning of all love.

The voice I heard sounded more like wind than man. *Raleigh, open the rocks.*

I looked down. At my feet, round granite rocks pillowed a dry river bed. The stones stretched up the mountainside, following the topography with supernatural rhythm. I reached down, picking up two rocks. The brown clay beneath was parched, webbed with drought cracks.

Open the rocks.

The weight of the stones made my wrists ache as I tapped them against each other, chalking gray stripes on their black surfaces.

Harder. Open them.

I hit them against each other with a force that sent percussive waves into my elbows, into my shoulders. Again and again, I pounded the rocks, my ears ringing with the sound, sparks bursting between the stones, a flint that evaporated in the cold air like stray sulfur. My hands burned, my arms ached. And finally I gave up and dropped the rocks.

When they hit the ground, light flashed from the river bed and the fire erupted so quickly the heat singed my face. I stumbled back, scrabbling over the dry bank as the flames sliced through the emerald forest, the trees scorched and crimson. I looked down again, feeling the earth shake beneath my feet, the stones rumbling.

"Harmon!"

The gasp was mine—I heard it—and when my eyes flew open, I saw the vinyl dashboard, the windshield framing the night. My neck snapped. Jack's face, in the partition.

"Danato! She just said, 'Danato'!"

I pulled myself over to the driver's side—the MP5 was gone—sharp briars tumbling down my right leg. I stepped on the brake with my left, shaking my right leg to wake up, and turned on the ignition. The van was rocking side to side, and in the rearview mirror a crouched figure flew through the red glow of the brake lights. Another dark figure stood by the back bumper pulling on a Kevlar helmet. I lowered the window, pain needling my shoulder.

"Who's still here?" I yelled.

"Tweedles!"

Jack raced across the street, heading for the alley.

I gripped the steering wheel, pulling myself higher. The van had the same rocking sensation as the dream. Only now I heard the van's shock absorbers squeaking like scared mice.

"Tweedles, sit down!" I called out.

The live tape was playing and I could hear the conversation, nothing to do with cards. The Meerkat was asking Lucia about the wedding. Friend of the groom or the bride? Lucia was pausing too long in her answers, and then the Meerkat said, "That's funny. I don't know no Danatos in Seattle. And I know everybody."

I picked up the handheld radio, thumbing the volume high, catching SWAT in progress.

Basker's voice: "Get the flash bangs!"

I turned my head, pain stabbing my neck. "Tweedles, turn down the live feed! Now!"

I heard one of them say, "What is she talking about?"

"Cover your ears!" I yelled.

But it was too late. The first thud rolled through the van, followed by two more, the sound so close the grenades could've been sitting between the Tweedles. I clasped my hands over my ears, yelled at the Tweedles again, and heard a sound like thunder cracking over my shoulder. Then I heard a scream coming from the back of the van as the metal roof seemed to tear open. On instinct I squeezed my eyes shut for what came next. Light. Blinding light.

When I took my hands off my ears, I heard: "FBI! Everybody down! On the ground!"

I leaned to the right, glancing through the partition. The Tweedles were quivering like gelatin, their fleshy palms pressed against their ears. With one hand, I signaled for them to let go. But they refused. Basker hollered on the live tape, telling the poker players to hit the floor, and a wave of relief swept over me, the peace that prevailed after the shock-and-awe paralyzed the perps.

"What are you saying?" Tweedledata asked, taking his hands off his ears.

"Turn down the live feed," I said.

"What? I can't hear you." He turned to his twin. "Can you hear what she's saying?"

They were deaf. I lifted the radio next to me and mimed the motion, raising my voice. "I've got the radio. You can turn down the live feed."

But just as Tweedledata reached for the sound board, I heard: "He's running—he's running!"

"Hold it!" I said. "Don't touch that!"

The live feed sounded frantic: "You got him?"

"No, I don't have him! Radio—runner!"

Tweedledump cried, "What is going on?"

My radio squawked to life. "All units, we have a runner! Small build, black hair. We lost him!"

I cocked my head. On the live feed, somebody was yelling in the background. Then the radio blared, "All units—take the runner alive! Say again, alive!"

Across the street, headlights flashed. A dark sedan squealed off the curb. My radio squawked again.

"This is SE-14. We see the runner. Heading north. Say again: he's heading north. We're in pursuit."

But just as suddenly, the car stopped, brake lights flashing, and a figure jumped from the side door, running on foot, disappearing in the dark.

I shoved the gearshift into Drive and stepped on the gas, bouncing over the curb. The Tweedles banged against the walls, yelling. The car stopped at the second intersection.

"This is SE-14," the radio said. "Who's behind me?"

"SE-12, Harmon with Tweedles. Do you have a read on the runner?"

Pause. "No."

Silence.

"We'll head west," he said. "Take the east."

"Roger." I turned right, leaning out the open window, my foot riding the brake pedal.

"Why is she slowing down?" asked one of Tweedles.

"How should I know?" said the other.

"She was driving fast then—what's wrong?"

"Get off me!"

"You get off! I was here first."

"Both of you, shut up!" I yelled.

The next intersection was a four-way stop. I took my flashlight off my belt and scanned the side roads. One was paved, painted with yellow lines, a through-way leading to a main artery. The other road was a narrow strip, pocked, veering off to the right. In the flashlight's beam, broken glass glinted below a crumbling curb. I turned down the road slowly, changing from headlights to parking lights, trying to read the shadowed sides of the road. When we hit a pothole, the undercarriage scraped, creating a long scar of metal.

"She hit something!" screamed a Tweedle.

"We're going to die!"

"She'll get us killed!"

I reached up, slamming shut the partition, then lifted the flashlight, aiming the beam just beyond the hood. The road disintegrated into chunks of black conglomerate, a gravel and tar mess that finally ended at an aluminum lathe fence. It was painted red and restrained rusted automobiles stacked like bodies in a morgue. Next to the dead cars, towers of rubber tires listed to one side. The painted white sign on the fence read SZAFRANSKI'S AUTO PARTS, NO TRESPASSING.

I raked the beam across the fence. Twelve feet high, capped with twisted razor wire, nobody was going over it without a pole vault. I shoved the gearshift into Reverse, backing into the junk-yard's gravel lip. But when I tried to turn around, the steering wheel felt rubbery, bouncy, resisting. I let go but it didn't unwind. Leaning out the window again, I shined the flashlight at the ground.

Left front tire. Flat.

I heard the murmured dissonance of Tweedles in back and picked up the radio. How far could I drive without ruining the rim? I wondered whether to call for help now or wait for the dust to settle.

I clicked on the radio's talk button. "Anybody got a read on the runner?"

Four clicks came back. Acknowledged negatives.

Picking up the flashlight again, I raked it along the curb. A long garland of crushed aluminum cans. Greasy paper with yellow arches. Torn plastic bags billowing like ghosts. Lifting the beam, I followed the buckling sidewalk. But it disappeared. There was a steel rail, brown paint peeling like a mean sunburn, and nothing below that. I ran the beam across the black hole in the ground. Some kind of handicap adaptation. Except no entrance anywhere.

My first thought was that some animal was pinned in the corner. Raccoon, rat. I saw wiry fur in the shadows, and when the radio blared, "Anybody, read?" the animal jumped. Then it ducked deeper into the shadows.

Picking up the radio, I lowered my voice, "This is SE-12. I'm east of the warehouse. Worden Road. Send back up. Immediately. I think I have the runner."

Laying the radio on the seat, I kept the flashlight beam fixed at the steel rail. The brown fur was gone.

Behind me, the partition slid open.

"We want to know why you're stopping!" Tweedledump hollered.

The man flew from the shadows.

I jumped out of the van, flashlight in my left hand, Glock in my right, but my legs struggled to catch up, stiff from sitting in the van. My left foot tripped. I glanced down, seeing the white letters FBI on my vest. Perfect target.

"Freeze!" I yelled.

The man raced up the stairs, turning at the rail. But the last moment, his head turned. I lifted my flashlight, aiming for his eyes. He stumbled, grabbing the steel rail to break his fall.

"FBI! Freeze!"

It was a split second—but the longest split second in law enforcement. My finger twitched on the trigger. I watched his hands, looking for his gun. Knife. A pipe to bash in my skull.

"Hands up or I blow your head off!"

He hesitated. My heart pounded.

"Hands up!"

They were small hands. And they were empty.

"Grab the rail, nice and slow." I walked toward him.

When he hesitated again, I swept my left foot into his right ankle, taking his balance. He fell, grabbing the rail with both hands.

"That's better."

I jabbed the barrel of the Glock into the area just below his ribs, once, then pulled it away before he could grab it. I reminded him that if he moved I'd either kill him or give him a colostomy bag for the rest of his life. Then I silently holstered the gun and yanked cuffs from my belt, pulling his right arm back, then the left, squeezing his small hands together, palms facing out to neutralize his grip. His skin felt slippery, clammy.

"Yer gonna be sorry, girlie."

His breath smelled of cigars and bitter fruit, and when the headlights came toward us, scouring the dark street, I ratcheted the cuffs over his narrow wrists. I kept my eyes diverted from the headlights and patted down the Meerkat's curved back, his narrow hips, ankles, feeling for a weapon. The ankles felt sharp, honed as arrowheads, and I found the .25 pistol in the ankle holster and I pulled it out.

He spoke over his shoulder. "Yer gonna pay, girlie. Big time."

I pushed him toward the car where Byron Ngo was stepping out, his narrow face set like a batholith, dark eyes shining. I leaned toward the Meerkat's ear.

"Ernie," I said, "don't bet on that."

chapter fifteen

Lucia Lutini's brown hair appeared coated with a thin layer of gray ash. Fine lines radiated from the corners of her agate eyes. It was 12:37 a.m., and her voice purred from a bedrock of certainty. She was unharmed. She had kept the money she started with.

And since no players would admit they bet one cent, SWAT collected the rest of the money. The Bureau would return to the VanAlstynes every last dime, and turn a profit on an operation that should have cost the Feds thousands of dollars. A smile played across Allen McLeod's worn face. Our surveillance—done on the fly—had gone terribly, profitably right.

"When the brush kept asking about the wedding," Lucia was explaining to McLeod, "I thought at first he was homosexual, so interested in the details. And he was letting the break extend, even longer than before. The other players seemed restless, watching him speak to me. I began to wonder why he wasn't returning to the table, then realized he knew something was wrong with my story. He would call my bluff. So I simply said: 'My grandfather once lived in Seattle, that's how we know the bride's family. Their name is Danato.' Then I walked toward the bartender, to the far side of the room, putting distance between myself and the door. It burst open moments later, and I must say, the flash bangs were spectacular."

McLeod's face carried a night's growth of beard. With the tasseled loafers, it gave him an odd roguish appearance: bureaucrat-turned-pirate.

"So what's your read on the players?" I asked. "Any suspects?"

"Each of them is what my father calls no-good-winks," she said. "We could run them through the system and discover deviations of some kind. The Korean high roller, the man they call Pusan Paul?"

Ngo looked up, interested.

"He's definitely organized crime," she said. "He's certainly worth looking into for that. But is he connected to the disappearance of the girl? I doubt it."

"Why?" McLeod asked.

"Because the VanAlstyne girl has money. Lots of it. And she enjoys gambling. The last thing the mob wants to get rid of is a paying customer, particularly when there's going to be more where that came from."

"Who else?" McLeod asked.

"The man I spoke to during the first break. He was introduced to me only as 'Mac.' He wasn't somebody Kit Carson knew. And he's strange, but he would need serious assistance to pull off a disappearance, particularly any kind of kidnapping like the VanAlstynes allege."

"Why's that?" McLeod asked.

"He's a messy card player, lacking focus. He wins occasionally, but simply due to others players' mistakes. Which tells me he's a messy thinker, not methodical. If this girl was taken from that parking lot, it was a clean abduction. The brush on the other hand . . ."

"Yes?" Ngo said.

"The brush is hiding something. And it's rather significant."

"Such as?" I asked.

"Difficult to say at this point. But he recognized my bluff quickly, and I believe it's because he's so focused on the subterranean aspects of life. When a man hides things, he looks for the same secrecy in others. And, of course, he ran. He's the first suspect we should investigate. Then, possibly, the man named Mac, though he's much less probable."

"Maybe they worked together, taking the girl," I suggested.

She shook her head. "This girl's been gone, what, nine days? I don't see this Mac as a patient man. And I can't see those two working together. He clearly despises Suggs. And if they took her, why haven't they sent a ransom note to the parents? They're greedy men. Why bother gambling if they have a sure thing? The parents will pay, we know that." She turned to McLeod. "Raleigh deserves some recognition for tonight."

McLeod nodded. "Harmon, you got any more questions for Lutini?"

I shook my head.

"Expect a call from upstairs," McLeod told her. "Get some rest."

Lucia left the room, Ngo followed. And I stood, gathering notes from my interviews of Basker, Ngo, Jack, the two agents who pursued the runner, and the Tweedles, who mostly offered exclamations of fear. Now I had to write an official log, the catalogue of procedural details that took place, why we chose certain procedures, at what time, what happened. After that, the FD-302s, documenting all the facts according to each agent—facts only: what the agent saw and heard, no insinuations, no hunches, no embellishments. All 302s read like dialogue from *Dragnet*.

"Write everything up tonight," McLeod said. "They'll want it upstairs first thing."

I nodded. I could hear the excitement in his voice. And I could feel the pinch in my spine, stabbing at my right shoulder blade, radiating down my arm. That is what I got for curling up like a pretzel in the truck cab wearing a bulletproof vest. It was a foolish error, nodding off, and during the post-surveillance interviews with McLeod looking on, I kept waiting for somebody to mention my mistake. But no one did. And it made me wonder how long I'd been out—five minutes, ten? Fifteen? Long enough to dream about a river of fire. Long enough to develop a crick in my neck. But perhaps not long enough for anyone to notice. At least, that was my hope.

"When I tell the SAC that Lutini took these guys to the cleaners . . ." McLeod chuckled, shaking his head, imagining the reaction from the special agent in charge. "He'll want Lutini undercover full time on poker games."

I shifted the notebooks to my left arm, dangling my right, alleviating one fraction of the pain. "Anything else, sir?"

I caught the "sir" too late and was too tired to apologize. I wanted to go home, take a shower, sleep.

He ran his hands over the short black whiskers, making a sandpapery sound. "Just so you're warned, Ngo wants to write up his own report."

"One less 302 for me." Besides, Ngo offered only meager information during his interview.

"I wish he was writing a 302," McLeod said. "But he's writing a memo. He's sending it to the SAC. It's about your screwup tonight."

A memo. Ngo wanted a memo. So the suits upstairs could read about my dozing off.

"I made an error," I said.

"Yeah," McLeod agreed. "He's got a point."

"I should have been more careful."

"It was a dangerous situation, Harmon."

"Yes, sir."

"If you're going to collar a runner, wait for backup."

"Pardon?"

"Especially with a disabled vehicle. That was dangerous. Ngo wants it on the record that he didn't advise you to take the runner by yourself. He says you acted without authorization—his words—and that you put yourself, and the Tweedles, in jeopardy."

I started counting to twenty but gave up on four. "The runner was a flight case. The order was to bring him in alive. That's what I did."

"But it was danger—"

"It was a good collar. Sir." My throat felt tight, cinched with anger. Ngo's memo was the same sort of over-regimented attitude that landed me in Seattle. Another addition to my personnel file, and it might keep me here. Or get me transferred to South Dakota.

"Harmon, the end doesn't justify the means."

"I'm not saying it does. But if I didn't get out of the vehicle, if I sat there thinking about protocol instead of doing my job, would Ngo write me up because I was a coward?"

He raised his hands, placating. "Harmon, listen—"

"I brought in the runner. That was the objective. I met it."

"We all make mistakes," he said. "You're still a little green behind the ears."

Once—just once—I wanted to correct his malaprop. "I would appreciate your support. This was a nearly perfect night for Violent Crimes. Maybe Ngo wants to ruin it by offering his version of events."

He stared at the tasseled loafers, leaning back against the

counter, crossing his ankles. Then pushed himself from the counter.

"I can't get in the middle," he said. "Ngo's not part of my squad. And Organized Crime does things their own way. If he sees a need for this, then he sees a need."

"What *need* are we talking about?"

"Harmon, take it easy."

"Ngo should have stayed with the van instead of rushing into the warehouse to look like a hero. He lost the guy. The *need* here is Ngo looking to divert attention from his own error. Why aren't we writing him up?"

McLeod sighed. "You got lucky. He didn't."

"I don't believe in luck."

He stared at me for a long moment. "Put the reports in my box. I'll be back in here at six." When he reached the door, he turned. "Look at it this way. Lutini made us money. That'll smooth a lot of rumpled feathers."

≈

I typed the 302s feeling an exhaustion that made even close objects seem distant and distorted. But then a thought of Ngo and his memo would slip into my mind, and a barbed surge of adrenaline would twist into my system, fury propelling me through the dry forms. After I slid all the paperwork into McLeod's office box, I rode the elevator down to the parking garage. My government ride was parked in the visitor's space, and under the dim underground lights the weird purple paint looked midnight blue, a color like the one I'd seen in my dream.

When the guard raised the steel gate that led to Spring Street, I drove through the deserted city, watching the wind lift sheets of loose newsprint, carrying it across the road like paper cranes. I got home close to 2:00 a.m. and took a hot shower, hoping the water's heat and force would beat the pinch from my back. Madame was lying on my bed when I got out, the digital clock reading 2:16 a.m. I set the alarm, curled up with the dog, and fell into a deep and immediate sleep.

The next morning, before anybody else was up, I pulled fresh clothing from the closet and tiptoed downstairs, scribbling a note on the kitchen pad, telling my mother and Aunt Charlotte that I hoped to see them for dinner. Before leaving, I checked the cupboards, hoping to find something to eat. But the shelves were bare.

I drove to the office under an autumn dawn like melted pewter. I avoided the freeway, taking Madison Street into the city's center, relishing every stoplight for the rest it provided. My legs felt weighted walking up the hill to the office, the wind buffeting every step. At my desk, I dropped my gear and walked to the conference room, money in hand, tossing two dollars in the wicker basket beside the coffeemaker, a donation that paid for Starbucks instead of Bureau-issued Folgers. I drank the first cup staring at the bulletin board—new incentives for Iraq, still not enough—then carried the second cup to my desk.

There was a folder waiting, a background check needed on somebody who'd applied for a federal job. I pushed the file aside and lifted my calendar, counting the days. Courtney VanAlstyne went missing Sunday, October 9. Today was Thursday, October 20. I stared at the orderly boxes on the calendar, a sick feeling in my stomach. McLeod came out of his glassed-in office holding the documents I'd typed up just hours ago. His face was cleanly shaven, the red tie in place. But dark circles shadowed the keen blue eyes.

"They all walked," he said.

"Excuse me?"

"Every one of them walked this morning," he said. "Lawyers sprang them before we'd even finished debriefing Lutini."

"What about the runner?"

"Slugs?"

"Suggs. Ernie Suggs."

He tugged on his earlobe.

"What?" I said.

"We *had* to let him go. He's filing charges against you."

"Charges—for what?"

"For breaking his wrist."

"Excuse me?"

"They had to pull off the cuffs in the interview room. His hand was blue. His lawyer's the happiest man in Seattle."

"I did not break his wrist."

McLeod evaluated my face, as though searching for mendacity. "Did you double lock the cuffs?"

I remembered the feel of the man's clammy skin, his nearly boneless elbow. How I clamped down the cuffs right before the Bureau car pulled up and Ngo took him away. But did I punch the lock, the mechanism that kept the nickel-plated hasps from closing completely?

"I always lock them, it's a habit," I said. "I keep my index finger hooked under the cuffs. When the metal hits, I stop ratcheting."

"But you don't actually remember pushing in the lock last night?"

I shook my head.

"This will be a fresh hill," he said.

He meant hell, I knew that. But "hill" wasn't far off. I was looking at a heap of internal memos and interrogations by management, subpoenas from defense attorneys, courtroom hearings, a fresh hill of paper to join Ngo's report in my personnel file. It could take years to clear my name. If that was even possible.

"You okay?" McLeod asked.

I picked up the background check on the new federal worker, tapping the file against my desk. When I glanced up, I could see McLeod's question had been genuine. But I avoided a genuine answer.

"Sure, I'm fine."

"What's wrong?"

"Aside from all this garbage, she's still missing. A couple days, okay. Maybe she's off somewhere. But at this point, no. And I keep coming back to the casino. This guy works there."

He shuffled the documents in his hands. "Here. I approved the search on the casino. Shoot the request over to the U.S. attorney, ASAP."

"Thank you."

"Then I want you to write up another affidavit," he said. "Let's gather some probable cause for this guy's house."

"The runner?"

"The parents don't care if his wrist's broken. They're still calling the Senator, he's still calling the ASAC, and we can't roll over because some defense attorney is about to get rich. If you say you didn't break his wrist, you didn't break his wrist."

"I didn't break his wrist, sir."

"Stick to that story, Harmon. You're going to need it."

chapter sixteen

Twenty-two minutes after the faxes blistered back and forth between me and the U.S. attorney's office, I walked north on Fourth Avenue to Stewart Street. The wind felt damp, full of a cool mist that seemed pressed out of the clouds. But it did not rain.

Inside the U.S. District Court House, I found the federal magistrate's office. Two suited attorneys ahead of me checked cell phones that were supposed to be turned off. When the attorneys left the magistrate's office, they looked equally frustrated.

The judge's chambers smelled of thick cottony paper, the kind bound with thread into old books, and I closed the door behind me, smoothing down my wind-beaten hair as the judge read the warrants. He was somewhere in his sixties and wore the long-suffering expression of a bassett hound, the corner of every facial feature drooping. When he glanced up, his eyes appeared green-gray, like glacial lakes. He nodded at an empty Windsor chair. I sat down.

Behind his teak desk, volumes of federal tortes bound in red leather stretched across the shelves, and I stared at a series of tugboat pictures in which the sturdy elliptical vessels pulled barges several times their size. His chambers felt like a ship—teak

desk, Windsor chair, large brass hook holding the black robe—
but my mind kept flashing to my father's judicial chambers. I
didn't understand why until the judge started scrawling notes on
a yellow legal pad, reading my minor petitions as if they were the
Magna Carta.

My father used to say his job description was "to seek justice,
love mercy, and walk humbly with God." When I joined the
FBI's mineralogy lab, I took his mission statement as my own, but
less than a year later, after examining forensic evidence that proved
beyond a shadow of a doubt what horrors man would inflict on
his fellow man—and woman and child—the words of the minor
prophet rang hollow to me. Murder. Rape. Child molestations
that made the term *perverted* sound too polite. Mercy? For a guy
who raped his three-year-old niece at knifepoint?

My father shook his head. "God sees evil, Raleigh. His wrath
is real. But his mercy equals his wrath. He won't send one without the other. And neither should we."

I protested; an entire industry took advantage of mercy,
purging psychopaths and pedophiles from prisons, extending
paroles, unleashing brutalities on the innocent in crimes that
grew worse with leniency.

"I agree," he said. "Mercy without judgment is pathetic. But
judgment without mercy brings despair."

"But how do you know, how do you figure out what they
deserve?"

He had smiled at me. "I pay attention to the last part about
walking humbly with God."

The judge cleared his throat. I glanced up. He stared at me
over his reading glasses.

"Indian land," he said.

"Pardon?"

He held up the affidavit for the casino search. "You're talking about Indian land here. We get into some hair-splitting legal boundaries where tribal rights are concerned. Indian land receives different interpretations under the law."

"Do we need more probable cause?"

"Just be prepared," he said. "Watch yourself. Don't stride in there thinking the FBI is some sheriff in a Wild West movie. I've seen how some of you agents operate. Respect the people's rights, but get what you need. Then get out."

"Yes, sir."

"Sir? Hmph." He held up the second warrant, for Ernie Suggs's house. "Not exactly clear-cut either, is it?"

"No, sir." I quickly told him about the previous night's surveillance, how Suggs took off, how we believed he knew something about the missing girl who gambled heavily in the casino where he worked. "He's a person of interest."

"Yeah, I got that. But a guy running from a surveillance operation? Let me tell you right now, the ACLU throws parties over that stuff. They'll say, 'Of course he ran, you're the FBI.' And the jury agrees with them because these days everybody's a victim."

"What else do we need for you to sign it?"

"Nothing," he said. "But the U.S. attorney needs to know they'll have to duke it out later in court. Watch your step on that search too, you hear?"

"Thank you, sir."

"Don't thank me," he growled. "Find that girl. I saw the story in the newspaper. Makes me sick. Used to be all we worried about was bears in the mountains. At least back then, we knew who the enemy was."

≈

Outside the courthouse I looked around for Jack. He was supposed to meet me here—McLeod's orders—and when I finally
spotted his black Jeep, it was because of the curvaceous backside
of a skirted woman. She leaned into the passenger window and
tipped over the loading zone's painted yellow curb, the ropy
straps of her sandals winding like asps up the tanned bare legs.
The wind caught the edges of her blue skirt. I heard her giggle.

"Excuse me," I said.

She turned around. "Oh."

I opened the car door, slipping into the leather seat, staring
straight ahead. Her citrus perfume hitched on the wind, a scent
that bit and beckoned at the same time, a smell like blood
oranges marinated in rum.

"You better call me, Jack," she said.

"I will, Becky."

She took one step back, wiggling her fingers. "You know
where to find me."

The Jeep peeled from the curb. He looked over. "You got the
search warrants signed?"

"Search warrants?" I said. "What search warrants?"

He braked, turning for the curb so fast I had to brace myself
against the dashboard. A clutch of smokers outside the courthouse turned, their faces startled.

"You didn't get the search warrants signed? Harmon, what
were you doing in there, catching another nap?"

"No, I was flirting. Isn't that why we visit the courthouse, to
flirt?"

He glanced at the rearview mirror, waited one split second,
and sped toward I-5. Following the highway south, he took I-90

east, and as we entered the long tunnel he reached between the seats, pulling out a plain manila envelope. He tossed it in my lap.

"That girl you just insulted? She saved you a ton of paperwork. Check it out. Suggs has a prior, of sorts."

I opened the envelope and found a Maple Valley police report dated eight years ago. It described an unnamed ten-year-old girl walking home from school, taking her usual short cut through an abandoned field, when Ernest R. Suggs stepped out from behind a stand of trees and pulled her into the forest. The girls' mother arrived home from work and found her daughter in the bathroom, sobbing, bleeding. The mother took the girl to the doctor, the doctor notified police.

But the case never went to trial. Two weeks later, the girl recanted her story; the mother asked the police to drop the matter, and the incident would have disappeared except for a prosecutor who asked a judge to order a psychologist's evaluation of Suggs. The evaluation was in there, too, a half page of abstract psychobabble. After reading the words "completely rehabilitated," I closed the file. No sex offender was ever completely rehabilitated. At least, not by the justice system.

We were crossing the floating bridge over Lake Washington and the road seemed to hover inches above the water, the concrete blocks fracturing the wind. To my right, lake water rippled with white caps. To my left, it stretched smooth as blown glass.

"You call it flirting," Jack said. "But you'd be surprised what it turns up. Becky's brother-in-law works for the Maple Valley police. They've kept a file on the guy ever since."

I turned my head toward the rippling lake, feeling the wind out of the south pulsing against the Jeep, sending a sporadic whistling sound through the door frame. We drove in silence until we reached the town of Issaquah fifteen minutes later, where the cloud cover had descended down the mountain like disapproving gray brows.

In the Burger King parking lot, two Bureau vehicles idled next to an Issaquah police cruiser and another cruiser from the state police, plus the gray Crown Vic I'd seen the first day out here, the car belonging to Detective Markel.

We followed the detective's convoy down Sunset Avenue, turning in at a manmade waterfall with the word "Talus" engraved on the polished black granite. If anybody cared, I could have explained that it was just about impossible for talus and polished granite to wind up together—talus being the broken rock found at the bottom of crags and cliffs—but I could see why the marketers had seized the word. Talus somehow insinuated wealth, exclusivity, a much better choice than its geological equivalent: scree.

We followed the newly paved road through what had once been forest but now carried trimmed shrubs and planted autumn flowers that wouldn't survive the winter. At the top of the hill, a group of new Craftsman-style homes faced east, like manufactured heliotropes ready to greet the rising sun. Down below, the blue mountains cupped Lake Sammamish like a cool drink between sturdy hands.

Ernie Suggs's house was three stories, with a driveway unsullied by motor oil stains. His neighbors' homes were similar palaces yet close enough that when I climbed out of the Jeep, adjusting my bulletproof vest, I could hear a phone ringing next door. It finally stopped.

After I got out, Jack drove the Jeep to the end of the street and parked, stationed on lookout, with another Bureau car closing the street's other end. The state trooper parked at the curb, walking toward the house. It was Lowell, the trooper I'd met in the Cougar Mountain parking lot. He nodded and we followed Detective Markel and two Issaquah deputies to Suggs's front door. We let the two SWAT agents knock.

Then a blue Toyota Camry raced down the street, pulling into Suggs's driveway. Byron Ngo leaped out, dark eyes flat as a delta, with about as much current below the surface. Ngo walked to the front door, nodding acknowledgment to the detective. The SWAT agent rang the bell.

The Asian girl who answered had silken skin the color of honey and my mind flashed to the court file, to the therapist's report about Suggs's "complete rehabilitation."

She stared at the SWAT agent, then looked at Detective Markel as he held up the search warrant. The girl shook her head, small eyes jumping from one agent to the next, lingering on me, the only female. Then on Ngo, the only Asian.

"No speak," she said. "I no speak."

Detective Markel turned around. "Can anybody here translate?"

Ngo stepped forward. "She sounds Thai."

I couldn't understand the words, but the gestures were obvious. The girl nodded vigorously, as though somebody was shaking her thin shoulders, then she held the door open as we filed in. SWAT went first, securing the house. Then the detective, his deputies, and I came up behind Trooper Lowell when Ngo leaped ahead of me. "Experience first," he said.

The living room was empty, the brown curtains were drawn, making the leather furniture look like skinned animals crouched for a kill. I smelled curry and bacon and cigarettes, and in one corner of the room the detective inspected a glass and oak gun case, testing the lock. One of our SWAT guys went upstairs, his footsteps soundless, while the other moved into the hallway, MP5 ready.

"FBI!" Ngo hollered.

"What the—" Detective Markel spun.

Ngo was already starting down the hallway with SWAT. The trooper started to follow, but I grabbed his arm.

"Stay with the girl," I told him.

"Why?" he said.

"Because the place isn't secure yet."

It wasn't enough for him, I could see that.

"SWAT needs you here. Wait for the agent to come back downstairs," I said. "Keep a close eye on everything. You're essential here."

The skin on his square face pulled tight, the muscles flexing in his jaw. But he stepped back, nodding. I walked down the hallway. The SWAT agent had secured a half bath, and Ngo was positioned outside the only other door. It was closed, and the detective stood on the other side of the jamb, his .45 drawn.

"FBI!" Ngo yelled again.

There was no reply.

Ngo glanced at SWAT, nodded, then reached out, quickly twisting the knob, flinging the door open.

The voice inside the room seemed to leak out. "You guys just don't know when to quit. Come on in, enjoy the show."

Ngo glanced into the room, pulled back. Then glanced again. With his left hand he signaled SWAT, and walked into the room.

Daylight leaked through the horizontal blinds, falling on the large platform bed sheathed with black satin sheets. The shiny material bunched around the oddly elongated torso and the two Asian girls on either side of him. The girls clutched at the satin, trying to pull the slippery material over their naked bodies. I looked away, from instinct, then looked back, from training, and saw Suggs's left forearm sheathed in white gauze.

"First yer breaking my arm. Then yer busting into my house," he said. "Man, I'll never have to work again."

The SWAT agent slid open a set of mirrored closet doors that made the room feel overpopulated. A sleeve of clothing dangled from the shelf inside, as though reaching for the wire hangers below that held lace outfits dyed the color of fake gems. I walked over, pushing aside the lingerie, until I found the shoes resting on the pale carpeting. When I glanced over my shoulder, Ngo was pawing through an oak dresser while the detective and his deputies stood beside the bed. The detective's thousand-mile stare was slightly fractured by the sight of Suggs and the girls. But Suggs continued to smile as though we'd arrived in time to witness his prowess with girls who still shopped in the juniors' department.

"You have the right to remain silent," the detective said. "Anything you say can and will be used against you in the court of law. You have the right to speak to a lawyer. If you can't afford one—"

"Afford one?" Suggs interrupted. "I got lawyers *begging* me to hire them."

"—one will be appointed to you without cost. Do you understand each of these rights the way I have explained them to you?"

"Yeah, I understand. You broke into my house right after the Feds broke my wrist. This is so bad, it's great. What's the charge anyway?"

"Abduction," Detective Markel said. "Possibly murder."

"What?" Suggs said.

The detective pulled out his cuffs.

"Hey, man, you can't cuff me." He lifted his left arm. The splint and white gauze ended at his knuckles, and his fingers looked like blue sausages. "That girlie over there, she broke my wrist last night."

Detective Markel looked at me.

"Cuff him," I said. "Just make sure the hasps are double locked."

"You got a problem with yer ears?" Suggs said. "I just told you, my wrist is *broken*."

"You're wearing a splint. Broken usually means a cast."

"It's cracked, the bone's cracked. The only reason they didn't put a cast on was they're waiting for the swelling to go down."

"So wait a few more days," I said.

"I don't believe this," Suggs said. "You know what? By the time this is over, you'll be lucky to scrub toilets fer a living. Hey, I know. You can scrub my toilet—in my new house in Maui."

The second SWAT agent appeared in the doorway. He spoke to Ngo. "There's an office upstairs. We secured a computer and file cabinet."

Ngo left. The detective ordered his deputies to cuff Suggs, then followed Ngo down the hall.

I turned to the closet again, lifting each shoe, examining the soles. Suggs wore lifts, one leg apparently shorter than the other, and his tennis shoes held a milky green soil inside the treads. I took an evidence bag from my back pocket, dropping in the tennis shoes.

The deputies had wrapped a beach towel around Suggs's naked waist. I helped the two girls dress, with the only available clothing—the ridiculous lace numbers—then I walked them down the hall to the living room.

The deputies and Suggs were already there, with Officer Lowell standing behind a large leather chair that now contained the girl from the front door. The trooper kept his back to the window, but his face appeared flushed, the skin like burnt copper. Perhaps embarrassed by the girls in their outfits.

I turned to Suggs. "How did you do it?"

"I don't have to talk to you," he said.

"Did you ratchet the clamps down on yourself? Or did you lean against the seat until the bone cracked?"

"You did this to me, girlie. I got witnesses. G-Men witnesses. My lawyer took pictures. By the time this is over, I'm gonna own the government."

"You're a desperate man," I said. "What did you do with Courtney?"

"I got nothing to do with that."

"With what?"

But he refused to reply, his thin lips pressed together.

I turned, hearing footsteps on the stairs, and saw Detective Markel carrying a laptop encased in a plastic bag, his thousand-mile stare gone. He was almost smiling. Ngo followed him, face still unreadable, and behind him the SWAT agent carried a small file cabinet.

"Do the girls have visas?" Detective Markel asked Suggs.

"Visas? They're citizens."

The detective looked at Ngo. "Ask the girls how old they are."

"You're fishing here!" Suggs yelled.

The girls from the bedroom sat beside each other on the leather couch, leaving the other girl alone. Ngo spoke to them in the strange-sounding language, his tone rising at the end of each burst of words. Before answering, the two girls whispered, still ignoring the other girl, and finally they said something to Ngo.

"They won't tell me their ages," he said.

"Take them all down to the station," Detective Markel said.

"Hey, what—"

But Suggs stopped. The detective turned to me.

"The Cougar Mountain trail connects to this subdivision. It's less than a quarter-mile walk from here," he said. "It's the same trail that goes directly to the parking lot where we found Courtney VanAlstyne's car."

"I'm calling my lawyer!" Suggs said.

"You can use the phone down at the station," the detective said.

chapter seventeen

That afternoon Jack and I walked through the casino to the management's offices downstairs from the gaming floor, where a receptionist honed her long nails with a glass file shaped like a butter knife. We asked her who was in charge and she said, "Second shift starts in fifteen minutes. You can wait here for the floor manager."

"Would that be Ernie Suggs?" I asked.

She was a chubby girl with hair that fell like ironed sheets of onyx down her back. When she ran the perfect nails through her hair, sparks seemed to dance from her fingertips. "You know Ernie?"

"We sure do," Jack said. "And Ernie won't be in today."

She frowned. "He's on the schedule. He didn't call in sick or anything."

"You probably weren't his one phone call," Jack said.

"His what?"

Jack flipped open his Bureau credentials. "Ernie's in jail. We're looking for whoever's in charge around here. *I* know that's you." He smiled. "But who do *they* say's in charge?"

The girl picked up the phone on her desk and punched in four numbers using a pencil eraser. She said, "Tell Mike to come to the office. Police-type people are here. Something about Ernie."

She hung up.

"Thanks." Jack sat on the edge of her desk and asked her name. I turned away. The walls were painted bright salmon and held shadow boxes that displayed Native American artifacts. Or what I thought were artifacts. Stepping closer, I realized the arrowheads had the milky texture of plastic and the masks showed the mechanical uniformity of crushed sandstone. Behind me, the receptionist said her name was Gayle.

"One of my favorite names," Jack said.

I was restraining my gag reflex when a lumpy man walked through the office's glass door. He wore a dark brown suit and the left pocket flap folded halfway inside as though he were the recent victim of an amateur pickpocket.

"Can I help you people?" He looked from Jack to me, then back to Jack.

I held out my Bureau credentials along with the search warrant.

Jack stood up from the desk and said, "We're going to search Ernie Suggs's office. We can hunt around for it or you can make it easy for everybody and show us where it is."

The man took the warrant from my hand. His ruddy eyes scanned the type quickly, blindly.

"Sir, may I ask your name?" I said.

"Mike." He looked up. "Mike Holland."

Jack said, "Okay, Mike, here's how this works. The warrant's legit, so don't bother spouting off about that. We're not asking, we're telling. Take us to Ernie Suggs's office."

Mike Holland looked panicked. "You're investigating us?"

Before Jack jumped in, I said, "We can't discuss that, sir. But we would appreciate your cooperation in this one matter."

"What did Ernie do?"

Jack said, "Let me put it this way. If you don't take us to his office, we'll definitely want to investigate this whole place. So you decide how you want to play it."

Mike Holland glanced at Gayle. His left hand reached back, touching the half-folded pocket flap, rubbing the brown cloth. The material had the waxy and threadbare appearance of an adored stuffed animal.

"Can I call my boss?" he asked.

Gayle picked up the phone.

"No," Jack said.

Gayle hung up.

I said, "You can call him later, Mr. Holland. Your cooperation won't go unnoticed by the Bureau."

He glanced once more at Gayle and then we followed him out of the office. I didn't need to turn around to realize Gayle was burning up the phone lines as we walked down the subterranean maze of hallways and Mike Holland stopped at a simple hollow-core door with a black sign that read ERNEST SUGGS, MANAGER. Pulling a metal ring from his belt, hands shaking, he tried several keys before opening the door.

The compact room smelled acrid and poisonous, like carpet glue. Jack walked over to a pressed board desk, sat in Suggs's chair, and turned on the computer. Holland watched him, eyes jumping, glancing at me, still beside him, then back at the computer, back at me.

Fear had so many permutations, so many nuances, that deciphering the root was always a challenge. From what I was seeing, Mike Holland's fear seemed natural. The Feds came to search, he might lose his job for helping us, might go to jail if he didn't, and unlike people with real crimes to conceal, he didn't attempt any nonchalance. He was scared. It showed. When I touched his forearm, he startled.

"Let me ask you something, Mike. Can I call you Mike?"

He nodded.

"Does the casino keep film of the poker area?"

"Film?" His upper lip beaded with sweat. "Film?"

"Any visual record of the poker area, for instance. Our search warrant covers recorded material. It needs to be turned over to us."

"But, but—but we tape over every thirty days." His eyes widened, as if we would ask him to reconstruct every scene from memory.

"Let's start with this month," I said. "It's October 17, so where would you keep those seventeen days of film?"

His hand reached back, waxing the suit flap. "Down the hall?" he said, as if I knew better than he did.

I turned to Jack. Ernie Suggs kept his rolling chair ratcheted down for a meerkat's short legs and elongated torso, and the chair placed Jack so far below the computer screen that his face was tilted up, childlike, as he clicked the mouse, a blue light from the monitor flashing across his face.

"I'll be right back," I said.

He glanced over. "Huh?"

"I'm going to get the film."

"Yeah, sure." His eyes were glazed.

Mike Holland walked with extraordinary speed, particularly for a heavy guy, but I suspected he crossed the casino this way all the time, his job one brush fire after another. We turned down a hall, the white sheet linoleum squeaking under his rubber soles, and passed walls of black metal lockers. He stopped suddenly, pulling out the key ring again, unlocking a dead bolt on a steel door. The room was nothing more than a storage closet with metal racks of CDs in clear jewel cases. White labels taped to their spines gave the locations: Slots, Roulette, Restaurant, Bar 1, Bar 2 . . . I walked over, pulling out the CDs.

"They start over at the first of the month?" I asked.

Holland's hand remained on the doorknob. He offered a weak sigh. "Somebody reviews this stuff daily, but they keep it here for thirty days in case something comes up."

"These say 'September.'" I picked up a bundle of CDs. There were at least a dozen, rubber-banded together, set on the upper shelf above the October CDs.

Holland almost ran over. I showed him the bundle, but didn't let go.

"I guess—I guess they didn't erase those yet. Or—" He stopped.

"Or what?"

"Or they wanted to look at something again," he said.

"That happen often?"

He shook his head. "Are you taking them?"

"Yes."

I found a box in the corner of the room that held the white labels for the CDs and emptied it, stacking the labels neatly on the floor. Then I placed the CDs in the box, lining them up by date. Holland watched, waxing his suit flap. Finally, he said, "Guess you got lucky."

I decided there was no point explaining my theory about luck to Mike Holland. Considering where he worked, he probably didn't believe in it either.

≈

We walked back to Suggs's office, but in a different direction, the hallway appearing to be some kind of circle running under the casino. We arrived back at the management offices where a cadre of stern men was now gathered around the receptionist's desk. Gayle was talking, gesturing with her lovely hands.

Mike Holland opened the glass door.

I kept walking.

In Suggs's office, Jack had unplugged the computer and was wrapping the cord around the tower.

"Jail's too good for the guy," he said. "The kiddie porn on here would turn Michael Jackson's stomach. You got the film?"

I lifted the box, and we walked down the hall. A tall scowling man stepped from the management offices.

"If Ernie Suggs did something illegal on his own time then we have nothing to do with it," he said. "You put that stuff down right now."

"The warrant's signed by a federal judge," Jack said, trying to get past him. "Get out of my way."

"What did you say to me?" The man stepped into Jack's path, baring his teeth.

It was one of those primal confrontations, where you can hear the fuse getting lit, hissing toward detonation. I wasn't about to let Jack ruin this search.

"Excuse me, sir," I said. "We're looking into a very serious crime, one that involves innocent lives. You wouldn't want the public to think you were part of any heinous crime that Mr. Suggs might have committed, would you?" I stopped. "Pardon me, I forgot to ask your name."

"Paul Wannamaker."

I moved the box under my arm, taking out my card. "Mr. Wannamaker, I'm Raleigh Harmon, special agent. If you have any questions, that's my cell phone number. I'm available anytime."

He stared at the card, the embossed gold-and-blue seal of the

Federal Bureau of Investigation glittering under the ceiling lights. Then he reached into his wallet. Paul Wannamaker was vice president of management and operations.

I thanked him. And we left.

Outside, the afternoon light stung my eyes, the way it did after a matinee. Four p.m. and the parking lot was starting to fill. We loaded the back of the Jeep, the hard top locked in place, setting the CDs and computer tower beside the evidence bag containing Suggs's tennis shoes. I walked to the passenger door.

"Where is she?" Jack asked.

"Who?"

"Felicia," he said.

≈

I kept my face empty as we walked inside the casino. But a light flutter was dancing under my ribs, an elation that came whenever the elusive target suddenly became visible. Suggs was in custody, evidence was mounting, and we seemed several significant steps closer to figuring out what happened to Courtney VanAlstyne—but Jack wanted to see Felicia. Arguing with him would only waste more time. He was ready to bust management heads, a mood that enjoyed an argument.

I turned down the now familiar row of slots, Jack following, and saw Felicia at a machine pulling the lever. Her low-rise blue jeans were giving out at the seams, her T-shirt exposed the pale padded belly.

She took one look at Jack and said, "What does *he* want?"

I took a deep breath, letting my gaze gravitate toward the ceiling where dark glass domes watched our every move.

"Felicia, he came to see if you're all right."

"Oh, I'm just great," she sneered.

Jack grabbed her elbow, pulling her hand off the wand. "Knock it off, Felicia."

She yanked her elbow back, then grabbed the wand with an ugly childish defiance.

"I didn't send you back in here, Felicia. You walked in. Don't blame me."

"Blame you? For tearing my life into little pieces? Why would I blame you?"

I sighed, glancing down the aisle. The old woman from last time was here again, rolling tokens into the machine. Then I realized this woman had the same dull expression in her dark eyes, but her black hair was longer and the silver rings were different. The best odds in the house were that these sad circumstances were replicated throughout this casino. Forget blankets contaminated with small pox. Forget the Trail of Tears. Native Americans were being systematically wiped out by a profit-making scheme set up by their own tribes.

"Leave me alone," Felicia was saying. "Go ruin somebody else's life."

"Can't you see I want to help you?" Jack was pleading now. "Can't you see that?"

Her eyes welled up, about to cry.

I couldn't watch anymore.

"Jack, I'm going to the bar near the poker pit," I said. "Meet me there. Felicia, take his advice."

Then I walked away, my elation gone, replaced by a heated frustration that burned through my heart as I walked through the poker pit, watching the jumpy men with their oily mannerisms at the green felt tables. In the bar, I found Stacee Warner coming on shift, tying the black pouch around her slim waist.

She picked up her tray, chatting with the bartender until he nodded in my direction.

She turned, blanching.

"Don't worry. Your manager's not coming in tonight."

"What?"

"Ernie's gone for a while," I said. "So why don't you tell me about the game at Sea-Tac?"

"I have no idea what you're talking about."

"Kermit Simms said the same thing, right before he decided to spill the truth. So let's try again. Do you ever work that game, as a favor to your manager? Or maybe a favor to Courtney? The tips must be incredible."

She spun away, her small mouth twisted to utter a parting shot just as Jack came up behind her. They collided, her tray slicing the air, her stilettos slipping on the floor.

"Oh," she said. "Oh!"

Jack reached out, catching her before she hit the ground. He lifted her as easy as a rag doll, holding her arm until she balanced herself. He barely flinched. But I saw an expression cross Stacee Warner's face, something I couldn't place at the moment.

"I have to work. I have to go. I have to—" She raced out of the bar.

Jack watched her go.

She stopped at the first table beyond the bar, where a startled man holding a round of cards looked up at her.

Jack said, "Who's she?"

"Courtney VanAlstyne's roommate."

"Really?"

"I told you last night in the van. I said she worked here."

He looked back at me. "You did?"

I nodded. Out on the floor, Stacee was having trouble writing down the drink orders at the table. She kept snapping her pen on the tray, scribbling in a flustered manner, shaking the pen for ink.

Jack was still watching her when he said, "You suspect her of something?"

"Suggs is her boss. I thought she might like to know he wouldn't be in today."

He nodded absently, then glanced around the bar. His blue eyes filled with the habit of law enforcement, surveying every crowd for potential threats. But he appeared to come to the same conclusion I had: the barflies were a threat only to themselves.

"You ready?" he said.

We walked single file through the noise, the tense voices, the pulsating anticipation of loss and loneliness and greed. I climbed into the Jeep, and as we headed toward the Interstate, Jack checked his cell phone for voice mail. I stared out the window. I was getting used to driving in silence, even grateful for it.

chapter eighteen

Dinner that night was barley kugel drowned in miso sauce. "Nadine, this is simply delicious," my aunt said.

Pearls of barley surfed waves of whole wheat noodles, swimming in a sea the color and texture of rust. I drank another glass of water.

My mother smiled. "Raleigh, we've certainly missed you."

"I think you're working too hard," Aunt Charlotte said. "You're not even returning Claire's phone calls."

I forked some sea goo. It tasted like ground vitamins. Under the table, Madame rested on my bare feet.

"Why don't you give Claire a call," my aunt said doggedly. "Her feelings are really hurt."

"Raleigh Ann," my mother said, "are you being rude to your aunt's friend?"

Manners were paramount to Southerners, and I sometimes wondered if part of the reason was because after the War of Northern Aggression—as my grandmother called it—"rude" provided an excellent code word for "Yankee." During Reconstruction, the word must have been particularly helpful as the fast-talking vanquishers ripped through the defeated Confederacy like dull scythes, brusque and bloated souls, carpetbaggers and self-righteous utopians, all of whom prided themselves on never owning slaves, yet by their poor example made it clear they did not differ from the enemy they now vilified; human nature was human nature, and we all fall short.

"Claire takes it personally when you don't call her," Aunt Charlotte persisted. "At least listen to what she's saying about that fire."

"Fire?" My mother put down her fork.

"Claire's got this idea for Raleigh's case—" Suddenly, my aunt stopped. "Not that I have any idea what Raleigh's working on. I have no idea. None."

Human nature was human nature: my aunt forgot her promise.

"*Case?*" My mother turned to me. "You're working on a *case?*"

"No."

She glanced at Aunt Charlotte. "You told me Claire's a clairvoyant. Why would she see fire in Raleigh's life?"

Aunt Charlotte stared at her plate.

"She means a legal case," I said quickly. "Somebody's suing a manufacturing plant because of some . . . arsenic; they used arsenic. We're looking into it. Claire thinks there was a fire at the plant. That's all."

My mother looked at me for a long moment. Then glanced at Aunt Charlotte. My aunt's doughy face appeared frozen, her eyes wide open, unblinking. It was an expression of pure bovine deceit. I might be a bad liar, but Charlotte Harmon was worse. Much worse.

"That's exactly what I'm talking about," Aunt Charlotte said. "What Raleigh just said, that's the truth."

My mother turned to me. "In any event, please do not insult your aunt's friend. Do you understand?"

"Yes, ma'am."

"People reveal themselves by their smallest gesture, Raleigh, and returning phone calls is one such a gesture."

"Yes, ma'am."

"I haven't done right by you," she continued. "Here you are, working around the clock, and I didn't have the foggiest what it is about. Why, that's just plain selfish of me. From now on, Raleigh, you have my word. I'll pay close attention to your work."

I glared at Aunt Charlotte. She offered another mooing expression.

"In fact, why don't I come see where you work?"

"Really, that's not necessary—"

"Raleigh's always out in the field," Aunt Charlotte jumped in. "Even for lunch. It's pretty dirty out there."

My mother looked horrified. "You're eating with all the rocks?"

Aunt Charlotte was on a roll. "Rocks are good company. You'd be surprised. And they have better manners than most people."

"Raleigh, you're not eating near that arsenic, are you?"

"Arsenic?" I said.

"The arsenic that the company is being sued over."

"Oh, *that*. No, ma'am. I'm not."

"And you wash your hands after you've been there?"

"Yes, ma'am."

"Your sister once had a close call, scared me out of my mind," she said. "We were in our first apartment in Richmond, not a nice place either. She was two and came toddling down the hall holding a box of rat poison. Somebody had left it in the closet."

"So that's what happened to Helen," I said.

"Pardon?"

"Nothing."

"Raleigh, I'm serious. If any of that arsenic gets into your system, it could kill you. It can work into your ovaries and your children will have low IQs."

"As long as they're polite," I said.

My mother paused. Significantly. "Have you talked to DeMott Fielding recently?"

A family friend in Richmond, DeMott Fielding was the man my mother most wished to graft into the family tree. "Why would I be talking to DeMott?"

"Why? Oh my lands!" she cried. "I *have* been negligent."

Aunt Charlotte said, "Fielding? Not those traitors out on the James River?"

During the Civil War, the Fieldings had offered their plantation to Union troops. General McClellan lived in the family's mansion, his army spearing canvas tents across the wheat fields that ran alongside the James River. Richmond burned in pride-filled loss, but the Fielding estate came through the war with barely a scratch. And the embers of resentment still smoldered.

"Don't you dare marry one of those FFVs," Aunt Charlotte said, referring to the First Families of Virginia, the state's blue bloods. "I married one and look what happened. I'll be in recovery the rest of my life. I'm telling you, those people are inbred. Have you taken a good look at their earlobes?"

"Charlotte, please," my mother said.

"Hey, I know a nice guy for Raleigh," she said. "He comes into the store. Nadine, you met Gary."

"That round man with the little glasses?"

She nodded. "I think he's single."

I stood suddenly, Madame fell off my feet.

"What's wrong?" my mother said.

"I have to get to the office."

"The office!" she cried. "But it's past seven o'clock. Can't it wait until morning?"

"No." I felt a rush of relief. Finally, an opportunity to speak the truth. "No, it can't wait until morning."

≈

A little after 8:00 p.m. I walked across the casino parking lot searching for a specific vehicle and license plate number. The bright orange neon sign reflected along the back windows of sedans and pickups, and I finally found the old gray Honda wagon parked along the building's side, where the pavement turned to sand and gravel. Red signs designated reserved spaces for high-level employees, including P. Wannamaker whose car was gone. When I circled back, looking for hidden cameras, I found one affixed to the corner of the stucco building. It was pointed at the public lot in front. Apparently, employee parking didn't have surveillance.

I snapped on latex gloves, slipping a seven-inch flat bar up my left sleeve; then I went to work on Stacee Warner's Honda. Her muffler was coated with rust, the same color as the miso sauce now giving me indigestion. The car was parked next to a Ford F-250 truck, the cab jacked up on fat tires. With the flat bar, I pried loose the Honda's right rear hubcap. The wheel well contained a fair amount of soil—coarse, with half-inch pine needles—and I deposited the sample into an evidence bag. Replacing the hubcap, I ran my flashlight over the tire treads where the rubber was worn down to steel threads.

Suddenly I heard a man's voice.

"Juss for that, you kin walk home."

I crouched, heading for the truck's front wheel.

"And you'll what, fly?" said another voice. "You're hammered, Hank. You shouldn't even be driving."

"Juss find my car," the man slurred.

I could see their legs, the truck's undercarriage high enough that they were visible from feet to waist. They stood just beyond the back bumper, and for several long minutes I listened to them debate the car's location, who should drive, and whether a certain girl was really interested in joining them. Then, just as suddenly as they appeared, they turned and wandered toward the public lot. I stood up, shaking out my knees, and quickly jimmied the flat iron between the Honda's window and door, popping the lock before a stab of conscience could stop me. And if I did feel one, all I had to do was remember the expression on Stacee Warner's face when she saw Jack this afternoon, when he'd caught her and pretended not to know her. When he acted like I'd never told him, even though I'd mentioned it just last night in the surveillance van.

There was a bundle of clothing on the front passenger seat and I scooped it up, dropping inside and closing the door to turn off the dome light. Her clothes smelled stale, a faded scent of sweat and stale perfume, and my feet kicked against something on the floorboard. A pair of hiking boots. I tossed the clothes on the driver's seat and lifted each boot, taking soil samples from the soles.

Then I picked up the clothes again because I'd felt something hard inside the pile of blouses and slacks. It turned out to be a yellow leather date book, several inches thick. Each day was laid out in half-hour increments, although her simple entries scrawled across full hours. One day read: "Nails, 2:00 p.m."

I flipped through the pages, discovering a tally of tips. Some nights Stacee Warner cleared $250, others $350. The page for the

Sunday her roommate disappeared read: "Mount Si with JS, 11:00 a.m."

Other pages held names of places she apparently hiked: Paradise Lake, Rattlesnake Ridge, Tiger Mountain West. But none of them had initials. I laid the book across my lap and picked up the cell phone, resting in the cup holder. It was an older model without a camera and I decided not to risk listening to her voice mail, in case I couldn't save them as new messages, and in case I got busted for not having a search warrant. I clicked open the phone book and found Courtney VanAlstyne's cell phone. I punched the button to dial the number and got nothing but twenty rings, no voice mail. Mrs. VanAlstyne was in there, along with four people whose last name was Warner, probably family. And I found "Ernie S," a number that connected me to Suggs's voice mail at the casino. Ernie Suggs was away from his desk at the moment—no kidding—and then I found "JS," also in the *S* entries.

I hit dial.

He picked up on the fourth ring. He didn't say hello.

"You okay?" he asked. "That was a close call today."

I hung up.

Seconds later, the phone rang. But the number did not show up on her caller ID. It was blocked by the sender.

Because all those numbers were blocked. Mine. Lucia Lutini's. Byron Ngo's. Every special agent in the FBI had a blocked ID.

Including Jack Stephanson.

JS.

chapter nineteen

A hundred miles into my drive to Spokane, the painted yellow lines on the highway began floating off the black pavement and flying into my windshield like javelins hurled by an invisible adversary. I leaned my head out the open window, breathing in the scent of sage that tumbled across the hard basalt of eastern Washington. The draft snapped me awake, I pulled my head back into the car.

But the javelins returned and I finally surrendered on the outskirts of Ritzville, parking at a truck stop. When I turned off the engine, the Barney Mobile shuddered violently, hissing like a snake. I told myself to check the fluids, then leaned my head back and closed my eyes.

When I woke up, it was past 2:00 a.m. and the parking lot was deserted. Inside the restaurant, a lone waitress in a dingy tan uniform slapped inverted ketchup bottles, squirting the remains into one bottle. She carried it to my table by the window and took my order for a cheeseburger, fries, and chocolate shake. I ate the meal without ketchup, listening to the call-in radio program playing somewhere behind the counter, then carried an extra-large coffee to the car.

Dawn was still hours away, but the lights around the truck stop created a false gray sky. As I passed the gas pumps, one of them was beeping, beeping, beeping, apparently signaling the pump was ready. But there were no cars around. And there was no attendant in the cashier's booth between the concrete islands. I pulled a paper towel from the box by the pump, listening to the tinny sound speakers embedded in the metal roof, a wordless tune playing a repetitive rhythm like the song was stuck. I glanced around. At the far edge of the concrete pad, a black eighteen-wheeler idled, its amber auxiliary lights glowing. But I couldn't see a driver in the cab.

Setting my coffee on the ground beside the Barney Mobile, I lifted the car's hood, feeling a desert breeze blow across my shoulders, sending a shiver down my spine. I pulled out the dipstick, wiped it on the blue paper towel, reinserted it, and found I was a quart low. I glanced at the attendant's booth, still empty. Maybe they sold oil inside. I grabbed the hood, letting it drop to close.

Then I turned.

The man stood behind me. He wore a checked flannel shirt. His white beard had the fibrous appearance of torn cotton bolls.

"You by yourself?" he asked.

I didn't answer.

"Middle of nowhere," he said. "Stuff happens."

My right hand moved toward my hip.

"I'm parked over yonder." He pointed at the idling eighteen-wheeler. Something was in his hand, his gnarled fingers twisted around it.

I unsnapped my holster.

"Thank you for your concern," I said. "But I'm fine."

"Well now, I don't know about that. God told me to come over and talk to you. I told him, 'God, I just drove twelve hours and I got another twelve tomorrow; I want to sleep.' But God just kept kicking me and kicking me. Finally I got up and walked over here. You can't argue with him."

I leaned forward, pretending to look at his truck again, my palm on the hard stippled butt of the Glock. I still could not read his face, and when he moved his hand I lifted the gun, the barrel pointing at his forehead.

"Whoa, there." His right hand was raised. "I'm not looking for any trouble."

"Turn around and walk toward your truck."

"Hey, listen, I just want to give you something."

"Step away from my car."

"But God said I gotta give you this. Don't you understand?"

"You don't understand. Move away from my car."

He raised his hands, peering up into the night sky. He was nodding his head, the ragged edge of the white beard bouncing on his shirt collar. "All right," he said, "all right." Then he lowered his chin, looking at me. "You got a mighty nice gun and I don't know why you need this with it. But God's telling me he wants you to have it."

"Turn around," I growled. "Keep walking until you reach your rig."

"Now hold on, sister."

"I'm not your sister."

"Okay, okay. I'm just gonna put this on the ground. Okay? I promise, that's all. And then I'm going to turn around, real slow, and walk to my truck. You can pick it up when I'm gone. Just don't shoot me. I got a family. I got grandkids."

His hands stayed in the air as he bent his knees, lowering himself then setting the object on the concrete pad. His hands returned to the air as he straightened. "Now you got it and I'm leaving. I done what he asked."

He turned and walked bandy-legged across the pavement, past the empty cashier's booth, past the entrance to the restaurant. When he reached the eighteen-wheeler, he grabbed a vertical chrome bar beside the cab, hoisting himself inside and slamming the door. The Glock was still in my hand when I picked up what he left.

It was a knife. The wood handle was carved and shellacked, and one word had been burned into the handle, running vertically like an acrostic. TIGER, it said. I pressed the small button on the handle. Six inches of steel flicked out. Touching my thumb to the blade, it felt sharp, honed to slice. I stared across the parking lot.

The truck was moving, rolling across the pavement to the highway's entrance. I watched it drive away, headed west toward Seattle.

≈

I arrived at the state lab just half an hour later and waited outside, catching a nap in the Barney Mobile. When dawn broke, I opened my eyes to a morning that offered autumn's grace—sparkling frost and warm sun. I climbed out and walked into the lab, a uniformed trooper holding the door open for me, nodding his blue hat at my thank you. I signed in at the front desk, received a visitor's pass, and carried Suggs's tennis shoes and the soil from Stacee Warner's boots and car to the forensics lab.

If I had to pick one quality that distinguished great forensics examiners from the merely good, it would be intellectual curiosity. Every good forensic examiner was careful. They were diligent. Focused. But the great ones welcomed the unknown with enthusiasm. For them, the unknown was a thrill waiting to happen. Last night, when I called Peter Rosser's cell phone as I left the casino parking lot, I asked for another expedite. I told him it was new soil, and part of the puzzle I hadn't figured, and I needed answers quickly. He didn't hesitate. "Can you get here tomorrow morning?" he asked.

Now he handed me the chain of custody forms and accepted my handwritten note outlining the K and Qs in these new soil samples. He slipped on latex gloves and pulled white butcher paper off a roll bolted to the wall. When my cell phone rang, he didn't seem to notice. The puzzle had him and I stepped to the other side of the lab, where handmade posters listed every animal in Washington State along with a sample of its fur. Bear, deer, moose, raccoon, bobcat, cougar, skunk . . .

I looked at the caller ID. I repressed a groan.

"Hi, Claire."

"Your aunt said you're ready to apologize."

"At the moment, Claire, I'm a little busy."

"Okay, I'll talk fast."

I glanced at Rosser. He was hunched over the butcher paper, spreading out the soil from Stacee Warner's boots with a sterilized scalpel. He placed a ruler beside the soil for scale, took several digital photographs.

"Hello?" Claire said.

"Yes, Claire, what do you want?"

"You're looking for a place of fire," she said.

"You already said that."

"But I didn't get to explain. It's not just fire. It's the *place of fire*, that's your answer. I'm having Technicolor spectacles about this, and they would blow your mind because you're not a trained professional like me. I have experience with these things, so I'm okay."

"Thanks for calling, Claire."

"And another thing," she said. "I keep seeing these rocks. They're all stacked up. I think it's a grave marker. Maybe she's dead."

"Goodbye, Claire."

"Are you on a cell phone?" she suddenly asked.

"Why?"

"Because I can feel the sound waves zipping back and forth. I'm getting a headache from it. I have to go, good-bye!"

I closed the phone. The lab had the steady background noise I loved, the sluicing rhythm that sounded like maracas. The sifter in action. Rosser had turned his attention to Suggs's mud-splattered tennis shoes, scraping the rubber treads and placing the soil into another brass sieve. When the first sample finished sifting, he took it out and used a pair of tweezers to lift one rock fragment from the soil. He placed a drop of epoxy on a glass slide, deposited the fragment on the glue, waving it gently in the air, drying the epoxy as he carried the slide to a stainless steel sink and flicked a switch before pressing the rock against the wet stone grinder. It spewed distilled water droplets on Rosser's safety goggles, and he ground the rock to paper thinness, then carried it back to the microscope on his desk. He took a seat.

"You've got a distinct coarse-grained igneous here." He spoke into the microscope, his back to me. "It's a peculiar green and I saw it in that other sample you gave me."

He twisted the scope's knobs and I waited. He didn't need questions.

"Same markers in this stuff as that other. Same insect exoskeletons."

"Insects?"

He spun around on the swivel chair, placing one pawlike hand on each knee where the corduroy had thinned from wear.

"Washington's had a drought for several years," he said, "and it's stressed out the trees to the point where they're susceptible to certain pathogens. Since our winters haven't been as cold as they used to be, all the hostile insects have a higher survival rate. Which brings me to this soil sample."

He got up, walked across the room, and pulled out a drawer full of U.S. Geological Survey topographic maps. He peeled off his latex gloves, stuffing them into the back pocket of his trousers, and licked a finger to turn the map pages.

"Here's the quadrangle east of Seattle," he said, when he came to the map. "You see this part, the western side of the Cascades?" He tapped his finger on the spot. "The forest over there is getting wiped out by the mountain pine beetle."

"The exoskeletons are from pine beetles?"

Mountain pine beetles, he explained, burrowed into the tree bark, killing the trees but leaving them standing, setting the stage for forest fires. The fires further weakened the forest, and the relentless bugs chewed into new vulnerable trees, repeating their destructive cycle until the forest was wiped out.

"That's what I found in both samples, pine beetles," he said. "That only narrows it down by so much. The key is that metamorphosed gabbro under the scope."

Gabbro meant dark and coarse-grained igneous rock. It formed when molten magma got trapped beneath the earth's surface and cooled slowly into a hardened mass without any definite crystal forms.

"But I thought coal and arsenic were the markers in my sample. You didn't say anything about gabbro."

"I'm talking about the other one," he said. "That soil you brought in for what was his name, Stevenson?"

"Stephanson? Jack Stephanson."

"Right. Stephanson."

I frowned.

"What's wrong?"

"I'm not questioning your procedures," I said. "But can you check the mineralogy in the soil from the tennis shoes?"

He pulled the finished sieve sample from the shaker. I didn't want to appear hovering, so I walked over to the window, staring out at the small courtyard. A maintenance worker wearing denim coveralls waved his leaf blower at the ground, his work boots melting the frost on the grass and leaving dark impressions from his steps. He worked dead leaves around a cultured stone table, and my mind flashed to the sound of Jack's voice on Stacee Warner's phone, "You okay?" And what did he mean it was a close call? Did it have something to do with the soil from Mount Si matching the soil in Stacee Warner's boots, in the wheel well of her car?

"Raleigh."

I walked over to Rosser's desk.

"This clay, I'd know it anywhere," he said, "I stepped in it once and it almost took my boot clean off."

"Where?"

"It was a case that came into the state police, some vandalism of mining equipment. There's a company that mines this clay for bricks, and I had to get the samples to link the suspects to the crime scene. It took me weeks to get this stuff off my boots. And there's only one place it's exposed. Want to take a guess?"

"Yes and no."

"Cougar Mountain in Issaquah. It's the same area where your coal and arsenic show up."

Most clays were notoriously indistinct; they were all basically sticky brown or gray mud, unless the soil carried a particular chemical element. "Do you have a marker for it?"

"Not yet. But I'm gonna find one." He stood up and placed some of the clay in a glass petri dish. Then he carried it into the small side room with the scanning electron microscope, the room that sounded like refrigerators working overtime. Just like he'd done with the fabric sample before, he placed some of the clay on a carbon plug and inserted it into the scope.

The Gateway monitor erupted with spikes of color, the chemical elements flaming into relative peaks and ratios.

Al for aluminum.

Si for silica.

S for sulphur.

And the final spike was As.

Arsenic.

The geologist grinned.

"Rosser," he said to himself, "you've still got it."

chapter twenty

I drove back toward Seattle following Peter Rosser's directions
to the north side of Cougar Mountain where stratus clouds
hung low enough to obscure street signs, including the
sharp left for the Anti-Aircraft Trailhead.

During the 1950s, the U.S. Army carved out compounds
like this one because the nation pulsed on high-alert against the
communist threat—and Seattle was within easy striking distance
for the Soviets. Ten years later, most of the missile compounds
were dismantled, and all that remained today on the Cougar
Mountain site was a set of concrete stairs that eerily led to nothing but the clouds.

I hiked behind the nowhere stairs into woods filled with fading oak and birch trees and ferns whose autumn fronds were
turning the color of baked tin. A mile later I came to a black
lagoon, the water forming a nearly perfect circle, the surface
covered with yellow leaves that floated like small boats.

From what Rosser told me, Cougar Mountain was mined for
coal long before it was a missile site. Rich beds of dense carbon
ran through the mountain, he said, traversing the terrain all the
way to the city of Renton, ten miles to the south. At one time,
miners could walk the lightless tunnels from one side of the
mountain to the other. When the mining tapered off in the

1920s, there was still enough coal to leach into groundwater and bubble to the surface like black ink.

I stared at the lagoon, remembering the black smudge on the fabric tied to the tree. At the edge of the water, I filled empty film canisters with sediment, then continued down the trail to a gravel road Rosser had told me about. The road descended into an enormous bowl with fine silt walls that rose a hundred feet, all of it scarred by mining. But even under the darkening clouds, the clay glowed. It was a luminous light blue color that looked as though light was shining through it from inside the earth. Despite the scarce rain, the basin held several puddles, which told me the mining equipment had hit a water table.

I walked into the basin, my shoes slurping out of the mud until my feet felt weighted with the clay. From a mining perspective, it was excellent clay, sticky to the point of annoyance. Nature's cement. I collected several soil samples, took photographs of the pit, and walked to the far end of the bowl where I found a pile of bricks in the dying weeds. The bricks were uneven, the colors inconsistent, busted seconds dumped by the manufacturer. When I picked one up, a large brown spider scurried out of the pile.

Facing east, the town of Issaquah lay in the valley below, which meant Ernie Suggs's house was directly to my right, south as the crow flies. *Could he walk here?* I wondered. Detective Markel said the trail from his neighborhood led to the parking lot at the bottom of the mountain. Suggs could walk here—then leave with his prey? There would be no trace of him, save for this sticky soil in his tennis shoes.

I climbed the hill behind the bricks, heading south, and I walked a ledge above the pit, searching the dry grass and the thickened forest, lifting evergreen boughs out of the way. The verdant limbs bounced against my hands and suddenly the ground went out from under me.

I lay still for several moments, waiting for the pain to register, then slowly rolled over.

It was steel, rusting rebar, soldered into a kind of grate. Behind that was a black hole, bottomless. The cold wet draft rising up smelled like a dead man's lungs.

Scrambling across the rebar, my muddy boots slipped on the metal. Clay fell off my boots, a silent drop through the black mine shaft, followed by a faint splash of water. I crawled—hand, foot, hand—and finally reached the grass next to the grate. I drew long deep breaths, trying to quiet my pounding heart, and pulled my flashlight off my work belt. I flicked on the beam. The light shook into the pit.

Coal-ripped walls curved into the abyss with no end visible. Picking up a small pebble from the grass, I tossed it between the rebar, then counted. *One one-thousand. Two one-thousand. Three one-thousand . . .* The stone splashed eight seconds later.

Walking the grate's perimeter, I found a rusting lock welded to the rebar and took a series of photos, then beat my way back to the Clay Pit Road. The wind was kicking up, sweeping leaves from the trees like fishing lures dangling from invisible lines. I ran, the ground sending up a scent of earthen decay of rich soil putting flora to sleep for the winter. The first drops of rain were sporadic, spaced far enough apart that they couldn't be considered rain. But within seconds the charcoal clouds seemed to open with sudden fury, and I had to wipe my eyes in order to see the trail. My boots sloshed through quick puddles, splashing the cuff of my pants.

At the parking lot by the nowhere stairs, I jumped inside the Barney Mobile, slamming the door and rolling up the windows.

Rain beat like fists against the car's roof, producing a noise so loud that I didn't hear my cell phone ringing, only felt the buzzing sensation against my hip.

Shaking water from my fingers, I flipped open the phone. The ID was blocked. "Raleigh Harmon," I said.

"Harmon!" barked Allen McLeod. "Where are you? I've been calling for an hour."

I hit the volume button, barely able to hear him over the pounding rain. "My phone was on, sir."

"Get to the VanAlstyne estate. Now. This thing's taken a bad turn."

"I'm on my way."

"They just got a ransom note," he said. "The SAC wants to know why we didn't believe them in the first place."

I backed out of the parking lot, throwing the wipers to full speed. "I'm on my way, sir."

"Another thing, the note came with a finger."

≈

The circular driveway in front of the VanAlstyne estate held the sheen of heavy rain come and gone and now a mist rose from the pavement, shrouding the wheels of seven unmarked sedans, three Issaquah black-and-whites, and one state police cruiser. There was also a white panel van—Bureau surveillance.

At the gate, two deputies from Issaquah checked my ID. I walked toward the front door, where the lake beyond steamed like dry ice. The officer at the front door had his thumbs hooked through his gun belt. I flashed my ID, heading inside.

"What happened to you?" he said.

I turned. It was Lowell, the state trooper I'd met in the parking lot with Courtney VanAlstyne's vehicle. I told myself to keep walking, don't engage, but in the foyer the grit on my boots ground against the polished marble floor. I stepped to the side, kneeling to untie my boots. My socks were soaked.

"What did you do," Lowell said, "take a shower with your clothes on?"

I rolled up my socks, placing them inside the boots, then set them to the side of the foyer.

"They let you walk around like that?" he persisted.

"Lowell," I said, standing up, "I've never worn a uniform and I don't ever plan to."

He cocked his jaw to one side.

I walked across the foyer, feeling cold marble against my bare feet, then came to the next room. The plush carpeting was soft as fur and the VanAlstynes were sitting on separate moss-green couches, facing each other over a coffee table. The table had scrolled wooden inlays that swept toward claw-footed legs. It was easier to look at the table. The pain on their faces was unbearable.

Mr. VanAlstyne's cool blue eyes gaped with fear, giving him the appearance of a man on the verge of sociopathic rage. His wife's face was even more distorted. Her glistening white teeth suddenly looked gray, anemic, her lips so pale they were indistinguishable from the skin on her face.

"I . . . I . . . " she was stammering.

At her side, Lucia Lutini cradled one of the woman's skeletal hands. When Lucia met my eyes, I saw the depth in her brown irises, extending to the pit of hell and back.

I walked to the next hallway, where three SWAT agents conferred with Basker. I didn't see Jack but McLeod stood off to one side, in an alcove with an antique oak secretary offering photographs framed in polished silver. Detective Markel stood next to him.

"Harmon, what the—" McLeod said.

"I didn't have time to change, sir."

"Your feet are wet."

"Yes, sir. You said to come right over."

"Well don't drip on their carpet. They've got enough problems."

I turned to Detective Markel. "I took Suggs's shoes to the mineralogy lab in Spokane. The state geologist linked the soil to the Clay Pit mine, up on Cougar Mountain. I searched for a direct trail to his house. I didn't find it. But I found a mine shaft."

"I wish it worked," Markel said. "But we've got a problem. Suggs was in custody when they got this note. If he's behind it, he's got an accomplice."

I looked at McLeod. "What did you say about a finger?"

"We sent it to the state lab, downtown. They're running the tests."

"What did the note say?"

The detective flipped open his small notebook. "'We have your daughter. Orders will be issued. Obey the orders, she comes home.'"

"We?"

He nodded, then glanced over my shoulder.

Mrs. VanAlstyne was still seated on the couch but she was looking up at a thin woman who stood in front of her. The woman wore latex gloves and held a long cotton swab between her right thumb and index finger. Lucia wrapped one arm around Mrs. VanAlstyne's narrow shoulders and like a small bird in need of food, Mrs. VanAlstyne opened her mouth. The woman placed the swab inside, scraping the cotton against the inside of her cheek. She dropped the swab in a plastic bag, sealing the top.

She turned to the husband.

Mr. VanAlstyne watched the lab technician with a bleak realization. His fury was gone, and when he opened his mouth, it was a quick mechanical movement, something from a marionette.

"Harmon, go home and change clothes," McLeod said. "We're setting up surveillance here on the phone and the house. Lutini's going to stay with the family. I need somebody to keep up with the lab evidence. If that DNA comes in positive for the finger, your first call is me. Got it?"

I made my way back toward the front door, picked up my boots and saw the lug soles had deposited wet clumps of clay on the marble. With nothing else available, I wiped the floor with my wet socks. But there was no getting rid of that clay, not without heavy mopping. It left a thin layer of pale dust.

Lowell watched from the door. "How're they doing?"

I stood, cradling the boots. "Devastated. How else?"

He nodded. Outside a man was approaching the house carrying a large black briefcase. More surveillance, my guess. Lowell checked the man's Bureau credentials, taking an extra-long time to examine the small card. He looked puffed up suddenly, as though he expected to follow this low level federal employee inside, into the action. But all he could do was force the man to acknowledge his presence, to treat him as a peer in law enforcement.

"You done?" the man with the briefcase said.

"You're clear." Lowell handed back the ID. "Let me know if you need any help."

The man gave a tight smile and walked into the house.

I sat on the wide slate steps outside, slipping my bare feet into my boots. They felt cold.

"Amazing," Lowell said behind me.

I didn't turn around. "What's that?"

"It looks like this picture-perfect life. All the money, the big house, nice cars. And then, *poof.* There's this flash and you can see how they don't have everything after all."

I stood up and walked away.

There was nothing to say.

chapter twenty-one

Except for the cats, who ignored me, my aunt's house was empty. I quickly showered, changed, scrawled another note for the fridge, and rummaged for food again. My stomach was so empty it had ceased growling.

But the cupboards were bare—not even a bag of flaxseed—and when I opened the pantry door, the painted white shelves held nothing but ragged scratches from where the canned goods should have been. In the crisper drawer of the refrigerator, I found a bag of brown rice cakes two weeks past their expiration date. I ate them in the car. They tasted like dehydrated tree bark.

Just south of downtown Seattle, I turned on a narrow road near Boeing Field and parked outside a squat building with reflective window panes. The building was sandwiched between a hangar containing airplane propellers and a commercial laundry operation where white steam curled from aluminum stacks, melting into the gray clouds overhead.

While the Spokane branch of the state crime lab concentrated on evidence produced by its rural setting—minerals, flora, fauna—the Seattle branch was buried by urban decay. I walked through the materials analysis lab with my temporary ID from the front desk and saw evidence of the city's most obvious enemies: drugs, DNA, drugs, firearms, drugs. And finally, forgeries.

The Department of Questioned Documents was on the second floor, its south-facing windows framing a view of the laundry operation next door. The room had a hushed quiet, the kind of absorbed silence that penetrated reference libraries, and it prompted me to whisper my introduction to the examiner, a woman named Mary Worobec. She was petite with skin the color of sunbathed sandstone, and when she turned her head, her blonde hair swung like a hammock. The ransom note was resting on the light table in front of her, near a microscope and several magnifying glasses. She wore latex gloves.

"Short and sour," she said in a loud voice, pointing to the ransom note.

The words were written in black ink on white paper. Ordinary notebook paper, with two inches of white space at the top and thin horizontal blue lines running across the page. The handwriting was block style, all capitals.

"WE HAVE YOUR DAUGHTER. ORDERS WILL BE ISSUED. OBEY THE ORDERS, SHE COMES HOME."

"What do you make of 'we'?" I asked.

Mary Worobec shrugged. "In twenty-seven years, half the ransom notes I've examined say 'we.' Then it turns out it's one guy trying to throw us. Or he has delusions. Either way, I don't put that much stock in 'we.'"

On the wall above her every letter of the Arabic alphabet, all the calligraphic bends and curls, was laid out on a poster, along with the Hebrew alphabet, similarly inscrutable. Then Turkish. Chinese, French, Japanese . . .

"How long has she been missing?" she asked.

"The last time anybody saw her was ten days ago."

She nodded, grim. "My immediate take is you're looking for a man."

"Why?"

"First these simple declarative sentences. Any time you have an abduction or a kidnapping, it's an emotional situation. Women tend to go on and on when they get worked up. They advise, hector, nag, so forth. And women tend to make it personal. But look at these sentences, see how they line up? Verb-noun, verb-noun, verb-noun. And then, there's the block lettering."

"What's special about that?"

She lifted a jeweler's loupe from around her long neck, pressing it against her right eye before leaning toward the document. "The terminations of these letters are solid. No trailing off. It's aggressive, forceful handwriting. I can smell the testosterone from here."

"Maybe it's a woman being careful."

"Always possible," she agreed. "But the way people construct their sentences reveals how they think, what pattern their thoughts follow. Psychotics ramble because their thoughts are confused and disorganized. But this note shows the exact opposite, somebody with extremely linear thought patterns. Obsessive. Always in control. I'd hazard another guess."

"What's that?"

"He's enjoying the suffering he's inflicted on her. And on the family."

"A sadist?"

"Yes. He believes she deserves this," she said. "Look at the words again. 'Orders' . . . 'issued' . . . 'obey.' It has the ring of armed services, maybe something in his background. He might have been discharged for some kind of insubordination. I realize I'm hazarding speculation here, but I heard a fingertip came in with this."

I nodded.

"Solid speculations won't hurt, if this is as urgent as it sounds. Just realize what it is."

"I'll make a note. Go on."

"He's dangerous. Very dangerous. And part of what makes him so dangerous is that he presents himself to the world as perfect. That's what this precise handwriting is about. It's presentation; everything is in order. But when you look at the content, what he's saying . . . it's chilling, cold."

She was staring at the note, tapping her finger against her cheek.

"What else?"

"He works in a position of authority."

"Management?"

"Management is a possibility. He needs rules, wants the rules obeyed. But then he breaks those same rules—because they don't apply to him, because he's above rules. That's his secret life." She shivered. "I wouldn't want to be at this guy's mercy."

My mind was trying to recall if I'd seen any handwriting from Suggs. And then, almost unbidden, I wondered about Jack, realizing everything he'd given me had been typed on the computer, then printed out.

I left my card, asking her to call me as soon as she finished checking the note for fingerprints and DNA. Then I walked down the sterilized white hallway to Trace Evidence, located on the other side of the building, where the windows faced the mammoth concrete belt of Interstate 5. Afternoon traffic was already backed up to Boeing Field and along the windowsill were sample plants: marijuana, peyote, poppies.

At one of the long black counters, a middle-aged man stared at a series of photographs wtih the fractured dimensions of crime scene pictures. He glanced at my ID, then looked back at the photographs. The most prominent picture showed the interior of a black minivan, the middle seat ripped out, replaced by a hot plate and scorched pans.

"The latest trend," he said. "Meth lab on wheels. Free delivery, just like pizza. All we need is somebody rear-ending that thing. The explosion will blow the car off the road." He stuck out his hand. "Tom O'Brien."

I asked about the FBI evidence that came in today, and Tom O'Brien said he'd personally scraped the soil from under the fingernail about an hour ago. He sent the soil by courier to Spokane, to Peter Rosser.

"He's the best with soils," he added. "I have photos of everything though."

He pivoted a half turn, lifting a stack of four-by-six color shots. At first glance, the object beside the ruler looked like something coughed up by the sea. Then I realized it was skin, black around the exposed edges. But the nail bothered me most. Its elliptical shape testified to months of expensive manicures, but in the magnified shots from the digital microscope, the new nicks and tears were evident and the nail bed was filled with compacted soil.

"Could be the tip of a right pinky," Tom O'Brien said, as I stared at the photos. "You can see how the nail's torn—abrasion tears, like the finger scraped against something hard."

"Was a fingerprint available?" I asked.

He shook his head. "Whoever cut it off was careful. We didn't even get a good partial print. We're using DNA for identification. You want to talk to the lab?"

He went to make copies of the fingertip photos, saying he'd leave them at the front desk, and I walked across the lab to the DNA section, one square room with an entire wall consumed by a white dry-erase board. On that, a running count of the state's DNA backlog, all 53,721 cases.

Two young women, each wearing white lab coats, stared into microscopes. On the floor between them a note was taped to a small refrigerator, reading, FOOD ONLY!

On television, the kind of shows that Felicia Kunkel adored, lab techs were often seen collecting evidence. But in real life, lab techs never participated in an investigation, and when it came to DNA, their sole purpose was to find the fourteen different gene locations and determine whether those alleles, as they were called, matched any other person's DNA. Provided it wasn't presented to the O. J. Simpson jury, DNA was straightforward science.

"I have three sets of DNA," explained the first woman, a compact Asian girl whose black hair was cinched into a tight bun on top of her head. She began to explain how the DNA examination worked when I interrupted.

"I'm familiar with the process. I just need the conclusion."

"Okay, great," she said. "You can break it to them."

"Break what, to whom?"

"Maybe they already know. One of them should."

"I don't understand."

"The DNA from the fingertip?"

"Yes."

"It matches the mother's DNA."

"Okay."

"But it doesn't match the father."

I took a moment. "You're saying—"

"I'm saying he is not the biological father. Not one of his alleles lined up with the girl's DNA. Hey, maybe it's an adoption. Sometimes people don't want to talk about that, you know."

~

When David Harmon married my mother, he adopted me and my sister, Helen. I was five and Helen was eight, and if people haven't experienced adoptive love, there was little use trying to explain it to them. Description wouldn't help them recognize the territory, since most people couldn't comprehend the depths and heights and wide-open wilderness that appeared whenever a heart transcended desire for its own kind.

Adoptive love was not natural; it was not manufactured within our DNA. No evidence of its existence showed up in our blood types or facial features or the quaint familial traits that ran through generations, the genetic tendencies toward duty or distraction or drink. In scientific terms, adoption meant people were unrelated. Period.

But in the aftermath of my father's death, I came to realize, once again, that science never fully explained the world's greatest mysteries. Science was a high calling. It was a noble and wonder-filled endeavor. But science had yet to provide satisfactory answers for our most beautiful unknowns—all the things that transcended understanding, the miracles that pervaded individual lives and stretched back to a majesty spoken into existence, to a sacrifice that continued to resonate within our souls thousands of years later. A sacrifice based on adoption: he chose us, he loved us, then he died for the worst within us.

That afternoon, as I pulled into the VanAlstyne estate, my heart was keeping a rhythm that matched the thoughts jumping around my brain. Maybe Martin VanAlstyne knew Courtney was not his birth child; maybe he felt honored to be her adoptive father. But then, why the charade of taking DNA samples? And what about the white mask of dread I'd seen on Mrs.

VanAlstyne's face? Lucia believed she was hiding something. Perhaps this was it.

A different state trooper guarded the front door now, and several Bureau figures had changed inside the house too. The atmosphere had downshifted slightly, a barely detectable emotional pullback from the earlier urgency. It had been six hours since the note with the finger had been discovered at the gate by the assistant named Sequoia. No further instructions had been given, and McLeod, I was told by another agent, had returned to the office, probably to brief the suits upstairs. Detective Markel had left to get a handwriting sample from Suggs.

The dark-haired assistant named Sequoia moved about the living room, pointing her severe gaze at various pieces of surveillance equipment, then barking her requests at the agents. As I stepped outside to phone McLeod, there was still no sign of Jack Stephanson. The wind was pulsing, lapping the lake water against the rocky bank. My hair blew across my face, and I pressed my free hand against my ear in order to hear McLeod's responses. I told him that Questioned Documents had examined the note. He interrupted me twice.

Then I said, "The mother's DNA matches the fingertip. But the father's DNA is completely different."

"What?" he said.

"Martin VanAlstyne is not the birth father."

"Then why'd he let us take his DNA?"

I let the question hang in the air, where the wind whirlpooled fallen leaves at the edge of the driveway.

"Oh, great," he said. "Another temple in a teapot. Let Lutini handle that information, Harmon. She's heading back there for the night, to stay with them. You focus on getting this girl back."

"Yes, sir. But I'd like to broach the subject with the mother. I'd like to observe her reaction, without Lutini there to comfort her."

He mumbled something incomprehensible.

I pressed my hand against my ear. "Pardon?"

"You're right, you're right. Go ahead. I was thinking about keeping the peace instead of solving the case. Too much time upstairs." He sighed. "Besides, if you make them mad, what do we lose? They already don't like you."

I closed the phone and walked back to the front door.

"She's upstairs," the trooper said. The nameplate on his shirt said Officer Dirk Duncan.

"Do you know where Mr. VanAlstyne is?"

"Downstairs, in the gym."

"Thank you, officer."

I walked to the curving iron staircase, the rail's cold, hammered metal against the palm of my hand. On the second floor, I knocked on the closed doors, waiting a moment before turning each knob. The rooms were empty and the furniture had a showroom quality, as though I could reach under any of the silk lampshades and find a price tag that would knock the air out of my lungs.

When I got back to the stairs, I looked down at the pink marble foyer, then up. The stairs made one last small pirouette. I followed it to a crow's nest resting above the mansion's main roof. An upholstered chaise longue the color of cinnabar stretched under the rectangular windows and outside, a falling dusk made the lake look like slate. The crown of her platinum hair was visible above the chaise's back.

"Mrs. VanAlstyne?" I walked around the side of the chair.

For a moment, I wondered if she were sleeping, she was so

still. But her eyes were open, fixed on the water, her irises mirroring the flat color of the lake.

I waited several moments. "We have the results back from the lab. The DNA."

She turned her head slowly, rolling it against the chaise's back, as though realizing my presence for the first time. "He doesn't know," she said.

"Yes, ma'am."

"He loves her so much."

"I'm certain that's true."

She didn't try to blink away the tears that rose in her eyes. The tears hovered, pooling against her strangely colored eyes. "How do I tell him? What do I say?"

I had no answer. Only more questions. "Ma'am, who is the birth father?"

She pressed her long white fingers flat against her eyelids, as though pushing the tears back from where they came. "Tell me, Agent Harmon. Does DNA carry a gene for gambling?"

"Ma'am?"

She lifted her thin legs, setting her black ballet flats on the carpeting. When she stood, one pale hand grabbed the windowsill. Her body swayed. When I took her elbow, it felt as delicate as a bird's wing.

"I'm feeling light-headed," she said.

"That's understandable."

A pink flush came to her cheeks. She walked down one flight of stairs, moving like a person in a somnambulant daze. On the second floor, she turned down the hall, her steps dirgelike to the third door. She opened it, walking inside, closing the door behind us.

The room had a peppery scent, like fading carnations, and

the pink walls held black-and-white photographs, each identically framed in silver. They seemed familiar somehow. And then I recognized them. The same photos I'd seen in the condominium that Courtney shared with Stacee Warner. The same stunning symmetry. Six-sided, perfect crystals. I couldn't help myself.

"Microscopic images of crystals?" I asked.

"Snowflakes," she said. "They're photographs of snowflakes. Courtney takes them all the time."

The facet of each flake was visible, down to the beveled edge on every termination. Not one flake was the same.

"You'd think they would melt, wouldn't you?" she said in her dull husky voice. "But her father invented a camera that keeps the flakes frozen under the magnifying lens . . ." Her voice trailed off. She set herself down on the edge of the large bed. "Her father," she whispered.

"Mr. VanAlstyne is still her father."

She looked at me for a moment. "I made a mistake. A horrible mistake. I've spent the last twenty years hoping nobody would find out. When Courtney disappeared, I knew it was my fault. I was being punished. My reprieve was over."

"Does the birth father know?"

"About Courtney?"

I nodded.

She placed her hands on the bed, bracing her thin body. She nodded.

"At the time, I was lonely," she said. "Martin and I had been married five years. It was difficult, it wasn't the marriage I thought it would be. Martin worked eighty, ninety hours a week. He didn't have time for me. I tried to cheer myself up by remodeling the house. The builder, he was here every day." She looked at me. "Have you ever wanted a man to pay attention to you? Just pay attention, listen. That's all I wanted."

I did not attempt to comfort her; that was Lutini's job. And as she wept, a quiet polite sobbing, I stared at the snowflakes that Courtney VanAlstyne had captured. She had managed to transfer the sensation of cold into the photographs, making them look as though a glacial blue existed between black and white.

When Mrs. VanAlstyne dropped her hands into her lap, she spoke staring at the floor.

"I love my husband. I've always loved him. And I didn't want to lose him. But I didn't break off the affair until Courtney was almost nine. I . . . I realize now I was getting back at Martin. I can see that now. He loved his work so much, and I loved him. I was jealous of his inventions." She threw a hand toward the photos. "I was even jealous of those cameras. Pathetic, isn't it?"

I gave a condoling smile.

"Then, suddenly, Martin suffered a health scare. They found prostate cancer. They removed it, but it scared him. He decided to retire, decided it was time to savor life. We began spending time together, as a family. And he took such a deep interest in Courtney, a real interest. Finally, we were what we should have been all along. Except, of course, we weren't. I knew the truth. And Courtney knew the truth."

"You told her?"

"Children have a way of knowing. The builder was here so much when she was young. And they developed a relationship."

"Did she ever say anything to you, to Mr. VanAlstyne?"

She shook her head. "She loves Martin. She would never want to injure him in any way."

"And the birth father?"

She chewed her lower lip. Then, realizing what she was doing, ran an index finger over the spot, as though searching for any injury. "My daughter is a genius with numbers. I don't know if anybody's told you."

"Yes, they've mentioned it."

"Everybody assumes she got her brains from Martin." She laughed mirthlessly. "And I can't correct them."

She stood, steadier, and crossed the room to throw open the double doors to the closet.

It was larger than my bedroom, and the clothing, just like the clothes at the condominium, was regimented by color and function. All the slacks in one section, then all blue jeans, all the white blouses, yellow dresses, green skirts. With a ferocity that stunned me, Mrs. VanAlstyne reached into the section of shirts and shoved the entire raft down the wooden rod, the hangers screeching.

Several dry cleaning bags hung at the back of the closet, their soft clear plastic shimmering with the sudden movement.

"They're all his," she said.

"Whose?"

"The birth father, those are his shirts," she said. "He used to wear them working around the house. If he took one off, Courtney stole it. When I realized what was happening, I worried she was planning to blackmail me. But then one day, years after I broke off the affair, I walked into her bedroom and found her sitting on the bed, wearing one of his shirts. She was sniffing at the fabric. When she moved into the condo in Kirkland she didn't take them with her and I had them all dry-cleaned. If I got rid of his smell, maybe she would throw them out."

But she hadn't thrown them out.

The mother continued talking about the connection between her daughter and the man who was her birth father, and I stepped forward, lifting the plastic bags. The shirts were identical weaves of wool, all various plaids. Lumberjack shirts. And they were enormous. The tag in the collar read, "Pendleton, XXL."

"He's a big man," she said, reading my thoughts. "Tall. Courtney gets her height from both of us. That's the one thing nobody attributes to Martin."

"Did it end badly?"

"Of course. I led him on for ten years, gave birth to his child, then threw him away when my husband decided to take an interest in me. Even worse, my husband claimed his daughter."

I turned, watching her closely. "How much did you have to pay him?"

She didn't hesitate. "Five hundred thousand dollars."

I tried not to react. "How long ago was that?"

"Nine years ago."

"You had the money?"

"My husband keeps a safe in the basement," she said. "There's always $500,000 in there. It's a compulsion of sorts."

"Mr. VanAlstyne didn't notice the money was missing?"

She lifted her right hand. Her middle finger held a diamond and emerald ring. My estimate was eight carats for the emeralds circling the ten-carat diamond.

"The best synthetic money can buy," she said. "I sold the real jewels to replace the cash in the safe. I flew to New York, worried one of the local jewelers would tell Martin." She sighed. "Now you have all my secrets."

Almost, I thought.

"After you paid him, did he ever contact you or Courtney?" I asked.

"He sent her birthday cards until she was fourteen. I always intercepted them. Once or twice, he tried to call. But that was years ago."

"Do you suspect he had anything to do with your daughter's disappearance?"

"It occurred to me, yes."

"You don't sound certain."

"I can't see him hurting her, not like this," she said. "He and Courtney had a close relationship. They bonded. He . . . he loves her."

"Were they in contact that you know of?"

She laughed, again without joy. "Welcome to the World Wide Web. I finally realized why he stopped sending cards. They were e-mailing each other. Precocious doesn't begin to describe my daughter. And I was left to hope she would come to see that Martin VanAlstyne was a better man, a better father." She brushed her hand toward the snowflake portraits. "What man invents a camera for his daughter?"

I turned back to the shirts. I counted nine. And ten hangers.

"Did she take one of the shirts?" I said, pointing to the empty hanger.

"I didn't see her take it." She stepped closer. "And it's been years since she even touched these things. She had him—she didn't need his shirts anymore."

There was a knock at the bedroom door; Mrs. VanAlstyne froze. I watched her face compose itself as she stepped from the closet, closing the door behind her, leaving me inside with Courtney's sentimental favorites.

I heard her say, "Yes, Sequoia?"

Then a mumble of words, followed by a response from Mrs. VanAlstyne.

"I'll be down shortly," she said. "Thank you for telling me."

When she opened the closet door, Sequoia was gone, the

door to the hallway was closed, and her mask had returned. The dead pale mask that was her normal appearance.

"I have some things to attend to," she said. "Your coworker just arrived. Ms. Lutini. Do you need anything else from me?"

"The name of the birth father."

"Bill Johansen," she said. "He's a gambling addict."

I walked downstairs and outside, the shirts over my forearm, and found Lucia Lutini stepping from her gold Camry, crossing the driveway. As I loaded the shirts into the Barney Mobile, my cell phone rang. I pulled it off my belt clip.

"Harmon," I said.

"Are you familiar with ESDA?" asked Mary Worobec, calling from the documents department at the state lab.

I wedged the phone between my ear and shoulder, securing the shirts to the hook above the car's backseat. I knotted the bottom of the plastic, so the particulate stench in my car wouldn't contaminate the material. "Yes, I'm familiar with ESDA."

In an ESDA test, the document in question is placed inside a sheet of clear Mylar, set on a Plexiglas plate, and electrostatic toner is sprayed over the plastic. The toner settled into any indentations on the paper, any divots left behind from the page that once rested on top of the questioned document. In the old days, detectives would run a soft pencil over the page, holding the pencil at a particular slant to create lettering in white relief. But that ruined the document itself.

"What amazes me is how many times people will write ransom notes on whatever paper's hanging around," she said. "But here's another reason I suspect we're looking for a man. A woman would buy a new pad of paper. Something fresh, something special for the brutal occasion. She would want the paper pristine."

"That's a good theory."

"I think so," she said. "And when the ESDA revealed this word, I first thought of the location. I picked up the phone to call you. And . . . your name."

"My name?"

"Raleigh. That's your name."

I froze. "Yes?"

"And that's what the ESDA revealed. 'Raleigh.' Somebody wrote the word 'Raleigh' on the page directly above this ransom note. Now it could still mean the city in North Carolina, there's always the possibility. But what if it means you?"

chapter twenty-two

I drove to the Seattle crime lab and waited at the evidence control desk inside, until the metal gate lifted and a young man with a blond goatee handed me a manila envelope from Questioned Documents. Another envelope contained pictures of the brutalized finger.

I took the envelope back to my car, cracked the windows even farther, turned on the dome light, and read the copy of the ESDA, along with Mary Worobec's notes from the examination. My name, written in the same block lettering as the kidnapping note, traveled across the page at an upward angle. Two parallel lines ran beneath it, for emphasis. Like a note. A reminder?

I climbed out of the car and found Tom O'Brien as he was leaving the Trace Evidence lab for the day. I asked to use one of the lab's computers.

"Does this involve forensics?" he asked.

"Not really," I admitted. "I need some background searches for this kidnapping case. It would save time if I could run the search here, instead of the FBI office." I also wanted to run a search on Jack Stephanson and didn't want a record of it on my computer. "I'll need access to the state and national records. Do you have those?"

His office was yet another compact room with another white

board, this one full of case notes and dates, and at the very bottom right corner, a set of words written so long ago the ink was deteriorating. The handwriting looked childish. It said, "I love you, Daddy."

O'Brien logged into the system and picked up his briefcase. "When you're done, double-check you're logged off. And lock the door. I don't have to tell you, I know, except the cleaning staff comes in at 11:00 p.m. and the defense attorneys are hovering over us like vultures. If I didn't tell you, some lawyer would smell blood."

In a city where Scandinavians and Norwegians pervaded the deepest foundations, the name Jack Stephanson didn't bring up much. And when it came to Special Agent Jack Stephanson, there was even less, except laudatory articles in the local press about his work on Violent Crimes.

Similarly, a name like William Johansen was too easy a reach in the Northwest. Several dozen possibilities for Courtney's father popped up in the crime system and it wasn't until I began narrowing the search with certain key words—gambling, construction—that I found three potential William Johansens. One was dead from a defective pneumatic gun that drove a three-penny nail into his brain. The second Bill Johansen also worked as a contractor, but was much too young to have fathered a nineteen-year-old daughter.

The third William Johansen sent me directly back to my car, and then a drive to Queen Anne Hill.

≈

Kit Carson's condominium was guarded by the same woman as before, her short dark hair like an animal pelt, the voice like sand sluicing through an oak barrel.

"You must like coming around here," she said.

"Not really. I need to speak with Ms. Carson."

"She's busy at the moment."

"Make her un-busy. Now."

She threw me a sullen expression but picked up the black telephone, murmuring into it. Moments later the clattering elevator descended, and the bodyguard held the metal cage for me. The blue tattoo on her arm, I realized, wasn't a cross. It was a sword.

"There a problem?" the bodyguard asked.

I didn't reply, and when the elevator door opened at the penthouse, Kit Carson stood front and center wearing a red silk kimono that stopped six inches above her bare feet. Her painted toes shimmered with oil, and the short hair appeared darker than before, held back by a scarf the color of mercurochrome. She smelled of lavender and cigarillos.

"I was in the middle of my daily massage," she said. "I get crabby when it's interrupted."

"I wouldn't have noticed."

She smiled. "Touché."

"You want to tell me about Bill Johansen?"

"Bill?" Her smile faded. "What about Bill?"

"I asked you about Courtney, that first day I was here. You said, 'Daddy knows everything.' But you weren't talking about Martin VanAlstyne. You were talking about Johansen. That's who you meant by 'Daddy.'"

"I left my massage for this?"

"Johansen's her birth father and you knew it."

She walked over to the Danish modern couch and sat heavily, tugging the silk kimono closed. She blew out a stream of smoke.

"Those icebergs on Mercer Island might want a lid on the truth but if you ever saw those two together, you'd know too. Courtney is Bill's clone. Or was."

"Was?"

"Drop the suspicion, Agent Harmon. I'm saying Bill let himself go. The resemblance is gone, and it's his fault."

"Did he teach you to count cards too?"

"Bill didn't teach Courtney to count cards. Some wonderful gifts get passed along family lines. Counting cards happens to be one of the better inheritances."

"When he went to prison for you, did you visit him?"

She took a moment, collecting a response. "Bill made a mistake," she said finally. "He did his time, he learned his lesson."

"What lesson was that?"

"Don't get caught—what else?"

"How about, never trust your partner in crime."

"Men do nothing for me," she said.

"That one did."

She tapped the cigarillo against the cut crystal, and I waited. But she was comfortable with interrogative silence and that was one of Kit Carson's greatest gifts: steely self-control. More than thirty years earlier, when a young Kathleen Carson was still learning the game of poker, she had flown to Las Vegas and met up with a man named William Johansen, a local building contractor who haunted the Strip at night. Not long after Kathleen Carson arrived in Vegas, a tourist from San Diego lost several hundred thousand dollars in one night at the Sahara. The next day, when he realized what had happened, the tourist filed charges against Bill Johansen and an unnamed woman. He accused them of collusion.

Collusion occurs when two or more players agree to share

secret signals, telegraphing an unsuspecting player's cards with words and gestures, leading the mark into ever-increasing bets. The pot grows, the mark gets excited, and then one colluder swoops in for the kill, scoring a "surprise" win. The mark, still pumped with adrenaline, still feeling confident after coming so close to winning, launches into another round at the "lucky" table, and the ruse begins all over again.

Las Vegas authorities searched the casino for a woman described as being in her late twenties, early thirties, brown hair, nice smile. The mark said her name was "Kitty" and he had met her in the casino bar, where Kitty reluctantly agreed to play poker, insisting she wasn't much of a player. Sure enough, Kitty played badly, she lost every hand. But the man later identified as Bill Johansen sat at the table too. And he cleaned up.

When police finally found Kathleen Carson, she was boarding an Alaska Airlines flight to Seattle. She claimed Bill Johansen was blackmailing her with naked photographs, that she was a victim, that she was new at poker and didn't realize the seriousness of her participation in the scheme hatched entirely by Johansen. For her total and complete cooperation with authorities, Kathleen "Kitty" Carson was banned from the Las Vegas casinos for life. She received no jail time.

William Johansen, meanwhile, spent two years in a federal penitentiary and was forced to repay the mark every last dollar. And while he was in prison, Kit Carson began her climb up the poker ranks in Seattle.

"What did you offer him, so he'd take the fall?" I asked.

"Your problem, Agent Harmon, is you see life as black and white. Life is gray. All gray. But if you knew that, you wouldn't work for the FBI," she said. "You want to know about Bill. I'll tell you. I doubt he had anything to do with Courtney's disappearance."

"Why's that?"

"He's her father, for one thing. And I can't see him doing anything to hurt her."

"How do you know she's hurt?"

"You wouldn't be here otherwise." She paused, pretending to think. "I said I hadn't seen Bill in years. I lied. The truth is I saw Bill this summer. He was standing on the corner of First and Pine. He handed me one of those dreadful tracts about the Bible. I thanked him, then rushed home to call my bookie. I laid ten grand on Bill's conversion. Six months, outside odds, in case he actually believes the garbage he's spewing."

"How did that bet work out?"

"I lost that particular wager," she admitted. "But I plan on winning. I always win."

"And you had no other contact with him?"

"None. We have nothing left in common. Bill won't indulge in sins of the flesh anymore. And that's the only kind I'm interested in. The man lives like a hermit these days. A regular St. Augustine."

"St. Augustine wasn't a hermit."

"No?" She raised one perfectly painted eyebrow, then stifled her yawn.

～

Twenty-five minutes after leaving Seattle, I came to the small town of Snoqualmie, driving five miles past the casino until I came to the main street of town. Tiny lights, like white pin pricks, outlined an old railroad station, antique club cars resting on the iron tracks that divided the center of town.

I turned right on Fir Street, into a neighborhood of older bungalows with the spare and purposeful appearance of company houses. Short porches, no window trim, no affectations. The road ended at an unfinished cul-de-sac shaped like a question mark. My headlights rested on a thicket of bamboo as dense as an Asian jungle, the yellow leaves concealing the last house on the street.

When I climbed out of my car and closed the door, a chorus of dogs started barking. The breeze kicked up, shivering the bamboo leaves as I followed a gravel path through the forest. The barks sounded closer with each step. It was mad, crazed hounding, and when I came through the thicket, security lights strapped to trees lit up a wide brown lawn scraped to suede dirt. Black mutts, yellow labs, snarling German shepherds, each chained to separate cedar trunks. I stayed on the gravel path, walking toward a one-story rambler. The dogs leapt, choking at the end of their chains.

The house's screen door bowed off its frame. Lights were on inside. When I knocked on the wooden jamb, a voice yelled, "Come in!"

An orange cat darted out, snaking between my ankles and setting off a fresh round of hostile barking. The cat darted around the side of the house, disappearing into the bamboo.

"You here for Barnabas?" the man inside said.

He was thin and tall—at least six-four—and his ragged hair was the color of pennies left at the bottom of a purse. In one hand he held a telephone. The other cupped his ear, as if trying to hear.

"Barnabas?" he said again. "That who you want?"

I shook my head.

He lifted the phone, speaking to whoever was on the other end. "No, they're not taking Barnabas. You get here with the money, he's yours. But you'd better hurry."

He continued listening to the phone, pacing the small kitchen, where the appliances were the color of dried mustard and the pine cabinets held black knots the size of fists. A plastic box on the ceiling framed fluorescent lights, and Bill Johansen ducked his head every time he passed under it.

"Yeah, yeah, yeah, I got it already," he said. "You don't have to tell me again."

He was glancing toward me, but looking from the side of his face. His eyes were set so deeply that I couldn't see the color clearly. Blue? Green? The barking madness continued in the yard, a sound that seemed to jump directly on my eardrums. Then I heard him say, "Listen, you want Barnabas, come get him." He hung up, then turned to me. "So you're here for Joseph."

I shook my head.

"Those two are the only dogs I got ready. The others, I can't guarantee they won't bite."

When I handed him my card, his mouth compressed into a thin line. He read it carefully, then threw back his head and yelled, "Dr. Strangelove strikes again!"

The barking took off again, invigorated, the metal chains snapping, claws striking hollow stainless steel bowls.

I raised my voice, but he couldn't hear my question.

He stepped across the kitchen in four long strides and whipped open the screen door.

"Zip it!" he yelled.

The dogs fell silent.

Letting the door close softly, he continued to face the animals, his deep-set eyes inches from the aluminum screen. I heard a faint whimper from the yard. Followed by a quick, defiant bark.

Bill Johansen pointed his finger at the screen. "I heard that,

Saul." He kept his eyes on the yard. "That old gasbag across the street," he said, "whoever gave her a PhD is insane. You know how she makes a living? Studies people's sex lives. She's worse than a fornicator. That's why I call her Dr. Strangelove. Took me to court twice about these animals. Both times I told the judge, 'The only animals you got to worry about are the ones she calls patients.' I got my permit, nothing wrong with what I'm doing. Even the cop who comes out here, he's on my side."

Then he turned to look at me. His eyes sparkled, a prismatic blue. "So now she wants the Feds involved. I say, bring it on."

"Sir, I'm here about your daughter, Courtney."

"What about her?" he said.

"She's missing." I watched his face.

He stared at me for a moment, then looked out at the yard again. The security lights shone on the dogs that stared at the house with stiff expectant postures, chains taut. Underneath the chains, the tree bark had shredded into ribbons of orange raffia.

I kept watching him. "Do you know where she might be?"

He shook his head. "She doesn't talk to me anymore."

He had shut down. I took a different tack.

"Do you breed the dogs?" I asked.

"Breed?" He whipped his head toward me, his eyes filled with sudden disgust. "Breeding outta be outlawed, all the dogs getting gassed every day. I get my dogs from the pound. They're on death row. I train them, sell them on the Internet. Girl called this morning wanting Barnabas. He's that lab over there. The black one? I got him in Yakima. Face was full of porcupine quills, welts all over his body. They were about to put him down. Now look at him. A new creature." He barely paused. "What do you know about Courtney?"

"She went missing on Sunday—"

"I was in church, praying for her."

"Which church is that, sir?"

The blue eyes burned. "You a believer?"

For some reason I hesitated. "Yes, sir."

The leathery skin on his neck was braided with tendons, and when he raised his hand, the forearm revealed a tensile strength, a shadow of his visceral self, the masculinity that seduced a lonely wealthy woman into bearing an illegitimate daughter.

"On the third day, God told the earth to bring forth grass," he said. "The biggest grass God ever planted is that bamboo. And I admit, I first planted it so Dr. Strangelove couldn't spy on me. Five years later, the stuff hadn't grown an inch and I thought something was wrong with it. But then, *BAM*!"

His hand hit the door, the dogs barked.

But his eyes stayed on mine, his pupils narrowing into black shards in an aquamarine sea. He opened the screen door, never taking his eyes off me, and slammed it closed.

It sounded like a shotgun.

The dogs fell silent.

"That was my life," he said. "I sat in dirt and filth and people took me for dead. But one day God touched me. I was delivered; I was lifted out of my sin; I grew. The old things passed away. I shot out of the ground, a new man in Christ Jesus."

I construed my face into a smile, but he was speaking without need of response.

"No more gambling, no more drinking. All I needed was God. And that bamboo grew five feet in one month. And the next month and the next, until I realized how much I'm . . ."

Bill Johansen continued to talk but I wasn't listening. I stared at the gray roots of his coppery hair, the true color pushing forward like sea foam taking the beach of his scalp. And his eyes, his eyes were filled with manic electricity, that steep and narrow passion that swallows a convert.

"I told her, I said, 'God wants your life, Courtney. God wants you to quit gambling, just like me.' But she wouldn't listen. And then, and then, she stopped talking to me. Oh, Lord, how I prayed for my girl. I fasted. Forty days. I repented. I cried out. It was my fault, I led her into that den of iniquity—I did that, to my own child! And now, now what's happened to her?"

I watched his hands puncturing the air, his arms lifted in agony. Bill Johansen was a man bearing so much guilt and shame and remorse that his repentance snapped with the sound of a tight banner whipped by torrential winds. The light had chased dark away, but darkness never went quietly. It always tried to return, appreciating nothing so much as a clean place to begin again.

"It's because I didn't answer God right away," he went on. "I found the truth but—" He stopped. "You have a question?"

"Yes," I said. "Yes, may I use your restroom?"

He frowned, confused. "You have to go to the bathroom?"

No. "Yes," I said.

He lifted one long lean arm, pointing. "Down the hall."

I walked slowly, sweeping my eyes left and right. Stacks of newspapers were piled in the hallway, gray stalagmites covered with cat hair that collected on the inked plateaus. What accumulated news did Bill Johansen find so essential, I wondered. Evidence of conspiracies. Proof of some kind. Three white doors lay open ahead of me, like dove wings folded back. I passed the bathroom.

"On your right," he said,

I nodded and turned inside, locking the door. The white porcelain sink was stained. The toilet bowl held a jaundiced pool of urine. I opened my cell phone and dialed Lucia.

"Do we have a profile for the perp?" I whispered.

"We've been trying to call you," she said. "Where are you?"

"Give me the profile."

"Raleigh, where—"

"I need it, now," I growled.

"We think he wants to teach them a lesson," she said. "It's not just about money. He's torturing her, torturing them. Raleigh, you have to—"

I heard a knock on the bathroom door.

"You all right?" Johansen asked.

"Yes, I'm fine." I pressed the phone to my shoulder and reached down, flushing the toilet.

I heard the floorboards creak, his footsteps falling away.

I lifted the phone. "I'll call you later."

"Tell me where you are."

"I'm in the birth father's house." I turned on the faucet. The pipes squealed.

"And?" Lucia asked.

I let the water run full blast and opened the medicine cabinet above the small sink.

There was a tube of Neosporin, one pink bottle of Benadryl, some generic-brand aspirin with the childproof cap missing, giving the bottle a headless appearance.

"He's crazy." I closed the medicine cabinet, turning off the faucets. When I looked at my reflection in the mirror, it was flecked with opaque drops from the mineral-hard water. Dark circles hung under my eyes, and I was about to look away when I saw the small white card wedged into the mirror's rusting edge. Water drops had melted some of the ink, making the letters look like blue tears.

But the block handwriting offered one word.

OBEDIENCE

He had drawn a box around the center of the word, severing three letters in the middle from the others.

DIE

I turned on the faucets again and gave Lucia the address, told her it was urgent, and then hung up, unsnapping my holster. I turned off the faucets, ran my hands over my hair, thinking, then opened the bathroom door.

Bill Johansen stood at the end of the hall, facing me. His back was against the screen door, and I could see the lights in the yard, the wild dogs.

"Are you sick?" he said, as I walked toward him. "You don't look well."

"Yes, I should go. Thank you for your time, sir."

I moved for the door.

"You can't leave."

"I have an appointment."

"I want to pray for you."

"My colleagues, they're expecting me, they're—"

"And you never told me what you know about Courtney."

I pressed my tongue against my bottom teeth, trying to relax my face. "Nothing, at the moment. If you hear something, please call us. You have my card."

I stepped forward and he did not step aside. Reaching around him, I pushed open the door. His body odor had a fetid cloistered scent, and from somewhere far away the dogs barked, the sound muffled and metallic, like oarlocks striking against a wooden boat. The night air felt crisp and I took the last step too quickly, twisting my left ankle, grabbing the handrail, an unpainted two-by-four. My heart jumped at the back of my throat.

"Be careful, Raleigh."

I looked up. He was staring out the screen door, his face

filled with angular shadows, the hash of metal over his ruddy skin like woven chain mail.

I counted my steps to the bamboo stalks. The dogs lunged. And the wind made itself known in the sibilant leaves, the canes striking against each other with a hollow knocking sound.

chapter twenty-three

I parked down the block, still on Fir Street, and called McLeod.
"I found the birth father," I said.

"Lutini just told me," he said. "What's your read?"

I described his background in gambling, and the religious conversion that separated him from the world of poker and his daughter. And then I told him about the note, tucked into the edge of the mirror.

"The handwriting looks identical," I said.

"You think it's him?" McLeod said.

"Something's wrong with the guy."

"Is Jack with you?"

"No, sir."

He paused. "Who's with you?"

"Nobody."

"You went in alone?"

"I was making a quick call, just to get a read. I wanted to make sure he was the guy my source said he was. By no means was he considered a threat. Nobody believes he's involved but I'm not so sure."

"So you went in alone?" McLeod repeated.

"You saw the finger. I'm not wasting time, sir. We've got to bring him in."

There was a significant pause.

"I'll get surveillance on the house," he said. "Lutini's already called the local cops; they're on their way. We'll get a search warrant ASAP, bring this guy in tonight. The notecard's in the bathroom?"

But before I could answer, there was a loud static crackle, followed by a muffled sound. Like the phone was being cupped. McLeod came back on. "Yeah, okay. Don't leave until the locals get there. Tell me again, the card said what?"

"The word 'obedience.' But the word 'die' was separated from the rest of the word."

"'Die' is in obedience?"

"Yes, sir."

"Let's hope he doesn't flush it. Anything else?"

I recalled my approach to the house, how the front door was open. And at my knock, he did not react with suspicion. He was expecting somebody to pick up a dog.

"If it's him, he's even more dangerous than we thought."

"What makes you say that?"

"An FBI agent in his kitchen, asking questions, and all he wants to do is preach. It fits Lutini's profile, about teaching lessons. And what the handwriting examiner came up with."

"'Obedience.'"

"Correct. He told me he wanted his daughter out of gambling. He might believe his own redemption depends on it. Kidnapping might seem like a justifiable means to the end."

When the police cruisers turned down Fir Street, I closed the phone and climbed out of the car, briefing two officers to watch the house; nobody was to leave it. But I didn't go into detail, since it was possible the local cops were buddies with Bill Johansen, at least acquaintances from all the complaints from Dr. Strangelove.

When I climbed back into my car, waiting for the Feds to arrive, it was ten minutes past 9:00 p.m. I stared out the windshield, the streetlights reflecting off the dark underbellies of the low clouds, the billowing shapes looking strange and tormented.

Twenty minutes later, the FBI showed up.

And I drove away, trying not to think about the fact that one of the agents was Byron Ngo.

≈

It was just past 10:00 p.m. when I drove down the VanAlstyne's long driveway, my headlights flashing on red maple leaves washed from the trees.

Two surveillance vans were parked outside, and McLeod stood by the front door under an enormous coach light. Next to him stood a state trooper, the door guard. It wasn't Lowell.

"Sir," I said to McLeod.

His white shirt was rumpled, the starched cotton fractured into acute angles. "We just got another note," he said. "I sent it down to the lab. But it named you."

I told him I'd already talked to the examiner about the ESDA that showed my name scrawled on the paper above the note.

He shook his head. "That's not it. We got another one. Come inside. The parents are restless."

He walked across the polished foyer into the living room populated by FBI agents and techies—I saw both Tweedles—and beyond to the dining room where an empty mahogany table would seat twenty comfortably, and then he walked into the kitchen. Martin VanAlstyne stood at the island wearing a dark nylon jogging suit with gray piping. The skin on his face had an unnatural shine. In one hand, he held a glass of orange juice, and when he set it on the black granite countertop, the burst of citrus color seemed extraordinary because the room had a mono-chromatic rigidity. Black counters, white cabinets, stainless steel appliances, black-and-white ceramic tiles laid in checkerboards across the floor.

The assistant, Sequoia, stood behind her boss, clothed in black. The expression on her face could have been taken from the freezer.

Mrs. VanAlstyne sat on the other side of the room at a white marble table, the window panes behind her obsidian with the night. Her pale hair was pulled into a ponytail. She looked haggard. Lucia Lutini sat next to her, brown eyes focused.

McLeod said, "Agent Harmon, as I told you, went to see the birth father. She believes there's some likelihood he's involved in your daughter's disappearance."

I heard Mrs. VanAlstyne swallow a section of air. I glanced across the room. The husband's face was set, like a slab of marble. It helped explain the physical distance between them; she'd told him the truth, and now warring factions had separated with their aides-de-camp.

McLeod explained how our surveillance would continue on Bill Johansen's house until the search warrant was signed and an arrest was made.

"When this last note came in, Harmon was in his house. So he's got somebody helping him. It would be a mistake to put all our eggs in one casket."

I glanced at Martin VanAlstyne. The wave of contempt that washed over his lean face constricted the muscles around his mouth. But this was a day of grand disappointments and Allen McLeod's verbal incapacity appeared to join the rest of today's trouble. Just as quickly as it arrived, the disdainful expression evaporated.

"Since we've got surveillance on the birth father, we'll tackle the note." McLeod turned to Mr. VanAlstyne. "You're certain you can raise the money by midnight?"

"I'm certain," he said.

"Mr. VanAlstyne, we are doing everything possible to get your daughter back," McLeod said, mistaking the expression he saw on the man's face. "You have my word on that."

I could see the cogs clicking past each other, all the latches of thought within Martin VanAlstyne's mind, rotating over the recent developments that had altered his well-ordered life. *My* daughter? *Your* word?

But he didn't reply.

And McLeod was already turning to leave, walking from the kitchen through the long opulent maze of the VanAlstyne residence. Lucia stayed at the table.

I followed McLeod.

We gathered on the lower level, in a room filled with pristine fitness equipment. Floor-to-ceiling mirrors reflected a view of the white Berber carpet, so spotless I could see the fine spray of black rubber shavings under the treadmill.

I sat on one of the padded black benches, near the triple rack of chrome free-weights, the dumbbells stretching across the wall, doubling in the mirror. Our SWAT guys fanned out among the other benches, and I counted eleven of the fourteen agents from Violent Crimes. McLeod stood at the front of the room with Basker. And just before he began talking, Jack came through the door, his face flushed. He made brief eye contact with McLeod, who nodded at him.

"Glad you could make it, Stephanson," McLeod said, "Now, everybody, I want this to be clear. It's not something I would say in front of the family, but if we have a choice between losing their money and losing our agent, we lose their money. Got that? I know it sounds obvious, but you'd be surprised what happens when you're talking about half a million dollars.

"Now the instructions are as follows," he continued. "The perp has singled out Harmon. We don't know why. But he wants her as the designated drop. The perp is mentioning her by name. So we take this guy seriously, got it? The note says she's to take the money up Tiger Mountain at 1:15 a.m. Sharp. Alone. That's less than two hours from now. If anybody follows, the note says the VanAlstyne girl dies and then Harmon dies. Of course, we'll follow.

"Second. The note says Harmon is to hike to the first signpost on the trail. We know from experience that this will not—again *not*—be the actual drop point. He'll bounce her from there to another spot. And he'll be watching for us. SWAT will be positioned in the woods around that first spot. And we'll have agents fanned out over the mountain."

He looked at Basker. Basker nodded.

"Three. Harmon will be wearing a transmitter. She can tell us what the next spot is, when she finds out. SWAT is going to track her—again, without detection—but this is going to be difficult, people. It's night, it's dark out there. That's his plan. He knows this mountain."

Jack raised his hand.

"Stephanson, go."

"Any other ways we can track Harmon?"

I stared at him. His face was unreadable.

"We're sending up a plane. The pilot has FLIR."

FLIR, or forward-looking infrared, meant a small camera was mounted on the front of the plane. Roughly the size of a basketball, the infrared camera was controlled by the copilot.

Jack raised his hand again.

"Stephanson."

"You don't think the perp will hear the plane's engine? If he says not to follow, the plane is a huge tip-off."

I still couldn't read his expression. I looked at McLeod.

"The pilot will stay far enough away laterally, it'll be difficult to detect the engine. And they're calling for rain, which will help with sound."

Basker said SWAT was driving to Tiger Mountain in the next five minutes, to fan out among the trails with topographic maps, wearing body armor, carrying radios, and packing M4s.

"It's too risky for Harmon to carry an HT," McLeod said, referring to the Handie Talkie that provided two-way transmission. "If he hears us talking to her, it's over."

He looked at me. I nodded. My hands felt clammy.

"When Harmon gets to the final drop point, wherever that is, we follow the pickup. Most likely, it will not be our mark, just some dope he hired. But we can't afford to lose him. We'll follow him to the kidnapper, who leads us to the girl. Preferably alive. And Harmon makes her way back down the mountain."

Just like that.

"All clear?" he said.

chapter twenty-four

Tiger Mountain was the third mountain in the Issaquah Alps, two hills away from Cougar Mountain, where Courtney's car had been abandoned. In the Tiger Mountain parking lot off I-90, McLeod held up an aluminum-frame backpack, grasping it by its upper edges, like a man offering to help a woman into her coat.

I slipped my arms through the padded nylon straps, shrugging the pack into place. Broken into twenties and fifties, $500,000 weighed a considerable amount and it forced me to lean forward to counterbalance. When I glanced up into McLeod's face it was lit by the headlights of his car, and it appeared that some of his characteristic abstraction was gone. No worries about protocol, no concern about regulation, no more bureaucratic distractions that tripped him into malaprops.

"Too heavy?" he asked.

"No, sir," I lied. "I'm fine."

He placed one hand on my right shoulder, closing his eyes. I stared up into the clouds, the western edges tinged by a diffused orange color, light pollution from the city. I would not have taken my supervisor for a praying man, but then he was a man who focused on power, where it resided in any given situation, always pointing himself toward it. He opened his eyes.

"Your transmitter is good for four hours," he said. "If you need batteries, we put spares in the pack. But be careful. Don't let him see you doing that."

I nodded.

"We've got eleven agents on this mountain, Harmon. The plane is tracking you overhead. We won't lose you."

I nodded, turning, and walked toward the trailhead. A damp chilly dew descended on the fallen leaves, causing my boots to slip on the ground. The backpack bearing down on my shoulders, I shined my flashlight up the trail, my breath appearing in foggy cumulus clouds before disappearing into the dark. I stopped once to drink water from the plastic bottle secured to the side of the pack, and listened for the airplane but could not hear it.

When I started up the trail again, sweat rolled down my back, and in the nocturnal solitude my mind performed mean tricks. The trees turned sinister, limbs reaching for me like grasping arms. The low bushes snarled. The rocks seemed as coiled as rabid vermin. Hiking at a deliberate pace, I tried to keep my breath steady. When that failed, I thought of my mother, of the times when her mind slipped into precipitous depths and sent back paralyzing delusions. I knew the power of tangible fear. It pressed against the crumbling wall of my mind, I pressed back.

"I'm past the one-mile mark," I whispered into my one-way transmitter. "I can't hear the plane. I can't see anybody."

I kept the flashlight pointed forward, my eyes on the light, following the switchbacks. I thought of Courtney VanAlstyne. I thought of the soil under her torn nail. The panic it represented, the clawing it would take to put it there.

At the first signpost, I found a piece of white paper. It was folded in half, gleaming under my flashlight. I pulled it out from under the thumbtack on the post, hoping a fingerprint would remain on the tack.

I whispered into my transmitter. "I have a note. It reads, 'LEAVE $10,000. PROCEED ON TRAIL TO NEXT SIGNPOST.'"

I slid the pack from my shoulders, feeling suddenly light, the cold air hitting the moisture on my back and sending shivers down my spine. I kept turning my head, thinking I heard something as I unzipped the main compartment and took out two $5,000 bundles of cash, setting them under the signpost.

I unscrewed the cap of my water bottle, still listening. Somewhere deep within the dark evergreens, an owl hooted. After that, the mountain sounded even quieter than before. In the far distance, I thought I detected a steady hum, an engine. I hoped. Hoisting the backpack onto my shoulders again, I continued the climb. My hands felt numb from the cold, though my back still sweated.

Half a mile later, I reached the next signpost. And another note. It gave identical instructions.

I unloaded another 10K, then followed the trail.

I found the same instructions at nine more stops, and when I reached the summit of Tiger Mountain, a soft drizzle had begun to fall from the clouds. The skin on my face was slick from sweat and rain and I blinked away the water, shining my light into the forest. I appeared to be on a rough granite outcropping, with a valley to my left where I could feel rushes of cold air pulling down.

On my right, more woods.

"Hello?" I said.

The area was so dark and narrow between the trees it was difficult to find any sort of clearing. I raked the flashlight beam, the pale yellow light striking the gray curtains of rain. And then

I saw the white square of paper. It rested on one long wet limb. I walked over, picked it up. The paper was dry.

"LEAVE THE MONEY HERE. RETURN TO THE TRAIL. OBEY. OR SHE DIES."

I read the note aloud. Then a second time, stressing the words "obey" and "die." Slipping off the pack, I placed the aluminum frame against the tree trunk, the boughs trembling, water falling from the branches, drumming against the pack's tight nylon.

My breath was too fast, fueled by adrenaline, and the rain was coming harder, faster, as though approaching from the sky. I quickly pulled the batteries from the pack's front pocket, slipping them into my jeans, and walked away, my head down against the rain, my ears straining.

Suddenly I turned and shined the flashlight.

The pack leaned against the tree, nylon dripping.

He wasn't that stupid, I told myself, turning around again. And we had people waiting for the pickup. I was supposed to leave. I was supposed to obey.

In low whispers, I informed McLeod that I was starting the climb down without the pack. No word about the girl.

I walked in silence, wondering if she would be standing on the trail, waiting. If he let her go. We had left the pack. He had the money. My mind filled with hope, with a happy conclusion that would bring this horror to a close, an end that would restore Courtney VanAlstyne to her privileged place in this world, the end that would allow me to walk away. To sleep again. I began running, mind and body racing, and when his hand grabbed my arm, I knew this nightmare was far from over.

I turned, pulling, trying to shine the light in his eyes. I reached for my gun. But his grip was vise-tight. Something stabbed my side. I doubled over.

"You move one muscle and your spine goes out your stomach." He yanked the flashlight from my hand, pulling my gun from its holster.

"Where is she?" I said. "What did you do with her?"

He pressed the sharp object deeper into my side. I bent again, the pain crossing one side of my body to the other.

"Is she here? Is she with you?"

"Shut your mouth," he whispered, yanking my hands back. I tried to ask something else, to get him to speak so I could hear his voice again, but the metal hasps closed over my wrists, and the gun shoved deeper into my side until I couldn't speak. One of his hands moved methodically across my shoulders, down each side of my body, across to the middle again until he found the transmitter. He lifted my sweatshirt and twisted the small box from the adhesive tape.

"Take the money," I said. "Just leave her. Don't—"

I heard a whipping sound and ducked. But he wasn't striking at me. It was the transmitter. It landed far to my left, toward the valley where the cold air rushed up the side of the mountain. Where was SWAT? The plane?

"Raleigh." He nuzzled into my hair. "I'm so glad you obeyed."

I wanted to pull away. But I resisted, still trying to place the voice. Get a sense of his height. Weight. That voice. I turned my head but he jabbed the sharp metallic nose of the barrel.

"Obey the orders," he whispered. "Then you can have the girl back."

Grabbing my right elbow, he pushed me forward, walking me toward the trees. We left the trail, and I had to lift my right shoulder to keep the wet tree limbs from swooping into my face. I stumbled forward, for what seemed miles, and then felt water rushing over my boots. Fast and sudden water, a stream washing down the mountain. I kept trying to turn my head and get a glimpse of him, but each time I did he shoved me forward again. My feet sank into another shallow gulley, with another stream.

He told me to stop.

I waited, listening.

Praying. Praying.

His voice was nothing more than a whisper, and I had to strain to hear him over the rushing water. He unlocked the cuffs, the gun still at my back.

"When I start counting, you start running," he said in the strange whisper. "I'll count to forty. That's your head start, Raleigh. Then the hunt begins. I play this game with Courtney. She loves it. You will too."

"One," he said.

My heart slammed against my ribs.

"Two . . . three . . . four . . ."

I ran. My boots slipped. I fell. My knee hit the ground. I leaned forward, trying to stand up.

". . . seven . . . eight . . . nine . . ." He was going faster.

I ran straight into the woods, branches snapping at my eyes. Rain hammered the ground, my lungs felt seared. My throat burned. When I stopped to listen, I was panting too hard to hear. I held my breath. And then I heard him. Crashing through the water.

I started running again, tripping, rolling down the mountain until I hit something. I stood up, one thought streaking across my brain. *The plane.* Could it see me this deep in the forest? I bolted right, making a blind run in search of that water, that clearing where the plane could spot me. A primal fear flitted between my thoughts like a blade.

Blade.

The blade. I stopped, looking up the hill. His flashlight was cutting through the forest like a scythe. I stepped behind a thick pine tree, the rough bark digging into my back, and squatted, searching inside my left pant leg until my fingers touched the wood-burned letters.

I pulled out the knife and pressed the small button.

The blade flicked out, a menacing sound, and for one split-second my mind saw the old man at the truck stop. With my other hand, I picked up a stick. His legs moved under the flashlight beam, his boots kicking through dead wet leaves. I wanted to run. Every cell screamed for it. But his advantages were too many, mine were too few. He walked down the mountain with calm purpose, with a plan. All I had was fear.

He was twenty feet away when he stopped.

I held my breath.

He started down the hill again, slowly, heading toward me. I threw the stick. It landed on the other side of him, the flashlight whipping toward the sound.

In the ambient glow, I could see his right hand raised above the beam. The gun. But I could not see his face. It was dark, obscured.

"I know you're here, Raleigh." He was still whispering. "And I'm disappointed. I hoped you would play longer."

He was stepping across the hillside. I could hear the leather of his boots creaking. But the flashlight was still pointed toward the stick.

I drew a deep breath.

Then he stopped. The beam began to turn in the other direction, moving toward me, and I watched the light become fractured by dark tree trunks, the rain falling from branch to leaf to dirt. He was eight feet away, coming closer, seven, six.

I jumped.

I hit him behind the knees. One of his boots struck my left hip, the other left the ground. I heard the heels clap against each other, the beam of light traversing a wide slow arc, ending in a hard bounce.

The beam shuddered on the forest floor as his body hit the ground, and I heard the sound of air bursting from his lungs and I sank the knife into his flesh. Felt the metal hit bone, an oddly delicate sound.

He howled.

I heard rage. No fear.

I pulled out the knife, sinking it one more time. Then I stood, and I ran.

I ran with a scream suppressed at my collar bone, my shoulders lifting to my ears, waiting for the sound of the gun, the barrel releasing the bullet into my back. I ran, my legs falling through gravity, tumbling down the steep incline, my body slamming into tree trunks, bouncing off. I ran until my boots splashed through the water. I ran the gulley, following the stream that soaked my jeans and tugged at my ankles like quicksand. I ran and the water puddled into a basin, the soil compact, flattening out. I ran, stumbling forward, and heard the earth echoing my footfalls. I ran until I saw the stroboscopic red lights flashing through the trees. I ran, a scared moth fleeing the darkest cave in the forest. I ran.

I ran.

chapter twenty-five

When I opened my eyes, the remnants of a dream hovered between sudden sight and lost sleep. I heard a familiar voice. It was coming from the figure trundling through a wide doorway, and when I realized who it was, pain twisted inside my skull, stabbing my forehead.

"I couldn't find any organic," Claire said. "But I got us some muffins. You don't like it, Charlotte, you go back. I'm about to take the fetal position after all the dead people I saw in that cafeteria—hey, look!" She pointed at me. "Raleigh's awake."

Claire the Clairvoyant set a tray on my bed and turned to Aunt Charlotte, who was sitting in a chair at the foot of the bed, her head bowed, her auburn hair looking as dry as false flames in an electric fireplace.

Claire shook her shoulder. "Charlotte, wake up!"

My aunt startled and something fell from her hands to the floor. She bent to pick it up, rushing over, lifting a blue pitcher from the table beside the bed. She splashed water into a paper cup.

"Drink this," she said. "All of it."

"Wait, I—"

She wrapped one hand behind my head, pressing my face

toward the cup. I lifted my hand, an IV pinching the skin on the back of my hand. Water dribbled down my chin, soaking the hospital gown.

She poured another cup; I drank that too.

"You're dehydrated," she said.

"Where's Mom?" My throat felt raw.

"She doesn't know a thing, don't worry," she said. "I'm never making that mistake again. How do you feel?"

"My head hurts."

Claire leaned over the bed. "You want me to get a nurse? I saw one next door giving shots."

I stared into Aunt Charlotte's eyes, pleading.

"Yes, Claire," she said. "Why don't you go do that."

Claire walked to the door. She turned left, then suddenly turned right. Seconds later, I saw her circular shape crossing in front of the door, heading left again.

"You don't like her," Aunt Charlotte said.

"If she's a clairvoyant, she should know if I want a nurse."

"She's got a good heart." Aunt Charlotte stroked my forehead. "She watched your mother for me this morning."

"What?"

"I didn't have a choice, Raleigh. Those people from your office called; it was almost three in the morning. They asked to speak to your mother. I said, 'Whatever it is, tell me, I'm the aunt.' When your boss said you were in the hospital I almost had my stroke right there. First thing I thought was somebody shot you. I lost your father, now I was going to lose you. What could I do, leave your mother alone, with this going on? So I called Claire, told her to stay at the house, and I drove right over here."

"Claire. You called *Claire*?"

"Raleigh, I didn't want your mother waking up to some stranger in the house. And the cats, they were acting very weird. Claire knows animal CPR."

"But Claire is here."

"Yes, well . . ." Her voice trailed off.

"What happened?"

"Well, your mother was very polite, talking with that Southern drawl, but she didn't mince words."

"What did she say?"

"She told Claire to get the hell out of the house."

I suddenly felt warm all over. My mother, my hero. "Did she wonder why Claire was there?"

"Yes. I had to lie. I said there'd been a break-in at the store, you were out of town for work again, and I needed to clean up the broken glass," she said. "Then your mom kicked Claire out and she came down here. I was starting to worry you'd never wake up, stay in a coma the rest of your life. I even started to—well, never mind—you seem fine now. Just like your old self."

I glanced out the window. The rolling topography of Capital Hill crossed under a sky so blue it was malachite. The autumn leaves glowed with a burnished beauty, and when I turned to Aunt Charlotte, staring into her familiar face, I suddenly remembered the dream, the dream interrupted by Claire's flat nasal voice talking about muffins.

I had been standing at the dry river rocks again, only this time my father was beside me, lifting a stone, speaking to me. I knew he was about to offer the key to unlock this vault of secrets, when I heard: "I couldn't find any organic."

"I had a dream," I told her. "Dad was in it. He was trying to tell me something."

"Something like, wake up? I was meditating on that. I'll bet you were touched by my thoughts."

"Aunt Charlotte, I keep having this same dream—"

"Dream!" Claire hurried back into the room. "Dream! You are not gonna believe the dream I had."

I closed my eyes.

"That girl, Raleigh," she was saying, "the one you're trying to find? She was in my dream. Know how I know?"

When I didn't reply, my aunt said, "How, Claire?"

"Because I saw a badger. That's right. I saw a huge badger. It was staring right at me. Foaming at the mouth. Like it had rabies. It was going to attack me, but I woke up."

"Pity," I mumbled.

"Claire," my aunt said, while throwing me a scolding look, "did you find the nurse?"

"On her way. Raleigh, this badger was so real I could've touched it. Just like my vision about the place of fire. We are talking animal sacrifices here. Live creatures, getting thrown into the fire."

"Would you just—" I began.

My aunt laid her hand on my arm. "Raleigh needs to rest." She leaned down, kissing my forehead, a scent of patchouli clinging to her tunic.

The object in her left hand grazed my forearm. Perpendicular planes of pale crystals intersected to form a perfect cross. Staurolite. A mineral cross, Mother Nature's crucifix. My aunt had been praying.

I looked up at her. "Check on Mom?"

"First thing," she said.

After they left, I waited for the nurse. After twenty minutes,

I pressed the yellow call button on the steel bed rail. Ten minutes later, I pressed it again. After that, I pressed it at every count to sixty.

Seventeen minutes later, the nurse appeared.

She wore a white apron over her white uniform, her white wedge shoes squeaking across the polished floor. Reaching up behind me, she flicked off the call button.

"You only have to ring it once," she said, brusquely. "What's the matter?"

"Why am I here?"

She stared at me. "What do you mean, why?"

"Is anything broken?"

She squeaked to the foot of the bed, lifting the electronic chart, tapping the LCD screen with a plastic stylus. Between stabs of the stylus, she pursed her thin lips. Her fingers carried no rings, no jewelry around her neck that said whether she belonged to somebody, anybody, and I imagined her going home at night, drained of good will. I took a deep breath, releasing it slowly.

"Multiple contusions, erratic heartbeat . . ." She looked up. "I don't see anything else, but the doctor can tell you more."

"When does he come in?"

"She. Dr. Michaela Smith's on rounds today."

"And when does Dr. Smith come in?"

"She's a doctor. They come when they feel like it."

The nurse walked out of the room.

I counted to ten, then pulled the IV from the back of my left hand. The quarter-inch probe dripped clear liquid onto the white bed sheet, and I pressed my right index finger against the burning vein, staunching the blood flow. I swung my legs over the side of the bed. My left ankle was mottled with purple bruises.

So was the right one. But they didn't hurt, which told me I was fine or full of drugs.

I shuffled to the bathroom, feeling dizzy and nauseated, and found my clothes stuffed into two white plastic bags on a metal hook. My jeans were wet, the cuffs full of sandy soil and torn leaves, and my white socks were brown, cold, but my sweatshirt was almost dry.

I finger-combed my knotted hair, looking at myself in the mirror. Under the fluorescent light, my pupils waxed and waned. I splashed cold water on my face, then walked down the hall, feeling less dizzy but more nauseated. Nobody was at the nurse's station. I walked back to my room, sat on the bed, and pressed the call button six times.

When the nurse appeared again, standing in the door, her large face bore an expression of peevish offense. That was followed surprise.

"What do you think you're doing?" she said.

"I'm checking out."

"You can't check out. The doctor has to check you out."

"Will you call her, please?"

"No, I won't call her."

My memory of last night was vague, but I recalled talking to someone who wasn't there. I presumed it was by cell phone. "I'd like to have my cell phone back, too, before I leave."

She placed her hands on her hips. "Who do you think you are?"

"Nobody. I just want to go home."

"This is unacceptable, totally unacceptable. I'm calling the doctor."

Funny how that worked, I thought, as she pivoted with a rubber squeak and left the room. I counted to fifteen, then walked down the hall in the opposite direction of the nurse's station, deciding that McLeod would have taken my cell phone, if I'd had one.

Although my vision was blurry, I squinted and saw the green EXIT signs for the stairwell. Following the stairs down to the lobby, I came out next to the gift shop. A bank of pay phones waited on the wall. I asked the operator to make a collect call, then heard the operator ask Lucia Lutini if she would accept the charges.

The operator thanked me for using AT&T.

"Raleigh, are you all right?" Lucia said.

"I'm fine. Can you pick me up?"

"They're releasing you?"

"Pretty much."

In the background, I could hear a flurry of voices, the emphatic inflected Italian that Lucia answered almost as emphatically. I waited. She came back on the phone and said, "I'm down at Danato's. My dad wants to know if you want a sandwich."

≈

The warm foil in my hands smelled of sage and caramelized onions, and I decided that if I was salivating, I must be fine. Lucia drove her Camry down Madison Avenue, the hills so steep I had to press my feet into the floorboard to keep from sliding forward on the leather seat. My left ankle throbbed.

"You left without the doctor's permission?" she said.

"What makes you think that?"

"No wheelchair. They wheel people out, particularly in your condition." She glanced over. "Do you remember anything from last night?"

"The sound of water. Red lights. Somebody screaming."

"That was you."

"I was screaming?"

She nodded. "You're lucky to be alive. After the perp tossed your transmitter, we lost you. The plane reported two images, then the figures split up. One ran down the mountain. You."

"Did we get him?"

"We lost him. We didn't get the money either."

"We had eleven agents out there. How did we lose him?"

She stopped at the light on Second Avenue. "All those $10,000 bundles he told you drop along the trail? It was brilliant. It meant one agent stayed there, waiting for a pickup. He split our forces. By the time you got to the top, we had one guy left and he was neutralized."

"Neutralized?"

"The perp didn't kill him," she said. "But he knocked him out, then took his gun and radio and cuffed him to a tree. The lab is running the cuffs, trying to source them, along with the duct tape."

"Didn't the plane's infrared catch this?"

"The plane was following you, remember? McLeod's orders were to save the agent, not the money."

"But where did we lose him?"

She gave one of her Italian gestures, signifying an unknown. "Somewhere on that mountain."

"He just disappeared?"

"It sounds better than saying we lost him, and the money. The VanAlstynes took it as you might imagine. The kidnapper got away with the money, didn't release their daughter, and now there's absolutely no reason to expect we'll hear from him again."

She pulled into the parking lot by the waterfront, stopping behind the Barney Mobile. Somebody had driven it over.

"What about the birth father, we connected him to this?" I said.

"It was a good theory," she said. "He's in custody, denying any involvement. And . . ."

"And what?"

"I watched tapes of his interrogation, Raleigh. He's got some weird religious convictions, certainly. But he was in custody while you were on that mountain. And I don't believe he's capable of working with an accomplice."

"What about the handwriting?"

"The state lab is examining the note, maybe there will be something to it." She looked at my hands. "You should eat that sandwich before it gets cold."

I nodded, taking a moment, weighing my words. "What's your take on Jack?"

"Jack? He's an egomaniac."

"But have you ever considered him unstable?"

"Unstable." She glanced toward Puget Sound. A green and white ferry pulled away from the pier's creosote-coated pilings, water churning under its engines. "Years ago I turned Jack down for a date. After that, he ignored me. No stalking. No persecution. But he has a massive ego, the personality of a showoff. Of course, the same thing could be said for half of the guys in Violent Crimes. They all want to slay the dragon, save the world, win the princess's heart." She paused. "What are you asking me, Raleigh?"

As carefully as possible, I told her about Jack's number appearing on Stacee Warner's cell phone. How he answered the phone when I dialed the number, what he said about a close call. And I described the moment we ran into Stacee at the casino, how Jack pretended not to know her.

"Maybe he didn't know her then," she said.

"Lucia."

"Okay, so Jack's dating somebody who's also part of a case. It's a big no-no. He should have reported his involvement. But it's also a big no-no to walk out of the hospital without a medical release."

"The dating occurred to me too," I said, ignoring the comparison. "But there are some other factors. The soil in her boots matches what Jack had me collect on Mount Si. And then Ernie Suggs, he's her boss at the casino, he works the card game at Sea-Tac. And she just happens to be the roommate of the missing girl? Lucia, it's like I can see the web, I just can't find the spider."

"Then bring her in," Lucia said. "Ask her some questions."

"And Jack?"

"I wouldn't mind seeing Jack squirm." She smiled. "Let's keep an eye on him."

≈

On the way to Aunt Charlotte's, I drove with one hand on the wheel, the other on the sandwich. Danato Lutini, I decided, was a miracle worker. After eating his food, I started to feel almost normal.

But when I walked into my aunt's bungalow, the house smelled of smoke and soot. In the front room, the wall looked as if a black tongue had licked the mantle. Aunt Charlotte was scooping up ashes with an iron hearth shovel. Her face bore a striking resemblance to my father. It was the expression in her eyes, the look of somebody who loved and ached in equal amounts at the same moment.

I stood in the doorway. "What happened?"

She turned to look at me. "I came to check on her. Claire and I pulled up, and the smoke alarms were going off. My neighbor, Mr. Chin, was running down the sidewalk and I ran in here.

Claire was with me, screaming about 'the place of fire' and your mother was ramming the broom handle into the ceiling, trying to destroy the smoke alarms."

I waited. "Was anybody hurt?"

She shook her head. "The fire department showed up. They found the flue was closed. Your mother was burning things in the fireplace, a lot of smoke. The firemen lectured me and left."

"I'm sorry, Aunt Charlotte. I—"

"Honey, it's not your fault. It's mine."

"Yours?"

"I sent Claire over here this morning. It upset your mother. She told me Claire wanted to steal something, so your mother decided to burn it all before Claire could get it. She even burned some of your father's things. Oh, Raleigh, I had no idea she was this bad off."

"I'll give you money for damages."

"Don't you dare." She shook the shovel at me.

Opal, one of the cats, sauntered toward Aunt Charlotte, slow and begrudging, front paws crossing over each other, bushy tail straight and high. Aunt Charlotte picked up the cat, burying her face in the thick fur, murmuring apologies. Opal stared at me, unblinking.

"Where's Mom now?" I asked.

"She went to lie down, in her room."

I first went to my room to change clothes, my ragged appearance sure to disturb my mother further. As I pulled clean clothes from the chest of drawers, I tried to ignore the newly bare spaces on my walls. I walked down the hallway to her bedroom, knocking on the door. Madame gave a quick bark.

My mother was sitting on the edge of the double bed, staring out the window to the back yard. The breeze outside was lifting brown leaves from gray branches, scattering them across the grass.

"The trees, they look like bare hands," she said. "Like they're reaching for something."

"Yes."

She turned to me, her eyes saturated with color. "Have you noticed how many homeless people there are in this city?"

I nodded.

"They're everywhere, Raleigh. The walking dead, like the people that horrible woman Claire keeps talking about." She glanced out the window again.

"Aunt Charlotte's staying home for the day. I'll be home this evening."

She turned. "Come with me to a service?"

"Sure."

"I found a wonderful place downtown," she said. "You'll like it."

I gently closed her door and walked back to my bedroom. The walls offered faded shadows of my father's accomplishments, a series of blank squares to represent his life on earth. When I stepped into the closet, I smelled a damp chthonous odor rising from the wet clothing on the floor. Lifting my face, I spoke to the one who knew everything, the one who knew this mortal life. Who knew love, and how it always brought suffering.

chapter twenty-six

It was just after noon when I drove to Issaquah.

Eleven days had passed since my first trip to the small town in the mountains, for what had seemed at the time like a routine call. Today, thin strips of white clouds curled against a blue sky. I heard my cell phone ringing, somewhere, and finally found it locked in the console between the two front seats. I must have put it there last night, before I went up Tiger Mountain. The battery was low.

McLeod was calling.

"Harmon," he said, "I should suspend you for this."

Hospital authorities, he continued, had telephoned him this morning after I left. They also faxed him a release to sign because patients who left without permission were no longer the hospital's responsibility and nobody was answering the phone at my house.

"Yes, sir. I understand."

"You've got a strange way of showing it, Harmon. The whole reason you're working here is because of a disciplinary transfer from Richmond. If this is you understanding, I'm worried."

"Yes, sir," I repeated. "Have we received updates on the soil taken from the girl's fingernail?"

"Harmon, I'm going to turn a blind ear to what just happened at the hospital. You're upset. We're all upset. But this is an order. Stay home. Do not come into the office. This mess was a lot easier to explain with you in the hospital. It looked like we at least tried."

"I'll stay away from the office," I promised. "And the soil?"

"Like talking to a wall," he mumbled. "Yes, the geologist in Spokane faxed in a report last night. Then he called this morning looking for you, something about coal and arsenic. I told him you were out of commission." He paused. "I'm serious, Harmon. Stay away. I got enough trouble."

I parked behind the Issaquah Police Department one block off Front Street and found Detective Markel inside, sitting in a makeshift lunchroom—half-kitchen, half-squad room—eating a sandwich. On the table his brown paper bag lay on its side, looking like a rectangular cave as he read a copy of the *Seattle Times*. When I pulled out the chair next to him, he barely glanced over, already looking away when he recognized me.

"When I was fifteen," he said, "I broke my arm. The doctor wrapped it in a cast and said it'd be six weeks before it healed. Two weeks later I cut it off with pruning shears. Baseball season, I wanted to play." He lifted his right arm, the sandwich in his hand. "Arm still doesn't work right. What's your excuse?"

In the corner a television sat on a rolling cart in the corner and showed a golden-haired news anchor looking grave and glittery all at once, like the well-paid publicist of the Grim Reaper.

"I keep coming back to the geology around here," I said. "All the coal and arsenic."

"If this is about the VanAlstyne case, forget it."

"Why?"

He grunted. "You didn't hear?"

I shook my head.

"They're suing us. Yeah, that's right. Another juicy lawsuit. Don't look so surprised. You Feds are next." He bit into the sandwich—I smelled peanut butter—then lifted the newspaper, obscuring his face. I stared at the back of the folded section where a story jumped from the front page, about a South Seattle shooting in which the police were being investigated.

"If the VanAlstynes are suing," I said, "we've got nothing to lose."

He rattled the paper. But he didn't lower it. My eyes drifted back to the television, which showed a young black athlete standing like an ebony plank between two white guys in thousand-dollar suits. The black kid was reading from a prepared statement while cameras flashed and the crawl at the bottom of the screen explained his apology for getting into a brawl, an apology that would allow the agents to continue wearing thousand-dollar suits.

The detective lowered the newspaper, his eyes on the TV. He said, "That kid's what, eighteen?"

"About the same age as the VanAlstyne girl."

He didn't look at me. "What's your idea?" he asked.

≈

The Issaquah public library was two blocks west of the police station on Sunset Avenue, close enough that we walked down the sidewalk, crossing over Front Street.

The librarian was a prematurely gray woman who wore a blue cotton jumper. She nodded vigorously as the detective explained what we were looking for, and we followed her through the channels of books, the bottom of her jumper flapping against her pale calves, a sound like heavy bird wings. She flew through sections of ancient history, cookbooks, and pop psychology where bright bold titles offered stinging rebuke

sibella giorello | 269

sibella giorello | 269

combined with commissioned compassion. *The Idiot's Guide to Self-Help* for instance.

When the librarian stopped, she stood at a bookcase filled with green binders. Tilting her head sideways to read the typed titles inside plastic sleeves, she muttered, "Planning commission. Transportation, arts commission, water use restrictions . . . I know they're here because we received new copies just the other day."

"These are copies?" the detective said.

"Of course they're copies!" she snapped. "You can't touch the originals. They're down at the state office under lock and key— here we go!" She reached in with both hands, pulling out a four-inch binder and dropping it into the detective's open arms. "The original maps are fragile; you need gloves. Speaking of, are your hands clean?"

We opened our palms, the detective juggling the heavy binder into the crook of his arm.

"All right then," she said crisply. "But these do not leave the library. Do I have your word, detective?"

He nodded, looking like a schoolboy reprimanded by his English teacher.

"Does the library have a problem with theft?" I asked.

"In this particular case, yes. And I wouldn't have known, but a building contractor came in several weeks ago wanting to check on some land near the Rim. Imagine how embarrassed I was, discovering our maps were gone."

"Did you happen to get his name?" I asked.

"Certainly. I told him we would call as soon as we replaced the pilfered copies."

"By any chance, was his name Bill Johansen?"

"That doesn't sound correct. He was Asian."

The detective said, "Do you know what land he was looking at?"

"The Rim," she snapped. "Aren't you listening?"

"Right," he said. "On Squak Mountain?"

"The gentleman wanted to know if the land was solid, or if it was susceptible to cave-ins, from all the mining that went on up there. I knew people were stealing our first editions, our magazines. But coal mining maps? What in heaven's name would somebody want with such things?"

She yanked out another binder, dropping that into the detective's arms too. "You can use the conference room in back. Unless the high school truants are in there. In which case, please arrest them."

She flapped away.

The conference room was empty but the oak table was covered with truant graffiti. I opened the first binder. The maps offered simple geographic details—creeks, hills, valleys—written by coal miners, not cartographers, whose sole priority was to show where on the mountain the black carbon slumbered and how much was there.

"Muldoon, Dolly Varden," the detective read aloud. "Dolly Varden? They named a mine after a fish?"

"They probably ran out of names. Look how many coal veins they tapped. Hundreds."

There were entries from the Carbon Hill Coal Company and the Red Devil Coal Company, the Blue Blaze, the Black Prince. Burn-it, Stoker, Reliance.

"Here's another good shaft," Detective Markel said. "The Shoo Fly. Imagine working the Shoo Fly Shaft all day."

"Except these aren't shafts."

"What are they?" he asked.

"They're tunnels, See how they run uphill? Shafts go down into the ground. Like that grate I fell on over at Cougar Mountain. But these wandering lines on the map, they're creek beds, and these are drift mines beside them. Geologists call them water-level mines. Miners would walk along the creeks, looking for places where the water cut through the ground, exposing the coal beds. Then they'd start digging, tunneling into the mountain and following the coal seam until it ran out. Gravity hauled out the water, keeping the mine fairly dry."

"What's it mean for us?"

"That scrap of material I found on Cougar Mountain had bituminous coal and arsenic on it. The geologist found the same thing under the fingernail. You don't find it walking through the woods."

"You think she's in a shaft?" He shook his head. "I told you, the mines are capped. You saw that yourself. The state locked them all up."

"Yes, the state capped the major mine shafts. But look at these maps. Mining was a free-for-all back in the 1920s. Anybody with a pick and a shovel could walk into these mountains and start digging. And if it turned out the vein wasn't profitable, they just walked away, found another creek. Those abandoned tunnels might not even be on the map, because they weren't considered real mines. Some were just caves."

The detective ran a hand over his black hair, staring at the map. "We had a big earthquake six or seven years ago. The houses on the hillside collapsed. Nice houses too. But it turned out they were built over mine shafts—okay, tunnels, not shafts—but nobody knew it because the forest had grown over the holes in the ground. And the state didn't have a record of the holes. That contractor the librarian mentioned probably came in to see if he could get a permit to build, depending on the mine situation."

"The Rim, where is that?"

He flipped the pages. "The top of Squak Mountain. The middle mountain, between Cougar and Tiger."

"My map says something about 'Sqwauk Hill.' Is that the same thing?"

"Let me see."

I turned the binder, showing him the map from the Blue Blaze Coal Company. Hand-drawn lines showed an anvil-shaped mountain, the creeks carving into steep valleys.

"That's it, same one," he said. "Squak gets spelled different ways. It's an Indian word, means 'water.' See that plateau there, just down from the summit? That's where the Rim is. The houses back up to state land, couple thousand acres worth. The Bullitt family donated it."

"Bullet—as in gun?"

He spelled the name. "Old Seattle family. They kept a cabin up there. But sometime around the 1970s they decided to give the land to the state, for a park. The old homestead is still up there. Or it was. Vandals tore it down."

The state survey, done in the 1980s, showed some of the topographic details, such as rock outcroppings, names of creeks, the elevation changes on the mountain, all the hiking trails that coursed over the hills. And at the center, the cartographer drew an outline of the old Bullitt homestead.

I leaned into the map, reading the details.

"It must've been quite a place," the detective said. "Too bad the only thing left is the fireplace. Just a big stone wall, out there with the trees. But I hear the fireplace still draws. Hey, why are you looking at me like that?"

~

We started hiking at the hairpin turn off Mountainside Drive: me, Detective Markel, and Issaquah's K-9 officer, whose trained German shepherd was named Rommel.

Rommel paid no attention to the squirrels and chickadees that skittered across our path. Periodically, the officer waved the scrap of fabric under the dog's nose, the fabric I'd found tied to the tree, the fabric I suspected came from a Pendleton shirt size XXL. At the three-quarter mark, where the trail split, we saw a man hiking down with ski poles.

"Is that dog gonna bite me?" He froze, eyeing Rommel. His voice was reedy and he wore a yellow windbreaker. "I don't care if you are cops. If that dog bites me, I'll sue you."

"Get in line," the detective mumbled.

"What?"

"Do you have the time?"

The man pushed up the cuff of his windbreaker, exposing his watch. The officer released several inches of Rommel's leash. The ski pole dangled from the strap around his wrist. "It's about two thirty. Get that dog away from me."

The detective took down the man's name, address, and phone number, asked him several more questions, then told him he could leave. The man stabbed his ski poles into the soil, working his way past us. We continued up the trail.

Ferns blanketed the forest floor, shielded from sun by towering cedars with moss hanging from their limbs in long curtains like gray-green yarn, and it billowed in the uncertain breeze. Twice,

Rommel pulled the officer into the woods. But the dog returned to the trail both times, whimpering with frustration.

We climbed until the moss disappeared, replaced by bare deciduous trees and birch bark that peeled in swaths.

Then I saw the fireplace.

The house was gone—no walls, no roof—but the rounded river rocks rose twenty feet to blue sky.

The officer dangled the fabric under the dog's nose again. Rommel circled the concrete pad, which must have been the house's foundation.

Then the dog sat beside the officer's left foot.

"Great," the detective said. "Now what?"

I walked north, stepping off the concrete and into the woods. The fireplace was at my back, and the forest in front of me was so thick that it obscured the view of Issaquah below. I turned, staring at the long scar down the homestead's concrete foundation. The earth had settled beneath it, trying to fill in on itself.

I asked the officer to bring Rommel.

The dog walked fifty yards into the woods, then stopped.

I glanced at the officer.

"Give him a second." He waved the fabric under the dog's nose again.

Rommel's ears pricked forward.

"Rommel, find!"

The dog leaped, snuffling the leaves and the fading ferns, pulling the officer into the forest. I jogged behind them, my memory stirred by the sounds. An image kicked up. I saw the perp's feet slicing through the underbrush. Rommel was barking up ahead, and I ran faster. When I caught up, the dog pulled against the leash as the officer tried to balance himself on the uneven ground. Moments later, Markel came up behind us, panting.

A mound of pine boughs were stacked against the mountain. Rommel pawed at the base, whimpering. The officer pulled him back as I came closer and lifted the branches. The green needles were already faded to brown, and the sawed-off limbs leaked sap from their wounds. With the detective beside me, we threw the branches behind us while Rommel barked—hoarse, frustrated— and the clean scent of pine sap mixed with another odor, leaking out from behind the boughs. The smell turned my stomach.

When all the branches were removed, I flicked on my flashlight, asking the detective to wait while I went inside. Rommel's bark clapped against the rock walls. The floor climbed at a ten-degree angle, following a coal seam that stretched back some forty feet. But the tunnel was empty. I traced my flashlight along the far wall and saw another coal bed, jumping at a fault line. The miners had dug out that seam, too, following the sudden steep turn, hoping to strike it rich carving a ledge about fifteen feet above the main floor. I found easy footholds below and pulled myself up to the rocky plateau, shining my flashlight into the dark crevice. The stench was worse, a pungent odor of dead blood and rotting meat, and when my flashlight found her, she was curled up with her back to the tunnel.

I called her name. She did not respond.

Her emaciated bare arms were wrapped over her head and handcuffs circled her wrists, chained to a steel rod that stood like a flag pole in a gray pool of freshly poured concrete.

"Courtney," I whispered.

The smell rising from her body gagged me. I coughed. Her right hand was a green balloon, the final finger black, truncated at the last knuckle.

"Courtney." The Pendleton shirt hung in filthy rags, and when I touched her arm her skin felt cold, clammy. At my touch, she turned her head, dirt ringing her neck. Her eyes were glassy, like a cheap doll.

"Courtney," I said softly, "we've come to take you home."

She didn't seem to understand the words. I repeated them, slowly.

And a moment later, she lifted her hands, automatically, like a small child who had grown accustomed to begging.

chapter twenty-seven

Personal experience had shown me there's an inverse relationship between what people think I should feel and how I actually feel, particularly in the trenches.

After my father was murdered, I applied to Quantico and people extolled my courage. But deep inside I felt only a desperate need for action, nothing heroic about it. When my mother suffered a breakdown, I moved to Richmond in order to take care of her, and the praises I heard had the staggering weight of unearned compliments, as duty was mistaken for valor.

Those same feelings rushed into my empty heart the week after Courtney VanAlstyne was returned to her parents. I was standing at the cherrywood desk belonging to the SAC, the special agent in charge of the Seattle field office, a man whose seventh-floor windows looked out over Puget Sound. The SAC had the sinewy physique of a dedicated distance runner, graying hair, and a starched white shirt that glowed with purity. His face was by turns placid and honed so firmly it appeared to have been created by a blacksmith. As we spoke, unbidden expressions slipped through his Bureau mask.

I tried to smile.

"The Bureau is grateful for your tenacious work, Raleigh," he was saying. "I've received a number of congratulatory phone calls, among them one from the director. He is extremely pleased with the results." He waited for my thank you, which I gave.

"Senator Avery's office phoned as well," he continued. "And, of course, the VanAlstynes, their appreciation goes beyond words."

Behind him, white caps whipped across the surface of the sound. The wind seemed to be coming out of the south, colliding with the tide from the north, where Puget Sound opened to the Pacific Ocean.

"Thank you, sir."

"The VanAlstynes want to give you a monetary reward."

He waited.

"That's not necessary, sir. Or appropriate."

"Correct," he said. "But I'm placing a letter of commendation in your personnel file. The letter goes to you alone."

"But there were other agents—"

He held up his hand, stopping me. "Yes, at one point, we had every agent in Violent Crimes working this case. But it was your tenacity that found Miss VanAlstyne. Alive, no less. That last detail can't be stressed enough. That's not the standard outcome on something like this. Your supervisor agrees, you deserve something beyond the usual atta-boy."

An "atta-boy" was a letter of commendation for good work.

"You will receive a $3,000 monetary award from the Bureau," he said. "It should appear in next month's paycheck."

"Thank you, sir."

I watched another curious expression sweep over his face. Leaning forward, he picked up a paperweight from his desk, a specimen of polished amethyst. It was the size of his fist.

"I understand you came to the Seattle office under less than ideal circumstances. Disciplinary transfer?"

I nodded.

"I have a letter on my desk from Agent Ngo, regarding the first surveillance operation. Can I presume you know about his complaint?"

"Yes, sir. Agent Ngo disagreed with my decision to collar the runner."

"Correct. Do you know why?"

"I've learned not to explore motive among my colleagues."

His lips twitched, almost a smile. "Ernest J. Suggs wasn't just any runner. He's our mole."

"Mole?"

"Suggs works as an informant for our organized crime unit. When you submitted the request for surveillance on the poker game, Agent Ngo became concerned. We were already watching the game, using Suggs, to crush the Korean mafia. Ngo was worried your surveillance would blow our cover. And then SWAT goes in after Lucia Lutini, Suggs runs, and Ngo rushes in, trying to preserve his source. Suggs, you can imagine, was confused, thought we were double-crossing him. But Ngo explained it to him in the car. Since the Korean mafia already suspects we're watching, we had to preserve Suggs's cover. Ngo took out the stop on the handcuffs, nearly breaking Suggs's wrist. Our mole launches a lawsuit against the FBI. We look bad." He shrugged. "But we keep our source."

I couldn't meet his eyes. Glancing out the window, I watched the wind throwing white sheets across the gray water, changing direction as suddenly as a matador's cape.

"But, sir, the soil in Suggs's shoes links him to the area where the girl disappeared. And he knew her, from the casino and the card game. He's still a possible suspect."

He put down the amethyst. "Ngo looked into the soil, after you had the house searched. Suggs admitted it, he went looking for the girl after her disappearance was reported in the paper, after the roommate told him where she went missing. He thought the rich parents would offer him a reward. The simple fact is, our mole is a greedy man. That's fortunate for us, since he'll sell out his friends at the right price. But Suggs is clear of any wrong-doing in the VanAlstyne case."

"The kiddie porn on his computer?"

He sighed. "It's disgusting. We'll handle that another way. But his greed, it's caused you some confusion."

He waited for me to respond. I felt a temptation to point out what really caused my confusion: Ngo's obfuscations, my colleagues not leveling with me. And if I pointed that out, I could kiss the commendation good-bye, along with the much-needed cash.

I nodded, as though this was all perfectly fine, as though this was excellent procedure.

"Some of our best agents push the limits," he said, "It's not what we want, per se, but Quantico is not real life. Your career development, Raleigh, will depend on crucial judgment calls." He paused. "How *did* you figure out she was in that cave?"

I watched the finely honed face, the intelligent eyes, and for one brief moment, I wondered what would happen if I mentioned the clairvoyant who spoke about a place of fire, and the river rock dreams where my late father appeared, speaking to me about what was inside the rocks.

My career came down to judgment calls.

"I took an educated guess based on my background in forensic geology," I said.

He nodded, satisfied. "I read about your background in the lab. I'm glad you chose to become an agent. Have you enjoyed working in Violent Crimes?"

"Yes, sir."

"Because if you would like to move to another unit, something more . . ." He searched for the correct words, the diplomatic terms that concealed the Bureau's view of agents who spent their entire career in Violent Crimes, the knuckle-draggers of the agency. ". . . something more long-term," he said, "it can be arranged. Your supervisor will support any request for transfer. Although I understand he would appreciate your staying in his unit."

I thanked him. He stood, extending his hand, and I left his office with a numb sensation that seemed to pervade all the way to my feet. I rode the elevator down to Violent Crimes where my desk was already blanketed with fresh manila folders containing new cases, new perps, new paths on an ancient map where X marked a treasure called Justice. And outside, in the wind-whipped autumn air, a man moved freely, bearing a conscience that allowed him to cannibalize a young woman's soul, to maim her in ways that might never be healed, to demand a bargain he never intended to uphold. Out there, a man lived without punishment, without consequence, just like the man who shot my father in an alley one cold November night and left him to die.

I picked up the phone, punching the extension for the Tweedles. The twin who answered identified himself by his real name, so I had no idea which one I was speaking to.

"This is Harmon," I said.

"Oh, *you*," he said. "What do *you* want?"

"Have you looked at the film from the casino?"

"Yes."

"Did you find anything?"

"We found something and we sent it to Lucia Lutini. She's a *lady*. She treats people with *respect*."

"She's a saint," I said, hanging up.

I walked to Lucia's desk where a Post-It note stuck to the dark computer screen said she was in the second conference room. I walked down the aisles of cubicles, past Jack who was talking on the phone, his feet propped up on his desk. As I passed, he gave me a nod, and when I opened the conference room door, Lucia didn't turn around. She was gazing at the television. Staccato images flickered in black and white.

"The Tweedles said they found something," I said.

Her brown eyes appeared polished, her expression distant. "Yes. They had a lot to cover. Twenty-four hours times two weeks, plus the September records you found. They isolated three scenes with the girl. She's stunning."

Picking up the remote, she pressed the rewind button. On screen, figures rushed backward, stopped, then moved forward as Lucia hit Play. The camera angle seemed to be above the corridor leading to the main restaurant and bar, the wide alley where I'd seen Stacee Warner coming in and out with her tray.

"There," Lucia said. "See her?"

Her flaxen hair appeared white on the screen, rippling down her back. She walked with confident strides, reminding me of a leggy young colt. Nothing like the creature I met in the cave.

"And here comes . . ." Lucia said. "There."

Courtney had stopped at the edge of the wide alley, apparently waiting, her head turning left and right, the long hair flickering under the bright lights. Then a man appeared. He was taller than Courtney, she had to lift her head to look up at him. But his face was obscured both by the camera angle and by the bill of his baseball cap. He took her elbow, she smiled. They walked away.

"Let me see that again," I said.

Lucia hit Rewind. Courtney walked backward, away from

the man. Then back to him. I watched him wrap his fingers around her arm. And I could feel his hand on my own elbow. "He used that same gesture on me," I said. "On the mountain when he walked me into the forest."

Lucia was silent. "Unfortunately, this is all the Tweedles found of him. He's not in anything else. The other shots show the girl playing cards. She's a controlled player. Or was."

"It's not the father, is it?"

"I wondered that too, because of the height. But you saw her reaction. She was happy to see this man. And the father has a rock solid alibi for this day. Although there is one thing." Lucia set the remote beside the television, leaving Courtney and the man in the baseball hat frozen, mid-stride. "The mother says Courtney didn't touch those Pendleton shirts for years. And we know she wasn't on good terms with the father anymore. So why wear his shirt?"

I waited, not wanting to interrupt her thoughts.

"Women are essentially creatures of emotion," she said. "Even the more logical ones, like Courtney VanAlstyne. This man she meets at the casino is quite tall, reminding even the two of us of her father. If he reminds us of Bill Johansen, her reaction might be even more powerful. Let's assume she misses her father, the man who taught her everything about poker. She dates a father-type, goes hiking with him and wears her father's shirt, a memento."

"I like it. But it's still speculation. If we could just talk to her."

"Impossible." She shook her head. "The shrinks told the parents not to let us anywhere near her. The Bureau's not about to defy them with court orders at this point." She tossed her head toward the TV. "But let me ask you, didn't that look like a date?"

≈

I walked back to my desk. Jack was still on the phone, still had his feet propped up, ankles still crossed. There was a smile playing on his lips. I stopped beside his cubicle, sitting on the edge of his desk.

"You got it," he said into the phone. He winked at me.

I reached down, depressing the plastic triangle in the phone cradle, severing his call.

"What the—Harmon!"

"Let's take a walk," I said.

Outside the wind blew hard but carried an unseasonable warmth as Jack and I walked up First Avenue. The tips of my hair lashed against my face.

"If this is about Ngo," Jack was saying, "you need to take it up with him. The Suggs bit was not my call."

At the Italian market on the corner, I turned left, moving into the crowd at Pike Place Market. The chattering noise bounced off the metal roof. Jack jostled into position beside me.

"Did you hear me?' he asked.

"That night in the surveillance van," I said, "you already knew who Suggs was. Is that right?"

"Yeah, I knew."

"So when Ngo told me to come up with the Brush's name, and I climbed into the cab to think in quiet, how long did you two laugh over that?"

"You've got the wrong idea."

"No, Jack. I've finally got the right idea. And you've got three minutes to explain everything, including Stacee Warner. Starting now."

"Stacee?"

"Two minutes, fifty-eight seconds or McLeod hears you're on her speed dial."

"What?"

"Tick-tock. Two minutes fifty-five seconds."

"What does Stacee have to do with this?"

"The day we went to the casino, you two already knew each other. I saw it on your faces."

He stepped aside, giving room to a man who wore a down jacket and held a copy of *Hard Times*, the homeless newspaper.

"Buy a copy?" he asked Jack.

The sleeves of the black nylon jacket were torn, and white feathers escaped, only to drown in whatever sticky substance had been slathered over the tears. Spit, it looked like.

Jack yanked out his wallet, handing the guy five bucks. The man stared at the wallet. He handed Jack the paper.

"Keep it," Jack said, clapping the man on the shoulder. More feathers jumped from the coat. "You can sell it again."

The man thanked him and we walked down the crowded aisle, past the displays of dried cherries and fresh honeycombs and cut flowers tied with ribbons.

He looked at me. "You don't give to the homeless?"

"Don't change the subject. I want to know about Stacee."

"Harmon, you have no idea."

"You're down to less than two minutes."

"She's a source."

"Of what—pleasure?"

"You *do* have a sense of humor. I was wondering."

"One minute forty seconds."

"She's my source on a counterterrorism case. The hiker who saw the Arabs on Mount Si? They were climbing up at night in street clothes, with backpacks? She's the hiker. She called us about three weeks ago, and I met her out there at Mount Si. She even identified three of them by our surveillance photos. They run a barber shop in the Central District."

"Not possible," I said.

"What?"

"She's part of two cases?"

"I know what you're saying. We couldn't believe it either. She did a good job keeping quiet though."

We were standing in front of the fish market, where the guys wearing rubber aprons chattered like softball players.

"Why was I kept in the dark, Jack?"

"Because when we raided the barber shop we found dozens of automatic weapons, shoulder-launch missiles, bags of fertilizer. That barber shop was quite the haul. These guys are going to lead us to the real monster, the source of funds. None of it can leak."

"Understood. But I'm not the media. Why not just tell me Stacee's a source on something else."

"Because, Harmon, you came here with less than glowing references. Disciplinary transfer? A chick in Violent Crimes? We thought you were another loose cannon, one of those libbers who screams about equal rights because they can't pull their own weight. And you weren't exactly friendly."

"Jack—"

"Okay, we were wrong. Really wrong. You just closed a kidnapping that's on par with the Lindberg baby. I stand corrected."

"It's not closed," I said. "The perp is still out there."

Behind us, one of the fish guys hoisted a king salmon from a bed of crushed ice. When he launched the fish through the air, the tourists gasped. Cameras flashed, the fish's scales glittering silver. The man at other end caught the fish. The tourists laughed, clapping.

"Why are you on her speed dial?"

"That's a problem." He nodded. "Women fall in love with me."

I gave him a look.

"Every woman except you," he said. "And Felicia."

"Yes, you can't hand Felicia five bucks and feel better about yourself."

"Don't be smug," he said. "You're on the hook too."

"Me?"

"She talks to you. You could actually convince her to get into a program. But go ahead, leave her out there at the casino. Free drinks, after all."

"You're pinning this on me?"

"No, Harmon. I see how it works with you. You won't give money to the homeless on *principle*, but when it comes to offering real help, you can't be bothered either. How's the view from the high horse?"

I felt heat flushing my neck. "What do you want, Jack?"

"There's no money in the budget to pay for rehab, but there's a shelter down in Pioneer Square. It's totally free. They have a good program. If you could get her in there . . ."

The tourists shuffled past. In the absence of new orders, the fish guys began chattering again, waiting for the next pitch. I glanced down the aisle. Clusters of fresh beets, the skins still dusted with soil, lay beside cut red dahlias whose blooms looked as bright as bursts of blood.

chapter twenty-eight

The brass token slid down the metal channel. I stood beside Felicia, watching the tarnished yellow light bathe her green eyes until they almost looked blue. While I spoke, there was no way of telling whether she heard anything. But she didn't argue. She didn't nod in agreement either.

"Two jokers, one ace," she said. "What's wrong with my luck?"

"There's no such thing as luck."

"That's what you think."

The white paper bucket was empty but she clutched it, refusing to let go. I picked up her torn duffel bag from the carpet, shrugging the strap on my shoulder.

"This is it, Felicia. I won't come out here again, and Jack is ready to wash his hands of you. If you want to take a gamble with your life, your kids, that's your business. But you've got an offer, and it's one time only."

I turned, heading down the bright and garish corridor carrying her duffel bag. I had no idea if she was following, and wondered what I would do if she wasn't—leave the bag? Take it back to her? When I got to the exit, I opened the door, feeling a small seed of hope in my heart, then turned.

Felicia walked outside. I knew better than to say anything,

and unlocked the Barney Mobile, setting her bag on the passenger side floor, holding the door for her.

She sat down, wrinkling her nose. "Man, your car stinks!"

I closed the door, walked around the rear bumper, and decided that for one night, I could keep my mouth shut. She rolled down her window and we drove out of Snoqualmie on I-90, the draft blowing through the car, the last light of day leaking across the western sky, an inconclusive end to a long day. I turned on my headlights. Felicia reached for the radio, scanning stations until she found some rap. She cranked the volume. The beat rattled the dashboard.

I reached over, turning it off.

"Hey!" she said.

"I don't like rap."

"How come?"

Because it sounds like barbarians pounding at the gates. Because it sounds like a prelude to tribal warfare. Because if music speaks to the soul, and rap speaks to so many people, what are the chances beauty will survive?

But I didn't say anything of that to Felicia. Maybe I was tired. Maybe I was done with lectures for the day. Maybe, maybe, maybe. "I just don't like it, Felicia. Why don't we talk instead?"

"About what?"

"You."

She looked out the window. "I'm dumb."

"You're not dumb."

She was stubborn, yes. Sullen. She carried a self-destructive hatred for her father that ensured low-life continued his abuse. But these were matters of the heart, not the mind.

"You're not dumb," I repeated. "Where did you get that idea?"

Headlights from oncoming traffic painted her skin with

strobes of chalk. "I wouldn't be living this way unless I was dumb."

"Felicia, you put yourself in this situation, you can take yourself out. Where we're going tonight, they serve hot meals, they have counselors. I hear they even have a free dentist."

There was no response. And I didn't have energy for another lecture, a lecture that might lose her again. Finally, I said, "You want your kids back, right?"

"I can't explain it to you."

"Try."

"You'd never understand."

I opened my mouth to protest, but the sound under the hood interrupted. *Whap-whap. Whap-whap. Whap.* I cocked my head, then glanced at the console. No blinking dashboard lights. The sound was gone. I said, "Why don't you explain it to me."

Her face was stolid, set like granite.

"I got a war inside my head," she said. "I got all kinds of thoughts and none of them line up. I think about my kids and the next thing I need is a hit. A drink, a shot. Anything. I want to hit the jackpot, just once, and get us a real house, with furniture, but the next thing I know, I'm strung out and hung over and still broke." She looked over. "You know where I been sleeping? In the ladies, on the toilet. You're wrong. I'm dumb."

The whapping sound returned, louder, and now we were losing speed. I pushed the gas pedal to the floor. The speedometer drifted down . . . forty-five . . . forty . . . thirty-five . . . Snapping on my blinker, I drifted over to the right shoulder, the car's wheels sinking into the soft sediment.

The engine clunked, once. Then died.

"Why are we stopping?" Felicia said.

We were fifteen miles outside Seattle, two exits before Issaquah.

Cars whipped past, the speed drawing the frame of the Barney Mobile, then releasing it. The car shuddered. I punched on the hazard lights. It was dark now, sunset was gone. I pulled out my cell phone.

"You don't have to tell me no more." Felicia sounded scared. "Just keep driving. I'm ready to go, really."

"It's the car, Felicia." I wondered who to call. Technically, it could be argued that I had a civilian in my car—against Bureau rules—since Bookman Landrow's case was closed and Felicia was no longer a source. I could call Jack since it was his fault I was in this predicament, but if he came to get us, Felicia would turn mulish, refuse rehab, and the whole ordeal would be a wash.

"Oh crap," she said.

A sudden blue light filled the car. I heard the siren wailing, followed by one blat of warning. In the rearview mirror, the police cruiser's headlights were blinding.

"Oh crap oh crap oh crap." Felicia kicked the duffel bag under her seat.

"What's in the bag, Felicia?"

"Nothing."

"Felicia—"

"Don't talk—he's coming!" She froze, hands clasp in her lap, and stared straight ahead, the picture of false innocence.

The officer rapped on my window. He stood behind my left shoulder, his body turned defensively. Two cars whooshed past as I rolled down the window before slowly raising my hands, holding them above the steering wheel.

"Officer, I'm with the FBI. My badge is inside my blazer, and I'm carrying a gun. It's holstered on my right hip."

He took one step forward, pivoting, almost lunging, and shined his flashlight into the car. The beam lingered on Felicia.

When I glanced over, her eyes were wide, she didn't blink. Combined with her pallor, the vapid stare made her look embalmed.

The beam moved to my face. I blinked, keeping my hands up.

"I guess you gals need a ride into the city, right?" He lowered the flashlight.

I looked up. It was Officer Lowell.

⁓

Felicia sat in the back of the police cruiser, clutching the duffel bag, and I sat in the passenger seat, watching Officer Lowell tag the Barney Mobile's rear window with a Day-Glo orange sticker, notifying the other troopers that the vehicle had been radioed in and would be towed within twenty-four hours.

He climbed in behind the wheel.

"Good thing I saw you when I did." His mood was buoyant, riding the white horse. "My shift ends at six. I was just taking my last cruise down I-90 for the night when I saw your hazard lights. Any later, I might've missed you."

I nodded.

We passed Issaquah, Felicia silent behind the grated partition separating the front and back seats.

"Must feel pretty dang good," Lowell said suddenly.

"What's that?"

"Everybody's talking about how you found that girl."

"She's home. It's a good thing."

"Who's home?" Felicia said.

Lowell glanced in the rearview mirror, eyeing Felicia carefully. He didn't appear to trust her. He glanced back at me. "Any idea who the perp is?"

"We're still working on it."

"Can't she tell you?"

"She suffered some real trauma, like a bomb went off inside her head."

Felicia grabbed the grate, her fingers lacing into the metal. "Who are you talking about?"

Lowell glanced over, waiting for a signal to elaborate, but I stared out the windshield. He was flying down the carpool lane at an easy seventy miles an hour. To my right, traffic backed up for the I-405 interchange.

"I heard he kept her in a cave, is that true?" he asked.

I didn't want to get into the difference between caves and shafts and tunnels. I didn't want to talk at all. But I owed him something, it was common courtesy. And he had worked part of the case as well. "From what we can piece together, yes, he kept her in a tunnel and then took her out at night and hunted her in the woods." Like he hunted me that night.

"What?" Felicia said. "You're scaring me."

It scared me too. And I was even more concerned that we hadn't caught him. Although we believed he abducted her from the Cougar Mountain parking lot, we still didn't know whether he appeared out of nowhere, or if she met him there, as Lucia believed, a kind of date. Stacee said Courtney never mentioned a new boyfriend, or anybody she was hiking with. And it would be a long time before we could interview Courtney VanAlstyne. If ever, given the psychiatric orders.

Lowell seemed to be reading my thoughts. "You guys don't have any ID on him, nothing?"

"Not enough."

"How did you figure out she was up there?" he said.

"Lowell, look," I said, trying to sound conciliatory, "the case is still open. I really can't talk about it."

"Yeah, sorry. I just want to help."

The highway curled to its conclusion, slipping down beside the steel arches of Qwest Field, home of the Seahawks. Tonight the stadium lights glowed blue and Lowell drove three blocks into Pioneer Square. Night had fallen like a black velvet cloak and the neighborhood's imitation gas lamps looked almost quaint. He circled the block until he found the load/unload zone near the shelter. I started to get out, then looked over at him.

"You really helped me out tonight, Lowell. Thank you."

He grinned. "That's what I'm here for. You want me to wait while you take her inside?"

I glanced into the backseat. Felicia's hands worried the frayed cotton handles of her duffel. Her skin had a putrid appearance. I'd seen that look before.

I quickly opened the back door, grabbing Felicia by the arm and pulling her out before she puked. She moaned. I leaned her against the load/unload sign, then turned back to Lowell.

"This might take awhile," I said. "You better take off."

"I don't mind waiting."

"What if you get a call?"

"I'm off in ten minutes," he said. "You don't have a car. Why don't I come back in what—an hour? Let me take you to dinner. You can tell me about the Bureau."

Felicia moaned again.

I closed the back door of the cruiser. Just days before, I had treated Officer Lowell with prideful disregard, fully convinced that my position in the Bureau elevated me above him. Now that pride tasted bitter in my mouth.

"Sure," I told him. "That'd be great. I'll see you in an hour."

I shut the passenger door and led Felicia down the sidewalk, hoisting the duffel strap onto my shoulder. She walked with the weariness of old age as we passed a group of men huddled against the stone building. Their restlessness was palpable, as tangible as the biting odor of urine that hung in the air. Their faces were florid, bruised, and distorted. They watched Felicia. She dropped her chin, sending the long greasy curtains of hair forward to conceal her face. For one brief moment, I thought I could hear the invading army inside her head.

When we reached the corner, I opened the door to the Gospel Mission. A bell rang.

Felicia stopped, green eyes narrowing.

"You've got to be kidding," she said.

She was staring at an area above the door, where a plaster cast of Jesus was affixed to the building. Jesus leaned out over the urine-soaked sidewalk, his robed arms open, his white garment dusted with city soot.

"No way," she said. "Uh-uh. I know how these Christians work. They start out all nice and loving, then they turn around and beat the living hell out of you. And you're supposed to thank them for it. I might be dumb but I'm not that dumb."

I let go of the door, the bell ringing with identical good cheer as it closed. I started walking down the sidewalk.

"Where are you going?" Felicia demanded.

"Back to the casino," I said over my shoulder. "You can probably still get your stall in the bathroom."

"Hey, at least the people in the bathroom don't pretend they're doing something nice for you."

And that's when I saw it, the precise mechanism that turned the crank on Felicia's behavior. Hypocrisy. Duplicity. It launched her into this spiral of self-destruction, beginning with the church-going father who abused his children, and the pimp named Bookman who promised to take her off the streets but put her to work on the corner. And the white knight named Jack Stephanson who coaxed her into testifying but never did get her kids back.

"Felicia, people will always disappoint you. Always."

"Oh, here we go."

"What?"

"This is the 'come-to-Jesus' speech, isn't it?"

I glanced down the sidewalk. The addled men along the wall grinned savagely, enjoying the show. Nothing better than a cat-fight. I walked back to where she stood, to where Jesus hung over a doorway that could change her life.

"Give it three nights, Felicia. After that, you decide what to do."

When I opened the door, the bell ringing, she spit out a curse. Then stomped inside.

At the front desk, a woman with two long braids of brown hair watched Felicia approach with a stomp that sounded like elephants. The place smelled of bar soap and boiled green beans.

"Hello!" the woman said. "You're just in time for dinner."

"Bread and water," Felicia grumbled.

"Just for the people in the dungeon. Everybody else gets spaghetti."

Felicia's mouth fell open.

The woman laughed.

I extended my hand, introducing myself. "This is Felicia Kunkel. She needs a place to stay for a while."

The woman was named Cynthia Youngblood and she placed a clipboard on the counter, explaining the rules to Felicia, who glanced around the room suspiciously while I filled out the forms, giving what information I had available. I put down my cell phone number for an emergency contact, then pressed the pen into Felicia's hand. She scowled. But she signed at the bottom of the page.

"Are you staying for dinner too?" Cynthia asked me. "We like guests."

"Actually, I have to leave—"

"Don't you dare," Felicia growled.

Cynthia reached up, tugging a long chain connected to a metal door, which she locked to the counter, and we followed her across an old fir floor worn down to deep grooves.

"Two meals, chapel daily," Cynthia was saying, tossing the long braids over her shoulders.

"I gotta go to church?" Felicia asked.

"You *get* to attend chapel every single day," Cynthia corrected.

"What'd I tell you," Felicia said.

"You'll have AA and NA meetings twice daily. I'll explain more later. If we don't hurry, you'll miss dinner."

Cynthia pushed against a set of double doors, banging them open to reveal an old gymnasium. Varnished oak floor, wooden rail around the upper perimeter of the room. Folding tables and chairs filled with men and women and children. A line formed at the cafeteria window, at the other end of the room.

"I need to get back to the front desk," she said. "The food trays are stacked next to the service window. Eat as much as you want. We have chapel after dinner." She stuck out her hand. "Felicia, we're glad you're here."

We watched Cynthia Youngblood walk away.

"She seems nice," I said.

"Just wait." Felicia walked to the cafeteria line, picking up a brown plastic tray. "Watch what happens when I screw up. You'll see what these people are really like."

"You've already screwed up. And she knows it."

She scowled, turning her back to me. We stood behind a Hispanic man whose baseball cap advertised a radio station. I picked up a tray, glancing at my watch. Officer Lowell would be back in about forty-five minutes. I heard the Hispanic man ask for extra food, then Felicia stepped forward, lifting her tray. The server stood behind a red heat lamp, half of the face in shadows, and steam rose from the aluminum bins.

"Good evening, young lady," she said. "Would you care for spaghetti with meatballs, or without? The meatballs are simply delicious. And homemade."

Felicia took everything—spaghetti, meatballs, garlic bread, green beans—and she said thanks. I pushed my tray forward, thinking this couldn't be happening. I had to be dreaming again. I lifted my tray.

"Raleigh Ann?" my mother said.

Her black hair was harnessed by a net, and the steam from the food laid a scrim of perspiration on her porcelain skin.

"Mom," I said, "what are you doing here?"

Behind her, swinging doors opened and a large black man, his arms like anvils, carried a bin of meatballs. He set it down on the steam tray.

"Comin' through, Nadine!" he said.

"Pardon me, Rufus." My mother stepped to the side, a long slotted spoon in one hand as the man exchanged containers.

"That oughta hold you awhile," he said. "Let me know if you get low again."

"Thank you, Rufus. I'd like you to meet my daughter Raleigh

Ann." She pointed the slotted spoon at me. "Raleigh Ann, this is Rufus. He's our cook."

Rufus, holding the empty bin, lifted his head in acknowledgement. "How ya doin?" He backed through the swinging doors.

My mother smiled. "Did Aunt Charlotte tell you I was here? I've been waiting to tell you myself but I never see you anymore."

"How long—" I began.

"I decided all these homeless people needed some help so I packed up all the canned goods and drove them down here. And I felt so much better." She waved the spoon. "Give and give and give, you'll always feel better. The next time I came down they asked if I wanted to serve dinner. And, well, here I am!" She cocked her head like a bird. "Is something wrong? Is that why you're here?"

"No, nothing's wrong. I brought a friend. She needs some help."

"*That's* why you've been so busy! Raleigh Ann, I am so proud of you. Your father is smiling down from heaven right this minute." Her eyes glistened. "Would like some spaghetti? Rufus makes the meatballs himself. They're delicious."

"You've eaten them?"

She waved the spoon. "When in Rome . . ."

I accepted three meatballs, two heaps of spaghetti, bread, and a large Coke from the fountain and carried my tray to where Felicia was sitting. She'd chosen an isolated table, across the room, the duffel bag by her feet. She was already sopping up sauce with the bread when I sat down. I tore open the clear bag of plastic utensils. No knife.

"You bring people in here a lot, huh," she said.

"Nope. You're the first."

"Then how do you know that lady?" She nodded toward the food line.

I twirled the spaghetti. "She's my mother."

She leaned back, trying to get a better look. "You don't look nothing like her."

I cut a meatball with my fork. "I take after my father, I hear."

I took a bite of the meatball. It was delicious. Rufus might have apprenticed with Danato Lutini.

"What d'you mean, you hear?" she said.

"My mother remarried, her husband adopted me. He's my dad."

"He's nice to you, huh?"

"Who?"

"Your new dad."

"He was the nicest man I've ever known."

"*Was*—something happened to him?"

I put down my fork. I didn't want to talk about my father. I didn't want to talk at all. I glanced over at my mother and tried to decide if she was really functioning, or just suffering some bout of mania. Her singing words rang in my ears. *Give and give and give . . .* "My father was murdered," I said. "We still don't know who did it."

Felicia's green eyes took on a gauzy hue. I went back to my meal, glancing up periodically to watch my mother. She smiled at everybody, her high cheekbones flushed with joy. When I finally glanced over at Felicia, she was still staring at me.

"I'm sorry," she said.

"Thank you."

I watched Rufus come through the double doors again, this time to help pull down a gate similar to the one that secured the front desk. The heat lamps clicked off, my mother's shape fell into shadow.

"When your dad died," Felicia said, "I bet you wanted to die too."

I looked over at her, and nodded.

≈

My mother was staying for chapel and raved about the singing, about the spirit-filled worship among street people. "Nothing better than finding God among the broken. Raleigh, you will feel your spirit open right up."

But I begged off, saying I would come tomorrow night, that I'd made plans for tonight. After I introduced Felicia and left the two of them at the chapel door, I walked outside.

The temperature had dropped several degrees, the wind was gone, and the clutch of men on the sidewalk had broken into two groups. At the curb I saw an older model, red-and-white Chevy Blazer, idling in the load/unload zone.

"How'd it go?" Lowell asked as I climbed in.

"Maybe we could do dinner another time."

"Yeah, that's cool," he said.

But the disappointment in his voice made me wince.

"Sorry, I'm a little beat—"

"How about a drink? One drink then I take you home. How about it?"

He reminded me of a puppy, freshly bathed. His brown hair was still damp, combed to one side, divided by a straight part. I could smell his shampoo, and the menthol in his shaving cream.

"Sure," I said. "I can do that."

He drove around the corner, parking on South Washington, and we walked down the sidewalk toward the Central Tavern.

But he was strolling, walking so slowly that I found myself pausing between steps to keep from getting ahead of him. We took a table in back of the tavern, beside a wooden stage painted black, and both of us positioned our chairs for a clear view of the entrance, another habit of law enforcement, so we were sitting side by side rather than facing each other. The cocktail waitress walked over, giving us a curious expression.

"Waiting for someone important?" she asked.

"No," Lowell said. "Bourbon and soda."

I ordered a Coke, no crushed ice.

"That's it?" Lowell said. "You don't want a real drink?"

"That is a real drink."

The waitress walked back to the bar. The tavern had the anticipatory feel of early evening, and I watched the waitress hook the heel of her boot into the brass rail.

"Who's the girl you took to the shelter?" Lowell asked.

"A former source."

"Is that part of being an agent?"

"We don't issue tickets and send people on their way." The words were out of my mouth before I could catch them. "Sorry. I didn't mean it like that."

"What did you mean?"

Whenever people appeared out of context, my mind struggled to catch up, as if I were meeting the person for the first time. Tonight, my mother's appearance as kitchen help in a homeless shelter had startled me, and now Lowell-as-civilian was having a similar effect. The severe trooper attitude was gone; he was almost amiable. And he didn't seem quite so imposing either. I decided he must wear a bulletproof vest under his uniform, giving him a beefier appearance on the job. He was actually lean.

"What I meant to say," I started over, "was, sometimes you can really help the people you meet on the job. I would think ticketing people and watching them drive away would get frustrating, especially if you want to help."

"You're right," he said. "It does."

The waitress set down our drinks, then walked away.

"Cheers." He lifted his glass.

But before I could take a sip, my cell phone went off. "Here's another part of the job, it's 24-7. Excuse me a minute?"

I took the phone outside, standing on the sidewalk. Traffic moved down First Avenue between the lights.

It was Jack.

"She's in the shelter," I said. "She's not happy about it, but she's in."

"Will she stay?"

I recalled the expression on Felicia's face as my mother described the wonders of chapel. Felicia had flinched when the phrase "glory of God" escaped my mother's lips. But the two of them were a good match. My mother thrived on evangelical challenges; Felicia needed parental guidance.

"She's got good people around her," I said.

"Harmon, thank you," he said.

I paused. So many old appearances were changing into something new tonight. My mother, Lowell. And here was Jack, sounding genuinely grateful.

"You're welcome," I said, taken aback.

"I owe you. Anything you need, just let me know."

I told him about my car, how Officer Lowell found the broken-down Barney Mobile on I-90 and drove us to the shelter. Although he'd come back to drive me home, I was concerned about the tow truck. "Lowell tagged the car on the side of the road and reported it to the State Patrol. But if McLeod finds out I had a civilian in my car, that this had nothing to do with work—"

"I'll take care of it tonight," he interrupted. "Don't sweat it."

I closed the phone and walked back inside. Lowell had a forlorn expression on his face, as though I had ditched him. To make up for it, I made a show of turning off my phone, although I only set it to vibrate instead of ring. The guy just wanted ten minutes of my undivided attention.

"Everything okay?" he asked.

"Super." I sipped my Coke. "What else do you want to know about the Bureau?"

He asked several questions, but talked more than he listened. I didn't mind. I was talked out and sipped my Coke, hoping to finish it before the ice melted and made it watery. Lowell started telling me all his reasons for becoming a cop and why he wanted to become a special agent. My attention drifted. Finishing my drink, I nodded and watched a skinny kid in black jeans climb up on stage. The jeans were so tight they seemed glued down to his ankles, and his T-shirt, also black, revealed love handles. He wore a belt for no obvious reason except that it was riveted with silver spikes. Standing on stage, adjusting the microphone stand, he moved across the dark surface like a black spider. When he crossed under the spotlight, his belt seemed to explode with light. Then it was dark again. But I could still see silver lights streaming like lasers. Maybe he was a spider. Spider boy, weaving his web of silver lights. I grinned.

Lowell stopped. "Did I say something funny?"

"No, no. That kid, up on stage, his pants . . . his belt . . . lights are shooting out . . ." My lips felt swollen.

Lowell went right on talking, saying something about police work, how grinding it was. Or grounding. Did he say grimy? My eyes drifted toward the bar. The rows of liquor bottles were bobbing up and down, floating at sea, and the waitress combed her hand through her long hair, lights flying off her gold rings. I felt a sudden wave of nausea, my mouth filling with saliva.

The meatballs.

Food poisoning.

"I don't feel—" I began.

Lowell waited. "You don't feel . . . what?"

"Home." The word took so much effort. "I want to go . . . home."

He stood, dropping several bills on the table, the paper floating through the air. Lowell came around from behind and pulled out my chair. I tried to stand.

"Here, let me help you," he said, taking my elbow. "I'll get you to the car."

I stumbled outside. We were shuffling, walking unevenly, Lowell limping beside me. The cars passing on First Avenue streamed white and red lights that shivered across the black night. I looked down, staring at the pavement, trying to shield my eyes from the neon in the windows, the street lights, the lights on the ends of cigarettes, lights flashing off Lowell's white teeth.

The food in my stomach climbed the back of my throat.

"Here we are." He leaned me against the back passenger door, unlocking the car. I closed my eyes.

"You better lay down," he said.

I felt him pick me up, wrapping an arm behind my knees, the other under my neck, as I collapsed across the backseat. He adjusted my arms and legs. Something like a blanket dragged my legs down. Then my hands.

"You'll be fine," he said. "Take some deep breaths, Raleigh."

I closed my eyes. One deep breath. I heard the car door close, the engine turning over. I took another breath. The car was moving, a gentle rocking motion. I took another deep breath and opened my eyes. The street lights were passing across the windows in perfect hexagons, purple magnesium and red iron and the bright yellow of pure gold. When the hexagons began cartwheeling across the black sky, I decided I was seeing the chemical compounds, the shifting shapes of molecular structures as they formed into new minerals and the color changed. I sat up, fascinated.

"Feeling better, huh?" Lowell glanced in the rearview mirror. "That's a good girl. We'll be there soon."

In front of us, two cones of white light tunneled down the highway. On either side, tiny lights danced. I tried to scoot to the side window, but couldn't get there and leaned over. The lights were moving to music. I could hear the abrupt pentachords the lights danced to, up and down, and realized it was water. Lapping water. Why was there water?

"Where . . . ?" I was confused. "My house?"

"I'm taking you somewhere better," he said. "You're going to love it."

I stared at the back of his head. He was nodding. When I looked down at my hands, they seemed foreign and familiar all at once. Two circles of gray metal wrapped around my wrists. I lifted my hands, the short chain clinking, secured to the car's floor. My heart jumped, as though trying to escape my body.

I opened my mouth. But what came out was not human. It was something guttural, the tortured response of a deaf mute.

"Now you're getting it, Raleigh. We're going back to the

mountain. Let's try again. I don't know about you, but that last time was no fun. No fun at all. It just frustrated me."

I pulled my hands up. The chain snapped. I pulled harder. Each effort more difficult.

"Look at that," he said. "Half gone and you're still going to fight. Man, I love that about you."

I kicked my feet across the floorboard, finding the chain bottom. Air seemed to leak from my lungs. I watched his eyes in the mirror, small blurry marbles, the shadows falling from his brow. He was speaking but I could not understand his words, his mouth seemed to move like somebody reciting vowels in an exaggerated manner, and I felt a distant buzzing sensation somewhere near the base of my spine. The sensation burred against my skin, running circles around my hips. Then suddenly, it stopped. And started again.

I threw my body against the seat.

He started laughing.

Paralytic, hands bound, mind firing with hallucinogens, I threw my body against the buzzing sensation. When it finally stopped, I leaned forward, resting my forehead on my forearms, my hands clasped together.

"Wh . . . wh . . . " I tried again. "Where. Where are you taking me?"

"If I told you that, Raleigh, it wouldn't be a surprise. And you like surprises, don't you? You liked surprising Courtney. And you liked surprising me, taking her away. Now I get to surprise you."

The Blazer swerved right. My body tumbled, caught by the chain before I hit the side door. Pain ripped across my face. I closed my eyes. No more fireworks, no more streamers. But even with my eyes closed, I saw molten lava running down a mountainside, bright red as blood.

He stopped the car and unlocked the chain, leaving the cuffs on. Pulling me off the seat, he yanked my head back, speaking into my hair, the same way he'd whispered on Tiger Mountain. Once again, he told me the rules of his game, how much fun we were going to have as he hunted me. I felt his hands, tearing at my waist.

The phone snapped off my belt.

"Did you call somebody?" he demanded.

I didn't reply. I couldn't.

"Don't want to play fair?" he whispered. "We won't play fair."

Fair. Fair. Fair. The word trailed across my mind as if written in electric green neon. I begged the lights to stop dancing. But when they did, I wanted them back.

The woods were solid black. He was counting off the numbers again . . . "One . . . Two . . . Three . . ." His wicked version of hide and seek.

I stumbled forward, my hands cuffed in front of me. The trees loomed, long-armed creatures with seaweed hair. I saw scabs of blood on the rocks. The quarter moon sliced a black curtain like a guillotine. I fell, got up, fell again.

He would find me.

I turned in a circle. Darkness, darkness everywhere.

"I'm coming, Raleigh."

Through the forest, I watched his flashlight flickering. I stared at the trees around me. They were dark columns, their high branches like umbrellas above my head. I walked behind one of the thick trunks and leaned my face against the bark. I could still see his strange light approaching, like a diaphanous white cylinder, falling through the forest.

I didn't want to die. And I couldn't fight him by myself.

When I lifted my head again, his feet were passing beside the tree. I didn't move. I didn't breathe. But suddenly he slowed, just as he'd done before, his predatory instincts those of a hungry animal. I watched him make a slow turn, sniffing the air for my scent, and I felt an odd resignation. Here. In the woods. No way out. It was beyond my ability to win. He still had his back to me, his sensory gifts telegraphing my close position. As I stepped out, he started to turn.

But he was too late.

My hands were already raised and I dropped the cuffs over his head, yanking the titanium links against his throat. A gurgling sound crawled from his mouth. He dropped the flashlight. With his free hand, he clawed at my skin. With the other, he beat against my arm with his gun. I twisted, pulling my body away. The gun waved through the dark, a spasmodic threat. I yanked harder, and for some reason I heard his gurgle as the color puce, an ugly smudge that disappeared into the dark. When the gun fired—white light—my arms burned. But I did not feel pain. Instead, I felt warm, an enveloping sensation that pervaded my arms, my heart, my legs. There was no fear. Because I could not win. I knew that. It was not my battle.

I felt a quick snap in his neck. He dropped, limp, dead weight that took me down with it. We fell as one to the forest floor and lay beside each other, close as lovers. I listened, not releasing my grip until he stilled, then shoved my knees into his body, rolling him, and removing my handcuffs from his neck.

I stood, looking down at Officer Lowell.

The flashlight lay on the side of the trail, burning like a box of sunlight. When I picked it up, it felt heavy. I tucked it against my waist, pointed it at the ground, and slowly made my way back through the trees, the rocks, the night. It appeared to be filling again with strange colors.

chapter twenty-nine

J ack Stephanson stood at the foot of the white bed.

"Get me out of here," I said.

He kept staring at me.

"Hello? Get me out of here. I hate hospitals."

"Raleigh, who am I?"

"You're Jack, a major pain in the—"

"Who do you work for?"

"The FBI. What is this, an interrogation?"

He sat on the corner of the bed. "You've been fading in and out all night. I want to make sure you're all there. You keep calling me Daddy."

My face burned with embarrassment. "Just get my clothes. They put them in the bathroom."

"McLeod promised to fire you if you walk out again."

I dropped my head on the pillow. Two IVs ran into my left hand. "How long have I been in here?"

"You're going on twenty-four hours," he said. "Your aunt just left with that crazy clairvoyant."

I waited. "What happened to Lowell?"

"He's in ICU. You crushed his windpipe, gave the guy a tracheotomy. Not bad for somebody on acid."

"Is that what it was?"

"Blood tests showed LSD. You were tripping so bad, they knocked you out so you could sleep it off."

The pictures came back suddenly, brutally. "I was sitting at a table with him. I ordered a Coke. My phone rang. I went outside—it was you."

He nodded. "Your car broke down taking Felicia into rehab. You asked me to get that junker towed. You said Lowell called it in to the state police, but they had no report of it. And then they said Lowell wasn't even working. That's when I got concerned. Did you notice him following you?"

"No. But I wasn't looking for him."

"I called your cell a second time, after I found out he wasn't working, it rang and rang. Then I heard you gasping. Harmon, you sounded like you were croaking."

I was. "How did you find me?"

"I was calling you from the office line. I used my cell to dial 911 and they got coordinates on your cell phone—Bureau phones have embedded GPS. The pings pinpointed your location, right off Sunset Way. Issaquah PD fired up cruisers, sirens blaring. And ten minutes later you come walking out of the woods like Gretel on acid."

"It was him. All along." I felt sick.

"Harmon, just because a guy carries a badge doesn't mean he's on our side."

"Badger," I said.

"What?"

Badger, I thought. Claire the Clairvoyant had seen a badger, foaming at the mouth. And this badge that turned. "This feels so personal," I said.

"Him coming after you?"

"That, and the betrayal. He acted like one of the good guys."

"Couple years back, we had an agent who double-dipped on drugs. When it all came out, I started to wonder who to trust. But I got over it."

"How?"

"Start counting the good ones, the really good ones. They outnumber the bad, by a wide margin. And you'll appreciate them more when you realize what it takes to stay good." He paused. "I'm going to call McLeod, see if we can spring you out of here."

He patted my leg and walked out of the room.

⁓

It took me four days to approach normal. When I asked to come into the office, McLeod sent me away. Finally, he told me to drive over to the VanAlstyne's estate.

"The wife wants to talk to you," he said.

All the unmarked sedans were gone, and Mrs. VanAlstyne answered the bell herself. The assistant Sequoia was nowhere to be seen.

I followed her through the foyer, into the grand living room, the house filled with a strange quiet. When we sat on the moss green couch, she placed an electronic baby monitor on the coffee table.

"She's having nightmares," she said, by way of explanation for the monitor. "The doctors said I need to be there as soon as she wakes up."

After somebody's worst secret is exposed and they realize they're going to live, the extraneous parts of their life tend to disappear. Only the elemental remains. In the case of Alex VanAlstyne, her hair appeared wiry now, strands of gray lifting from the shanks of platinum. She rested her hands in her lap. She needed a manicure.

"My husband and I want to thank you," she said.

"You don't need to."

"I realize we did not get off on the right foot at the beginning. But of course we were under such pressure. We were so worried. You understand."

"Yes, I do."

"I want to extend an apology for our previous attitude toward you. And toward the FBI. If there is ever anything— *anything*—we can do for you, please let us know."

"Thank you," I said.

But her eyes held a question.

"She's asking to see her father. I know she means her birth father. The psychiatrist believes it would be a good idea. But I haven't contacted him because, well, didn't you suspect him of being involved in all this?"

She wanted the wedge to widen. But Bill Johansen was nothing more than a wild-eyed born-again Christian, a believer modeling his life after John the Baptist.

There was a connection, however, and it was significant.

"Mr. Johansen has a neighbor who calls the police regularly about his dogs," I said. "The officer who came out on the complaints became a regular visitor. Mr. Johansen is a talkative sort, and he eventually told the officer about his concerns for Courtney, about her lifestyle. He asked the officer to talk to her at the casino, thinking it might scare her. The officer learned all the details of her life, including what she was worth, monetarily speaking. He befriended her, learned all about her life. And when he wrote the ransom note, he knew Johansen's penmanship. And then the shirt," I said.

"Yes. What about it?"

"We believe she wore it to go hiking with the officer. They had Bill Johansen in common. That's about all we can fathom, without her help."

Mrs. VanAlstyne waited, as though more information was available. But that part defied explanation. The part that answered why? Why somebody would torture another human being.

Suddenly she asked, "Do you believe she will ever be the same?"

No, I didn't. Courtney VanAlstyne would never recover. Not the way her mother expected. But I couldn't say that to a woman walking through the valley. What I wanted to tell her was that graphite and diamond were both made of carbon. One was so soft it could be used for sketching; the other was formed under tremendous pressure, its bonds nearly unbreakable, the most beautiful gem on Earth.

"She won't be the way she was," I said. "But she might be even better than she was before."

Her eyes welled. The woman who stared back at me bore little resemblance to the woman I'd met several weeks ago. It wasn't just the physical features—unkempt hair, chipped nails, lint clinging to her dark slacks—it was the weighted silence she allowed between us, a depth she would have avoided before this tragedy happened. And in that weighted quiet came a soft murmuring, a rustling static. The baby monitor flashed red.

She stood, picking up the monitor. "I have to go. Can you let yourself out?"

I walked through the foyer to the front door. Her quick steps ahead of me, then she turned to the stairs, her white hand on the black iron banister, all the somnolence gone. The brittle shell had cracked.

As I was closing the front door, I heard the mother's voice, slipping down the stairs, calling out in tones like bells, saying, "I'm coming, darling. Don't be afraid. I'm coming."

⁓

That afternoon my aunt spread crystals across the dining room table. She placed a small boom box on the sideboard and hit Play.

Angry rock and roll erupted.

"I have a new slogan!" she yelled over the music. "Seattle Stones, we rock your world! What do you think?"

"It's . . . what are the minerals for?"

She reached over, shutting off the music. "What?"

I repeated my question.

"A couple days ago," she said, "I was meditating and your mother was playing that classical music of hers. But instead of getting upset, I asked the spirit of the Earth to help me. And that's when I got my nirvana moment. I could see—actually see—the vibrations in the crystals, how they matched certain kinds of music."

"You mean the molecular vibrations, between the atoms?"

"Raleigh, forget that science stuff. I'm talking about psychic energy. I saw real sapphires floating through my mind, dancing to the rhythms of Bach."

"Aunt Charlotte, may I ask you something?"

"Sure, honey."

"Do you take drugs?"

"No. The next day I put on some hip-hop, started meditating, and Tiger's Eye came up. When I put on folk music, I saw turquoise. Rhythm and blues—now, you'd think it should be a blue stone, like azurite or cerulean, but here's a surprise. Blues is sandstone. I wanted to ask you about that. Do you see any connection?"

"Yes, I see a connection." The connection was that my aunt was loony tunes. "Is Mom around?"

"She's fixing dinner."

My aunt turned on the music again and I walked into the kitchen. My mother was reading a small white card with a handwritten recipe. The cats camped nearby, eyeing the Styrofoam tray of ground beef. Madame rested under the kitchen table.

"Rufus gave me his meatball recipe," she said. "Felicia's coming to dinner tonight and the only thing she'll eat is meatballs. Oh, I said you'd pick her up, since you're still on vacation."

I nodded. "What about Aunt Charlotte? She's a vegan."

"She's going out. Something about selling crystals at a rock-n-roll show tonight." My mother leaned in, her perfume smelling of orchids. "This new enterprise of hers, it seems a bit, well, *literal*, don't you think?"

It was more than an hour before I needed to pick up Felicia, and although the sky was dark with impending rain, I took Madame for a walk, making our way over to Broadway. We passed the punk shops and used-book stores and restaurants with one-syllable names, and at the corner of Broadway and Roy, we stopped to hear a street musician. He was playing a guitar and had a scraggly appearance, but his voice had a power that filled every minor key with meaning. The instrument's case lay open on the sidewalk, the blue velour interior freckled with coins. Suddenly I recognized his tune. That old Donovan song, about wanting to feel the warm hold of a loving hand, the elusive grasp that never holds, how it is like trying to catch wind. I waited for him to finish, then tossed money in his guitar case. Madame and I turned, heading for home.

acknowledgments

First things first: All errors are mine, and do not reflect on the knowledge and expertise shared with me by the following people: Special Agent (retired) Wayne Smith, a walking encyclopedia on the FBI and a superb writer; Special Agents Robbie Burroughs and David Thorp in the Seattle field office of the FBI; the superlative Washington State Crime Lab, specifically George Johnston and Bill Schneck, a great forensic geologist; state trooper Joe Ulicny, absolutely one of the good guys; and the officers of the Issaquah Police Department, including retired Chief Dave Draveling and Detective Chris Wilson. Also geologist Derek Booth, who explained the puzzle of the Puget lowlands with great patience. It is one thing to become knowledgeable, still another to be generous with that knowledge, and still more to use that knowledge serving your fellow man. Thank you all.

Gratitude abounds for my agent Brian Peterson, who never freaks out, no matter what my e-mails sound like, and the team at Thomas Nelson fiction, who hold the highest standards without losing their sense of humor: Allen Arnold, publisher; Amanda Bostic, editor; Jocelyn Bailey, a literary life raft with a red pen; and the rest of the crew in Nashville. Huge kudos to my editor, Traci DePree, a novelist who switches hats like a champ. You make me a better writer.

My friend Pat VandenBroek first told me about the world of poker and led me to Cat Hurlbert's book, *Outplaying the Boys*. Randy and Stephanie Harrison and Tim Timadaiski mentioned coal mining on Squak Mountain, and once things got rolling, I was sustained by a group of homeschooling moms who "get it," especially Monica Lange, and the many smart, funny women at Heritage Homeschool Co-op, particulary Stephany Mast, Leigh Hazen, Sarah Edwards, and Shari Hormel. Very special thanks go to Terry Brenna for her science class, and to Sara J. Ponte, who graced me with a CD by Sara Groves called *Conversations*. It was just that. Much-deserved shouts to my caffeine connection at Tiger Mt. Tea, Wayne Spence: Here's to all your Black Ceylons brewed at 4:00 a.m.

To God, whose mercies are new every morning. And Pastor Mark Driscoll of Mars Hill Church: Thank you for your honest preaching and rockin' sensibilities.

I would also like to thank all the people whose wedding receptions I showed up for on the wrong day, whose birthdays I completely forgot, whose mail I never responded to, or whose dinner I burned. I greatly appreciate your beautiful perspectives. For those who got huffy about these things, well, I probably never liked you that much anyway.

Perpetual thanks to my family: much-missed parents, the Honorable Roger G. Connor and Annabelle Simpson Connor, and Danny and Tessie Giorello. My brother, Roger Connor, Jr.; my uncle Fred Danz, who pushed me to write; and my other uncle, Dr. Robert W. Simpson, a motorboater who keeps a firm grip on the family rudder, and the rest of the Simpson clan. Janet and Dick Benson, for being terrific grandparents. And to Kris Robbs, my kinda cousin who drums up publicity. The Quinns, Giorellos, and Labellos—*eh, mangia!*

Many thanks to my sons, Daniel and Nico, experts on Transformers and Bionicles, for collecting rocks, asking the best questions, and laughing at my jokes. You guys are everything a mom could wish for, and all that she didn't know she needed.

Most of all, however, all my thanks goes to my husband, Joe. The Italian Stallion. The guy who makes it all happen and takes no prisoners. You make *la dolce vita*. Thank you.

Forever, thank you.

reader's guide

1. Jack Stephanson seems to make everything more difficult for Raleigh, and she seems to resent him for it. But do you sense a romantic spark between them? If so, where? If Raleigh and Jack were dating, what sort of couple would they make?

2. When Raleigh takes her mother to the charismatic church service, the preacher talks about the times in our lives when "the rivers run dry." Have you ever lived through spiritual drought? How did you restore your spirit? Do you have a personal "rain dance" that works? Every time?

3. Aunt Charlotte once belonged to the Episcopal church but now believes in crystals and charms and New Age philosophies. Why do you think she turned away from the church? Is her response reasonable? Typical? If you've known someone who did this, what was your reaction to their change of belief?

4. New places provoke new feelings, and Seattle presents a love-hate relationship for Raleigh. Can you see what she appreciates about this new place? What she seems to hate? Does her homesickness ever distort reality, or hold her back in some way?

5. Alex VanAlstyne has managed to keep a profound secret

from her husband. After he's learned the truth, do you think they'll remain married? What would that marriage look like? Do you know couples whose marriages have survived damaging revelations?

6. As a young single mom with really bad habits, Felicia Kunkel seems torn between her family and her addictions. Raleigh wants to help her, but can she? Are there some people who can't be helped, no matter what we do? Or do we have an obligation to never give up?

7. Courtney VanAlstyne has suffered. In the months and years ahead, what will her life be like? Will she recover? And how will she react to living with a physical deformity—will she ignore it or cover it up? Or perhaps do something else?

8. When Raleigh goes into her closet to pray, she sends up a prayer to the "one who knew love, and how it always brought suffering." What does she mean? And do you agree with her?

9. Mothers and daughters share a special relationship. What do you think of Raleigh's relationship with her mother? Are there any aspects that resemble your relationship with your mother?

10. At the end of the book, Raleigh and Madame "head for home." Does this mean she wants to stay in Seattle, or is she still hoping to return to Virginia?

about the author

SIBELLA GIORELLO began writing as a features reporter for newspapers and magazines. Her stories won numerous awards, including two nominations for the Pulitzer Prize. She recently won a Christy award for her novel *The Stones Cry Out*. She lives in Washington state with her husband and family.